The Journey Prize Anthology

Winners of the $10,000 Journey Prize

1989
Holley Rubinsky for "Rapid Transits"

1990
Cynthia Flood for "My Father Took a Cake to France"

1991
Yann Martel for "The Facts Behind the Helsinki Roccamatios"

1992
Rozena Maart for "No Rosa, No District Six"

1993
Gayla Reid for "Sister Doyle's Men"

1994
Melissa Hardy for "Long Man the River"

1995
Kathryn Woodward for "Of Marranos and Gilded Angels"

1996
Elyse Gasco for "Can You Wave Bye Bye, Baby?"

1997 (shared)
Gabriella Goliger for "Maladies of the Inner Ear"
Anne Simpson for "Dreaming Snow"

1998
John Brooke for "The Finer Points of Apples"

1999
Alissa York for "The Back of the Bear's Mouth"

2000
Timothy Taylor for "Doves of Townsend"

The Journey Prize Anthology

Short Fiction from the Best of Canada's New Writers

Selected by Elyse Gasco, Michael Helm,
and Michael Nicholson

M&S

National Library of Canada Cataloguing in Publication Data

The National Library of Canada has catalogued this publication as follows:

The Journey Prize anthology
Annual.
1–
Subtitle varies.
ISSN 1197-0693
ISBN 0-7710-4422-4 (volume 13)

1. Short stories, Canadian (English).
2. Canadian fiction (English) – 20th century.

PS8329.J68   C813'.0108054   C93-039053-9

We acknowledge the financial support of the Government of Canada through the Book Publishing Industry Development Program for our publishing activities. We further acknowledge the support of the Canada Council for the Arts and the Ontario Arts Council for our publishing program.

"The Cane Field" © Kevin Armstrong; "Karaoke Mon Amour" © Mike Barnes; "Machaya" © Heather Birrell; "The Present Perfect" © Heather Birrell; "The Gun" © Craig Boyko; "Anything That Wiggles" © Vivette J. Kady; "You're Taking All the Fun Out of It" © Billie Livingston; "Fishes" © Annabel Lyon; "The Way the Light Is" © Lisa Moore; "Little Suitcase" © Heather O'Neill; "In the Chambers of the Sea" © Susan Rendell; "Watch" © Tim Rogers; "Dream Dig" © Margrith Schraner
These stories are reprinted with permission of the authors.

The lines from "Morning Song" in "In the Chambers of the Sea" are taken from *Ariel* by Sylvia Plath, published by Faber and Faber Limited. Copyright © 1965 by Ted Hughes. Reprinted by permission of the publisher.

The lines from "The Green Insect" in "The Way the Light Is" are taken from *That Night We Were Ravenous* by John Steffler, published by McClelland & Stewart Ltd. Copyright © 1998 by John Steffler. Reprinted by permission of the publisher.

Typeset in Trump Mediaeval by M&S, Toronto
Printed and bound in Canada

McClelland & Stewart Ltd.
The Canadian Publishers
481 University Avenue
Toronto, Ontario
M5G 2E9
www.mcclelland.com

1 2 3 4 5   05 04 03 02 01

About the Journey Prize Anthology

The $10,000 Journey Prize is awarded annually to a new and developing writer of distinction. This award, now in its thirteenth year, is made possible by James A. Michener's generous donation of his Canadian royalty earnings from his novel *Journey*, published by McClelland & Stewart in 1988. The winner of this year's Journey Prize will be selected from among the thirteen stories in this book.

The Journey Prize Anthology comprises a selection from submissions made by literary journals across Canada, and, in recognition of the vital role journals play in discovering new writers, McClelland & Stewart makes its own award of $2,000 to the journal that has submitted the winning entry. This year the selection jury comprised Elyse Gasco, who won the 1996 Journey Prize for the title story from her debut short-story collection, *Can You Wave Bye Bye, Baby?*, winner of the QSPELL Hugh MacLennan Prize for Fiction and the QSPELL/FEWQ First Book Award, and a finalist for the Danuta Gleed Literary Award, the Governor General's Award, and the Rogers Writers' Trust Fiction Prize; Michael Helm, the author of *The Projectionist*, a finalist for The Giller Prize and the Trillium Award, who is also a regular contributor to *Brick Magazine* and various other publications in Canada and the U.S., and was a co-editor at *Descant* for a number of years; and Michael Nicholson, category manager for Chapters.

The Journey Prize Anthology has established itself as one of the most prestigious anthologies in the country. It has become a who's who of up-and-coming writers, and many of the authors whose early work has appeared in the anthology's pages have gone on to single themselves out with collections of short stories and literary awards. The Journey Prize itself is the most significant monetary award given in Canada to a writer at the beginning of his or her career for a short story or excerpt from a fiction work in progress.

McClelland & Stewart would like to acknowledge the continuing enthusiastic support of writers, literary journal editors, and the public in the common celebration of the emergence of new voices in Canadian fiction.

For more information about the *Journey Prize Anthology*, please consult our Web site: www.mcclelland.com/jpa

Contents

MIKE BARNES
Karaoke Mon Amour 1
(from *The New Quarterly*)

TIM ROGERS
Watch 22
(from *The New Quarterly*)

HEATHER O'NEILL
Little Suitcase 38
(from *This Magazine*)

SUSAN RENDELL
In the Chambers of the Sea 45
(from *TickleAce*)

ANNABEL LYON
Fishes 57
(from *Event*)

KEVIN ARMSTRONG
The Cane Field 64
(from *Event*)

HEATHER BIRRELL
The Present Perfect 84
(from *Matrix*)

VIVETTE J. KADY
Anything That Wiggles 103
(from *Prairie Fire*)

MARGRITH SCHRANER
Dream Dig   114
(from *The New Orphic Review*)

HEATHER BIRRELL
Machaya   122
(from *PRISM international*)

CRAIG BOYKO
The Gun   143
(from *filling Station*)

LISA MOORE
The Way the Light Is   152
(from *The Malahat Review*)

BILLIE LIVINGSTON
You're Taking All the Fun Out of It   168
(from *This Magazine*)

About the Authors   181

About the Contributing Journals   184

List of Previous Contributing Authors   189

MIKE BARNES

Karaoke Mon Amour

Foreign Shapes

Taiwan is shaped like an egg, an ovary, a tear. Korea is a stubby uncircumcised penis, one million soldiers stationed at its base. Japan is long and gently curving, tapering from a central mass into a chain of ever-smaller islands: it is the seahorse, tail unfurled, floating on ocean currents to the east.

The seahorse (*Hippocampus syngnathidae*) is a marine fish found in shallow tropical or temperate waters. The male develops the eggs and bears the young, incubating them in a brood pouch.

The hippocampus forms a ridge along each lateral ventricle of the brain. It is part of the limbic system, which is involved in the complex physical aspects of behaviour governed by emotion and instinct. The activities governed are those concerned with self-preservation and preservation of the species, expression of fear, rage, and pleasure, and the establishment of memory patterns.

The Two Sisters

English only! was their strict rule at the start, but George soon saw the sense of bending this a little. June, the younger of the two women he tutored on Tuesday, could speak English haltingly

– the Taiwanese school system had drilled her mainly in grammar – but her sister, May, could barely speak at all. As they sat around the carved cedar coffee table, George working with first one sister then the other, it was only natural for June to help out in Mandarin whenever he and May reached an impasse.

The house was May's. Or the first floor was. The basement was rented "to China boy" and the upstairs "to mother, her girl," which partly answered George's puzzlement at how two thirty-year-olds, one with five small children, could immigrate and right away purchase a house in North York. Not all of the mystery evaporated. The family business in Taipei seemed modest enough – "We are selling hats," June explained – and May's husband had no regular employment. He practised a martial arts discipline George had never heard of and couldn't pronounce. His trophies stood on the mantel and medals and diplomas hung above them, the only furnishings in the living room except for the table and the heap of children's toys in a corner. He travelled through Asia giving demonstrations. For free? George wondered. He had been gone on one of these junkets since George had met the sisters. Tomorrow he was due back.

"Husband . . . pick up," May made driving motions in the air.

"I am picking up my husband," George said, writing it at the same time on the paper he would leave behind. "Try."

"Try to say?" May made a comic song of the three words. She said something to June. They both laughed.

"What did she say?" At the question, June blushed and glanced at her sister. May was still laughing, her black eyes glittering.

"He say, your voice sound like music."

George smiled dryly, to show he didn't believe that.

Paper Cranes

Some of the paper cranes could sit upright, correctly balanced, but most lay over on one side; some were upside-down. It was as if a strong wind, which neither of them could feel, blew gusts through their apartment. Or perhaps – George had been taken duck hunting as a boy – a flock of the coloured birds had been

flying through and had met a hail of gunfire, launched by miniature marksmen hidden among the furnishings.

He showed one to Sonoko, his Friday morning appointment.
Shelley made this, he said proudly, bringing out the lime green
crane from a zippered pouch in his briefcase. It was only slightly
crushed by his sandwiches.

"Shelley? Ah . . . your partner." Sonoko spoke with slow pre-
cision. She had studied traditional tea ceremony at an institute
in Kyoto. Once when George asked if she would work at that
when she returned, her eyes went wide. "I have not served tea
for six months." *Out of date?* George thought, before remembering that the whole point of tradition was *never* to go out of
date. What did she mean then? That the motions of performing
the ceremony were so complex – he imagined slow sequences of
turns, clockwise, counter-clockwise, bows, subtle hand gestures – really, he couldn't imagine it. He and Shelley poured
water over Lipton.

"This . . . is . . . very . . . lovely," Sonoko said, turning the crane
delicately. "Origami. We made in junior school."

"Elementary," George corrected, his armpits flaming for
himself as well as Shelley.

Karaoke

*I am in love with someone. He is foreigner. It is impossible to
think. I will be insane.*

All the way home on the subway, he pressed the pocket of
his shirt, feeling the message on the slip of paper burn against
his heart.

But climbing the fire escape stairs to his apartment, he
remembered his friend Howard's words. *These Asian women,
they're like western women forty years ago. Marriage is everything to them. If they don't find a man, they're nothing.* Howard
was sexist, reductionist, casually racist; partly for these reasons,
George found his company bracing. He pricked balloons. Snug
in a regular teaching job, he found George's ESL gigs more
amusing than exotic.

Once, in a Forkchops on Bloor, George pressed him to try *kimchee*, the Korean national dish of aggressively spiced cabbage.

Howard, a curry devotee and foreign film fan, was not fazed by the fiery red flecks in vinegar. He chewed a large mouthful judiciously, sweat beading on his forehead.

"They bury it in a pot in the backyard," George told him.

"I believe it," said Howard.

There was a name printed in one very bottom corner of the note, so tiny it looked like a fly's footprints. *Kil Eun-Jee*. He liked the fact that the Koreans seldom picked a western moniker to avoid embarrassing struggles with their names. They let you try. Sometimes, mouthing substitutes like "May" or "June," he felt he was addressing a ghost self, like a hologram, shimmering between himself and the real person.

Losing Babies

George reckoned that he and Shelley had lost three children in six months. Shelley felt the same way, though George knew she went too far when she said, as she sometimes did, "It's just like they died." It wasn't *just* like that. As a language teacher he was sensitive to the dangers in the overly literal as well as in the overly metaphorical. Whatever sense he had of a higher power – and it was a very hazy, flickering sense, like early TV – he was sure that it involved at least a fine ear. Talk like that was dangerous. It could get you smacked with some real bad luck.

Not that he and Shelley hadn't had their share. First, they had thought Shelley was pregnant. Finally. Six weeks since her last period, and they had been tossing around names, when her doctor informed her that what she was growing was in fact an ovarian cyst, not a fetus. After her surgery, she was down, lower than even George had ever seen her before. At thirty-nine, and with her history of tricky menstruation, her doctor put her chances of another pregnancy at slim. It was George who first contacted the adoption agency. Four years, he was told, if everything went smoothly. Four *years*? He would be forty-five. Without even mentioning this to Shelley, he made further inquiries and finally found an agency that got – their blunt word – babies from Russia. An agency in Moscow took in homeless babies from all over that vast country, as well as from the former republics, Kazakhstan, Belarus, Georgia. "A clearing house," George thought unwillingly, and saw a van, like an old-style dog-catcher's van, roaming the muddy side streets. "Good health, parents and children," said a crisp young female, who was no less impressive when George met her in person.

Shelley was too depressed still to be very dubious or excited. She acceded.

"Igor? Vasily? Vladimir?" George joked gently, trying to bring her around. He still came home most nights to find her eating nachos in front of *Jerry Springer*. "Good-Time Grannies: My Mother Slept With My Son." She had gained twenty-five pounds, and was still gaining, even after returning to her part-time hours as a data entry clerk with a survey firm named, unfortunately, Matrix. Their sex life was nil, but had been dwindling for a long time.

"Katerina," she finally said one night with a weak smile. "We can shorten it to Kate."

Good Fortune

George was disappointed when, after the return of May's husband, May and June cancelled their next two appointments. It was business, partly; they were the last two sessions left in the package of hours they'd bought. But, also, he missed seeing them. He had come to think of the two sisters as an oasis of calm in his week. Peace, and something more. A hint of mystery, and promise of the most relaxing kind, since it need never be fulfilled.

They gave him cups of tea, green or black. Ginger tea once, when he was sick; it was sweet and spicy, the pale root slices floating in the pot, and after each sip it filled the head and chest with a surprising surge of delayed heat. And new food, too: red bean soup, which he found too sugary. Delicious warm buns filled with green onion or pork bits in a sauce. The house was always silent; strangely silent, for a home to eleven people. But the husband was demonstrating his martial art abroad, the children were at school; even the three tenants had vacated the premises, perhaps in deference to the arrival of "tutor-man," as May sang out when he rang the doorbell. The sense of stolen moments was what made him think of an oasis. The small delight of water and a palm tree, an hour of shade before the march again.

They sat cross-legged around the low carved coffee table, he on one side, the two sisters on the other. The silence felt to him like another language, a third tongue that murmured between the English and Mandarin. They laughed a lot. Giggled at mistakes, at deformed vowels and ribald consonants; at bad grammar. Words popped and fizzled and flared like a backyard fireworks display in the air around their heads.

There was an undercurrent. Of course he knew that. It came most forcefully from May, the married one. June was shyer. May would rattle off a string of Mandarin, several sentences' worth, which at George's prompting June would translate as, "She feel tired." May, black eyes dancing, looked anything but pooped. He kept asking just to watch June squirm, mumbling the double translation into a safe lie and then into English.

"Teacher hit," May suggested, holding out her hands when she had failed to do her homework. Her fingers were long and slender, pink from kitchen work, the nails clear and shapely. He felt a buzz of tingling energy in what Howard called "the lowest chakra."

They taught him a Chinese character that they translated as "Good Fortune." Its difficulty surprised him, sixteen strokes in a precise sequence. But then there were quite a few strokes involved in printing "Good Fortune" in English. During lulls in the lesson, he sometimes practised it, May and June laughing delightedly.

Naturally he had fantasies of sleeping with them. Taking the two sisters to bed in the echoing house. Such thoughts never occupied him for long; he enjoyed them in passing. During the first bald patch in their sex life, he and Shelley had visited a therapist, who asked them – five minutes in, which George recognized as a shock tactic – if they "got off on other people." George admitted he did occasionally (often, by that point); and Shelley, tearing up, said she thought she had "once." "Once, schmunz," the therapist, a tough-lover, jeered. He said, "Who

cares where you get your appetite, as long as you eat at home."
After three sessions they paid their bill and discontinued recovery. They went back to irregular snacking, from their own, or
each other's, hands.

The day May's husband returned, there were sounds in the
house at last. Deep breathing sounds from the kitchen, like
breezes in a poplar grove. George felt nervous. At the end of the
session, a squat young man in a burgundy track suit, with a
serene boyish face, planted himself in front of him and
announced, "I am Dave. I'm happy to meet you." His English
was fluent, lightly accented. George wondered why he didn't
teach his wife himself. "I would like to speak with you soon."

Soon, George promised.

Out of Business

Often it happened, an almost-expected miracle. "Nature's blessing," the doctor said, then, wincing at his own corniness, added
that it was probably hormonal. Happy expectation led to the
release of endorphins, which stimulated the production of
other, ah. . . . George heard confusion and perhaps ignorance in
the too-rapid delivery. But it didn't matter. Shelley was smiling.
Suddenly, two babies were on the way. Vladimir-Katerina would
be joined by Michael-Rebecca.

They would love them equally.

But, actually, both babies took a detour and wound up somewhere else. The Russian baby agency, or Canada's branch of it,
went out of business. *This number is no longer in service*, said
a sexy female voice each time George called. Then they received
a registered letter from a lawyer's office saying that their deposit
had been seized as evidence pertaining to a police investigation
and would be returned when, and if, etc. Vladimir-Katerina was
stuck in Vitebsk or Kustanaj or Batumi. George didn't know
why, but it made him feel better to find these names in the
atlas, give him/her a dot in the countryside at least. Michael-
Rebecca went down the toilet, a spontaneous first trimester
abortion. "Go down the toilet" was one of the idioms he taught
his students for a project failing; "go down the tubes" was

another. It was the horrible accidental exactness of language, no less than our fumbling attempts to control it, that oppressed him often.

Shelley didn't cry, not once that he saw. Her gently sorrowing face frightened him more than a Hallowe'en mask. She watched *Seinfeld*, *Springer*, and *Sally* with an unwavering attention, but was often hazy on details when he asked her the retention-testing questions he had developed in his work.

Eat Snow

When he asked his students what they had done on the weekend, the answer, if not "study English," was usually "karaoke." George had once joined a group that bellowed "Proud Mary" at a smear of cheering faces in a northern roadhouse serving half-price draft and chicken wings. That was fifteen years ago. Shelley had been one of the other drunken singers, swaying in a line with arms linked about each other's waists. He hadn't known her name yet. Six months later, they were living together.

But the Asian karaoke experience was, he gathered, different. "You must join us on a weekend, I insist," said Dae-Jung, a stylish architect from Seoul whom he met for "grammar refinement."

George was drunk by midnight when they reached the bar. Pitchers of draft were sloshing on top of a slithery supper of noodles topped with, first, a fried egg, then a glutinous black bean sauce. Tasty enough, though a bit much for his chopstick technique. The six Koreans, three of them clients, laughed good-naturedly. Shelley had begged off. Outside Christie station, George saw signs in Korean, the oblongs and circles less angular than Chinese characters. "Korean town," said the slight girl with the sombre, almost grieving expression who had been sitting next to him at dinner. He had forgotten her name, but at the hint of irony in her voice, he smiled.

Concrete stairs led down into the karaoke bar. Opium dens, George thought. It was not officially licensed, but at a word from Dae-Jung, the manager dipped below the counter and came up with a twelve-pack of Coors. An assistant showed them to one of the rooms. It was small, with clean white walls; an L-shaped black mock-leather couch faced the electronics stand in the corner; between them, a coffee table with songbooks, a remote, and two microphones. Faint thumps and laughter could be heard through the walls. Sex hotel, thought George, renting rooms by the hour.

The three girls were giggling as they flipped through the Korean and Chinese songbooks. He opened the English one. "Moon River." "What's New Pussycat?" "Do Ya' Think I'm Sexy?" Obviously selection was going to be a problem. "I insist you choose," pressed Dae-Jung, standing with mike in hand. He hit the dimmer switch and a small mirror ball in the corner began spinning, spraying dots of primary colours through the dusk. The lights spattered over and around the stand with its winking numbers, not quite reaching to where they sat. Electronics are the star, George thought; we have to emulate them.

Dae-Jung punched in the numbers of a Korean song. He blended seamlessly into the mix. So did the next two singers, each of them delivering a song without a glitch. That spooked George; he had been expecting a sing-along, but this was more like lip-synching. Another problem was the accompaniment, not the original tracks minus the vocals, as long ago in the road-house, but a peppy Muzak, heavy on synth and programmed rhythm tracks. The videos featured beautiful Asian women in filmy clothes, striking poses in front of a backdrop of stone columns, ocean sunset, or floral wallpaper.

Dae-Jung was pointing with the mike. George scanned the titles hopelessly. That was when he spied "Come Together" and remembered its tonic weirdness.

In the far corner of the black couch, the thin sad girl was staring at him. Grief and longing sloshed behind the mini-portholes of her glasses. No one sat very close to her. She had not sung, would not now.

With a sigh amplified into Apple wind, he began. Chanting the Lennonese, he was bolstered by the thought that it could not mean much less to his listeners than it did to him. When he reached the title phrase he was shouting.

For once, the group didn't laugh or clap loudly. After he finished rasping, a smattering of polite applause dispelled the silence. Dae-Jung clapped him on the back and launched into "Don't Be Cruel." He had a nice, light tenor.

Sometime toward the end of the evening, George had sung a few songs and drunk a few more beers, he was getting into it, not caring any more, when he heard a voice in his ear, at first he thought it came from inside his head, a woman's voice murmuring, "I like your deep voice. I wanna' –" Was he hallucinating? Around the urgent whisper, he heard a thin male voice, climbing an alien melody over a pounding beat.

He looked to his left and saw the grieving girl staring at her hands folded in her lap. He thought he saw her lips move – a silent prayer? She got up suddenly and left the room.

A short time later, he found himself on the street. New snow had fallen. The other faces looked as dizzy, as reeling under the streetlights, as he felt himself. The thin girl was looking away; she seemed impatient now, like someone waiting for a ride that is late. In the shuffle of going she had slipped a note into his pocket that he could feel with his fingers. A girl was scooping up snow and pushing it at her boyfriend's face. "Here, eat snow!"

737

Shelley had learned to make the origami cranes from a home decorating show on the Life Network. The show's host was a sort of Canadian Martha Stewart, less finicky and less impressive; often her instructions trailed off in a hazy ". . . or whatever." After she taught the viewers how to fold them, she showed the finished cranes to her gardening specialist, who happened to be Japanese.

"Ah . . . lovely," he said, as Sonoko had told George. He went on to relate the Japanese custom of making a thousand of the cranes as a form of prayer, for someone who was sick, for instance. He didn't mention that the technique was learned in elementary school.

"Wow! Well, if you're not up to a thousand, you can always enclose one in a Get Well card, since they flatten right out, or on a gift, or whatever," bubbled the host.

Shelley bought sheets of coloured paper that she cut into

two-inch squares. She had sheets of many colours: grass green, cedar green, ruby red, sky blue, cobalt blue, cotton candy pink, butter yellow, tangerine, burgundy. Deep, rich colours. She made a special expedition to the Japanese Paper Store to get sheets of gold and silver. These were George's favourites; they glittered like a king's ransom.

When folding the cranes, Shelley worked her way through all of the colours before returning to the first one. It was her own superstition. She did not use white or, of course, black.

At first, George knew, she was folding the cranes as a prayer for a healthy baby. She had seen the decorating show when her period was four weeks overdue. When that baby turned out to be a fibrous growth, he thought she must be folding the cranes for herself, substituting her name for the baby's in her prayer. He reminded her of the doctor's lack of concern, which they should interpret as reassurance. Finally he got up nerve to ask her.

"No," she said, folding deftly by now. "I want a baby."

All through the successive fiascos that followed, the loss of two more babies, each loss more actual, and thus more painful, than the one before, Shelley kept folding the cranes. By now George was confused about the reason, and to pray without purpose made him vaguely uneasy. Coloured cranes perched on the bookcase, the table, the fridge. They filled glass jars and bowls. Inevitably, with the wind of someone passing, they littered the floor, snagged in dust balls. George began to worry that they were unlucky.

"You didn't actually 'lose' the babies," said Howard over lunch one day. Then, remembering, he added, "Except for the miscarriage, of course." He didn't blush at his gaffe, though George winced inwardly; in his private sociology he had noticed that film buffs were not as easily embarrassed as most people.

"We didn't win," he said, demoting his feeling to irony. He thought that he had gone further than Howard in plumbing the meaning of loss. Loss was any missed chance or opportunity. It was the perception of absence, specific or generalized. It carried with it feelings, not only of sadness and anger, but also of guilt and confusion, blurred identity. Sometimes he felt he must have misplaced the babies; they would turn up if he only looked hard enough. Other times he felt that the babies were right where they belonged, and he was the one who had gotten turned around. He was a wanderer in a vast labyrinthine city, and he couldn't find a map or properly ask for directions. He couldn't even remember where he was staying, or who he was supposed to meet. Had the babies sensed that in advance and avoided such a befuddled dad?

"You don't have to see it all the way through," he said to Shelley one night. He had decided she was in superstitious thrall to a number, 1,000, and maybe he could help her free herself.

"No!" Her face filled with a foreboding he had never seen in it before. "I don't want us to lose any more."

So she did have a prayer. Not for gain, but against loss. Any, all, loss? And when she finally gave up folding, was that, he wondered, final resignation? He preferred to think it was boredom. Boredom was the commonest kind of bad faith.

But he wished she had given up earlier, or else finished the job. Seven hundred and thirty-seven miniature coloured cranes, constituting just over two-thirds of a prayer: that seemed like a definition of bad luck.

What happened at that theatre?

Some events are stubbornly surreal. It is as if they exist in an alternate universe and resist all our efforts to drag them into this one. All we glimpse here is odd, off-kilter limbs, sudden gasps, bits of a reality that somewhere else, perhaps, is correctly proportioned and breathing comfortably. It was like that the time George took Sonoko to the movies.

It began the night before, when he phoned to ask her. "Hello . . . hel-lo?" she kept saying, as if they had a bad connection. Then, dubiously, "George?" They had been meeting once a week for three months, but this was the first time he had phoned her. Occasionally she called him, to cancel or reschedule.

After a pause, Sonoko said, "It would be . . . Dutch treat?"

"Good," George said, "yes."

They met outside the Cumberland Theatre. Sonoko's normally pale face was chalk white, her black hair pinned back

severely. She wore a long black wrinkled raincoat. He thought
of Pound's lines: "The apparition of these faces in the crowd/
Petals on a wet, black bough." She had also studied kabuki
theatre; not performing it, of course, only men did that. But as
they paid for the tickets, he looked closely at her face, believing
he saw a layer of fine white powder blend with warmer tones at
her neckline. A sweetish smell rose from around her.

The ticket-seller and his companion – the manager? – were
middle-aged men who George assumed were gay. They were
well-groomed and they spoke in quiet voices, their heads close
together. It made the bare lobby strangely cozy, so unlike the
brisk hetero exchange – a boy or girl barking "Next" – at most
box offices. The ticket-taker also seemed homosexual, perhaps
just by association, but his personality was rougher, less com-
posed. A high school dropout beside university graduates,
thought George, configuring things. He was also a bit younger.

"Ah, you're going for the real stuff."

The ticket-taker spoke so quickly that Sonoko frowned in
puzzlement. Even George barely understood the blur of syllables.

"If it weren't for live flesh none of us would be here."

The comments seemed torn out of context, and George was
sitting down before they made any sense. The movie they were
seeing was *Live Flesh*, directed by Pedro Almodovar from a
novel by Ruth Rendell. Waiting in the dusk, he smelled
Sonoko's perfume, stronger at close quarters, a cloying scent
with something faintly metallic, a faint iron smell, underneath.
Sonoko was too fastidious ever to permit body odour. George
thought idly of sleeping with her, her strong legs – she rock-
climbed as fiercely as she memorized verbs – cinched around
his back. Partly this was automatic, having sexy thoughts before
movies. It was the dark, the screen about to come alive, the
nearby strangers.

A woman's scream began the movie. Briskly an older woman
bundled her into an off-duty bus where she gave birth to a
baby boy.

Sonoko leaned close to whisper something.

"Erotic?" he guessed.

"No!" Fiercely. "I know 'erotic.' Exotic."

The helpful woman used the driver's shoelaces to tie off the umbilical cord, and then, having nothing else sharp, she bit through it with her teeth. She sat in the seat behind the mother, her mouth red-smeared, like her hands and the baby she cradled. Tennyson's red-toothed, red-clawed nature. That was unusual in movies; usually newborns were shown born pink and glowing, as if bathed and talcumed prior to entry. The mother groaned deeply. "Keep pushing, it's the placenta," the impromptu midwife advised. George heard another soft gasp.

It was Sonoko. He turned to see her face floating ghostlike, drained and stricken. At once he understood her perfume with its ferrous undertone and the enhanced pallor of her face. It would be like Sonoko, with her blended masochism, to cover the evidence of her period with ministrations that actually drew attention to it. Mishima, he recalled, was her beloved author.

"Excuse me," Sonoko squeezed past without touching him. She never returned.

Afterwards he felt disjointed but refreshed, which from what Howard had told him was standard for an Almodovar movie. Shelley was in bed sleeping when he got home. He climbed in beside her and began stroking the small of her back. She responded slowly, with sleepy moans. Guilty but horny, he persisted. He came to a vision of Sonoko wearing a strap-on, fucking the sad Korean girl in the ass.

Who cares where you get your appetite.

"What happened at that theatre?" Shelley murmured before returning to sleep. He had told her that much.

Asshole

Dave was doing his breathing exercises in the kitchen next to the living room. George could hear him as he finished with the two sisters. He sounded like a soft engine starting up. Husbands, George thought, and wondered who would be more hopeless: a TSN addict who spent his days on the couch, or a martial arts expert who stood in rooms flexing and breathing. June poured more tea.

"My country is beautiful, yes," Dave was saying. George had asked about his trip. "It is my country. But it is crowded. Con . . . compressed? No. Congested?" George nodded. "Europeans called it Formosa."

Dave smiled as he spoke, a winning, boyish smile that lit up his handsome face. But George knew that he put too much stock in smiles. He always had; it was a weakness. He couldn't recognize aggression easily unless it came accompanied by scowls and grimaces and glares. But usually it didn't.

"I always called it Taiwan," George said.

May and June had moved back discreetly from the table. They were standing a few feet away, their faces meek and expectant.

"You are a great language teacher." George grinned at the exaggeration. "I am also a teacher. I could show you something."

Which is how George found himself standing rock-still in the centre of the living room for several long minutes, trying to relax and "go heavy" as instructed, feeling stiffness and soreness and restless energy migrate around his body. Feeling aches and pains. Feeling idiotic as he stared straight ahead out the window at the street, catching blurs of May and June and Dave moving around him, observing him as one would a museum exhibit. *Toronto man, 1998.*

Dave had showed him the place on the balls of his feet where the weight was supposed to concentrate. He told him the name, which George pronounced and forgot. By now he had great difficulty learning anything he knew he would never use. Dave's instructions were to "relax . . . go heavy," let all his weight flow down through the balls of his feet. Back into the earth. George tried, then – having read some Zen in his time – he tried not to try. Dave moved around him like a tailor, prodding him in the shoulder and stomach and thigh and buttocks. George was shamed by the mushiness of his muscles, but Dave muttered, "Not tight . . . let go." Finally, George succeeded in the sense that his various aches and pains merged into a general discomfort, and the energy of his body was concentrated mostly in his brain. He wondered if the froth of pink in the yard was a cherry tree. That would be almost as good as a lotus blossom. He also wondered what the best word would be for the way he felt, standing still in a living room among moving, watching people, his mouth falling open whenever he forgot about it.

He decided the best word would be "asshole."

Finally it was over. Dave looked at his watch. "Five minutes. Okay. Do it every day until you can do fifteen minutes. Very relaxed. If you feel pain, sudden pains, stop immediately."

"I will," George promised.

May and June were watching him seriously. It was a pleasure to be able to move his head again – *that* relaxed him. Soon he would leave and that made him feel warmly about May and June, the times they'd had together. He looked back at Dave and almost gasped. Dave's mouth was open, his eyes glazed; his arms hung limply at his sides and he leaned forward at a dangerous angle. He looked like a corpse tied to a stake. After a moment, George realized that he was being shown the correct procedure. He felt his own posture sag at the thought that the demonstration was not over.

"Feel my chest," the corpse murmured.

George put his hand on Dave's chest. It felt plump and still. "Through your stomach?" he guessed.

"Feel my stomach."

More plump stillness. Despite himself, George was curious.

"I'm breathing through my _____." The word for the balls of his feet. George nodded, as he did when a street person told him he could fly.

After watching for another minute or so – seeing nothing more – George said that he had to go. He bent to get his briefcase. "Let me show you something," he heard as fingers gripped his upper arm. Anger spread like a rash over his skin. Now he was being detained.

"Stand there," Dave said. He turned George's shoulders and positioned his feet so that George was advancing on him partly in profile, like a boxer. Standing very close, an inch away, he snuggled up with his head on George's breastbone. He adopted his limp posture, breathing through _____, his hands falling like soft plumb weights against George's thigh.

"Now push me," he mumbled.

George knew what was coming. Any man would. But he pushed anyway.

The result was still amazing. It was like pushing a rag doll weighing three hundred pounds. Dave felt soft and slippery, George could barely get a grip on his shoulders, as if he had been rolled in butter and then bolted to the floor. Despite himself, he pushed harder, straining. The head lolled against his chest, the small massive body rotated barely. The two sisters snickered. George felt duly humiliated and also, strangely, that this was deserved. "Push harder," said the other man. George stopped pushing.

Slugfest

"What kind of name is Kill?"

"Just one 'l.'" George usually did the laundry, but Shelley had been emptying his shirt pockets – why? he wondered – and had found the note Kil Eun-Jee had passed him at the karaoke bar.

"Whatever."

"It's just a name. Like Smith."

"Smith is like Kill?" They were looking at two different names in their heads, and he couldn't change her spelling. She had her hands on her hips.

"It is if you don't know the words."

A simmering silence followed. They retreated to opposite corners of the small apartment. Like most long-time couples, they argued with the practised rhythms of boxers, in rounds with inviolable rest periods in between. The combat itself took many forms: dancing, feinting, jabbing, slugging, hugging and resting. Or someone could drop his or her gloves suddenly, inexplicably, inviting the knockout punch.

"What do you think of me?" She was standing in the doorway. Why did she have to be in a doorway? he thought, with a sudden opaque fear. He put down what he had been doing, writing cheques to various creditors, while she repeated the question.

What right did he have to speak the truth? Lying seemed more defensible at the moment. But he began anyway. "You've let yourself go." An emptiness, a soft vacancy, came into her face. "At times you seem to have given up already. At thirty-nine." He could feel himself using these complaints as ladder rungs to climb toward an impossible statement. Finally he reached it. "I don't love you any more." It had to be the truth.

She went to her sister's in Brampton. At least it was closer to where she worked. Her new smile was soaked in irony. There had been no more scenes after the last one.

Word-of-Mouth

Dave was smiling broadly. "Each of us is a master of his own –" He sought for a word and then gestured at June. She knew it. "Discipline," Dave repeated.

They were standing by the front door. George had his coat on.

"You can learn any language," Dave declared, with how much intentional absurdity George could only guess.

He groped behind himself for the doorknob. Then, on impulse, he opened his briefcase and retrieved a piece of paper and a pen. Quickly and accurately, he made the series of strokes May and June had taught him. "Good fortune," he said, handing it to Dave.

Dave was a controlled man. His only reaction was the abrupt extinction of his smile, as though a candle had been blown out. It came back, but flickeringly, beset by an inner breeze. He turned and went down the hall.

George felt the brass of the doorknob, a cold globe; he just had to turn it. May and June were whispering, darting hurt glances up at him. Well, he had betrayed them. He knew, in a general way, what the character must mean, even if he couldn't translate it exactly. *Fuck? Fuck me?* Probably it was less aggressive, almost innocent. *Sex. Make baby.*

Then Dave was coming back, his face dense as a storm cloud. He advanced swiftly upon them. George assumed he was about to be given the complete demo.

What Dave did, in fact, was hand him his business card. Characters and numbers on a cardboard rectangle. *Fax* and a number added in pen. George inclined his head, but had nothing to give in return. He had no card. His business was strictly word-of-mouth.

With a groan of relief, he sealed himself in his car and switched on the ignition, windshield wipers, and Mix 98 (Oldies and The New). The eastern peace. He had to admit he didn't understand it. The comfortably slumped body, the calm eyes, took on another aspect as he watched them in memory. What he was seeing looked very much like what he would call stubbornness. Could it be a basic difference between east and west? He considered the possibility cautiously. Prejudice and stereotypes lay that way, but perhaps some truth as well. He was a western man, desperate to fly by any means, guile definitely not excluded, and as he drove down the drizzling road he puzzled over why anyone would deliberately court the forces pulling him back to earth.

Friends

Howard had been a lot of things. Had started being a lot of things anyway. A film studies major. A law student. He was one of those who became a teacher in order to have a steady platform from which to make leaps into the unknown, certain he will land somewhere safe again. Grey-haired now, he was thinking of applying for medical school. "Before the door closes." These days, there were some Doc U's that counted life experience almost as much as marks.

One day in May, George met him for coffee at the Manulife Centre. They sat at a wobbly little table with their cappuccinos. "Okay, so play doctor," George said.

"What do you mean?"

"C'mon, I know you. What've you been reading?" George did know Howard. "Reading up," in its preliminary phase of dreaming and loose associations, was what he did best, what he started things for.

Howard looked sheepish. "Geez." Then, with a frown of retrieval, he was off. "Well, I've been doing some reading on neurology. Brain anatomy and function. There's this little gizmo called the 'hippocampus,' which is sort of a mystery. I mean, it's involved in higher and lower functions in ways nobody understands exactly. The name comes from the Latin for seahorse. Actually, the Greek: '*hippos*,' horse, and '*kampos*,' monster. Some of those early anatomists must have been pretty wired to see a seahorse in a little bulge of grey matter."

Howard paused, and took a long sip of warm coffee. "You sound like a doctor," George said, untruthfully. A doctor would have bypassed the whimsical etymology and the wired anatomists for the serious memory work. Howard relaxed visibly. His shoulders sagged with a naturalness that would have pleased Dave.

"How's Shelley doing?" he asked.

George hesitated, then confided in the pseudo-doctor.

"I feel guilty, somehow."

"In what sense?"

"In the sense –" What was the sense? "In the sense of collaborating with the forces bringing her down."

"That sounds pretty abstract."

"It isn't. Not at all."

They left soon after that. Howard had himself on a schedule and had to get back to studying. George walked along Bloor Street; paper litter was eddying in semi-tropical funnels of air. Leaving friends, he often felt vaguely depressed. He made friends quickly, had found them wherever he lived; but, after seeing them, his dominant impression was of not knowing, or being known by, them. At times this could feel invigorating. It was like the bitter freedom he had sniffed reading Camus for the first time. But that was twenty years ago, and nowadays the scent was more elusive, its hints more apt to frighten than inspire.

Homeland

The coloured cranes, which he moved to safe places but did not discard, were like confetti thrown at the marriage of need and speed. He thought of the jets whizzing overhead, full of tourists, businessmen, students, the intercontinental flux. Seekers in their early twenties who thought nothing of stopping in Toronto *on their way* to Europe. The planet was small, but wind-swept.

He took out his datebook. The last page was graffitied with phone numbers. He looked at them, not sure which was the one he needed. The numerals swam, changed places. Finally he tried one:

Hello. I have returned to my homeland. If you want to talk to me you can reach me there. I hope you will contact me.

The hiss of tape unspooling after this was not a mistake. George realized this as he listened to it. The moving silence was full of whispers, of ghost voices, a conversational wind, decipherable if one had the key. Patience was the key, as was desire. Something else? No one had forgotten anything.

TIM ROGERS

Watch

At the instant of his father's death the noise of the world is halved. The heart of the world continues to beat: Tk'kanu's nephew, Oloro, maintains his tattoo on the minor drum, marking time for the practical purposes of the village. But the voice of the major drum, the sound that moves the feet of the hunters and the arms of the young wives pounding the grain and the circles of children spiralling about the small huts, the sound of the blood of the world turning its great wheel, which has not skipped a beat in Ppeprek's lifetime, has stilled at last and left an absence in the air.

Tk'kanu finds the boy by the still pool with his thumbs in his ears, crouched at the edge of the water, his eyes tightly shut, his lips pursed in a narrow pucker. When Tk'kanu calls his name, he does not respond. In the pool Tk'kanu observes a series of concentric ripples moving across the surface. They lap at the boy's toes in steady intervals. The ripples are caused by the branches of an overhanging *banja*, which taps the surface of the pond with drops of water from the evening's storm. The storms arrive and fade with a long but regular periodicity. Earlier they patterned the jungle with a complicated percussion of wind and falling branches, which has faded to leave this simple rhythm of the *banja* and the water drop and the waves and the little boy's toes.

Tk'kanu touches Ppeprek's elbow. The boy opens his eyes, and looks through the ripples to the holy man's reflection in the water.

"What are you doing, *ojo*?" asks Tk'kanu.

"I am listening," says Ppeprek.

The man nods.

"Come with me," he says.

They walk along a narrow path with which Ppeprek is unfamiliar. It leads away from the village and toward the sea. They walk for many thousand strides. Tk'kanu takes long steps with an easy measure, his feet whispering on the hard-packed earth: *shuf shuf shuf*. Ppeprek's paces are shorter, two for each of the tall man's, and his heels punch the ground like small fists. Together, they make a beat with the night drums in the village: *shupat pat shupat pat shupat pat*. The shadows of the trees around them swell like sea foam, until all Ppeprek can see of his guide is the gleam of the white bones strung around his neck and ankles. Occasionally a long, low keening stretches through the branches.

"*Daja*, what is that sound?" asks the boy.

"That is the jungle. It is mourning your father."

When the moon has reached its zenith Tk'kanu stops. He stares into the sky and rubs the back of his neck.

"A long walk," he mutters. "Are you tired?"

Ppeprek says nothing. The holy man sighs. From the bag on his shoulder he withdraws a small pouch and tips it to his lips. Then he hands it to the boy. Ppeprek drinks slowly. The liquid is cold and hot. He chews it like meat, swallows in a great gasp. He is drinking his father's spirit. The potion stretches long fingers through the length of his limbs.

"More," he says when he can speak. But the flask has disappeared into Tk'kanu's bag.

"We must continue," the old man says.

They walk on until the smooth feel of the path beneath Ppeprek's small feet gives way to the texture of twigs and vine. Tk'kanu seems to be listening for something. Ppeprek is concentrating on the jungle: very faintly he can hear the shorebirds calling their names, and he knows the moon has started down its hill. Even the cats have stopped their screaming. The only movement is the scurry of the night animals on their paths beneath the leaves, safe from the eyes of preying birds.

"Can you hear the drums?" asks Tk'kanu.

Ppeprek says, "Only in my mind, *daja*."

And the blackness splits open for a moment to show the white of Tk'kanu's teeth.

They search for a *banja* tree with branches close to the ground, but tall enough that the big cats cannot reach the apex. In the canopy of branches overhead Ppeprek sees his ancestors. The greyest light of early morning glints off their bones. Tk'kanu slings a cord around the lowest branch and pulls himself into the tree, then holds out his bony hand for Ppeprek. But the boy prefers to grip the bole with his feet, and clamber upward like a *chono*. He climbs swiftly, giddy with the liquor and lack of sleep, laughing at the ponderousness of the priest below him.

"Look at me, Tk'kanu! I am a spirit! I am my father's ghost, going to live with the moon!" He climbs until he feels the branches begin to bend slightly beneath his bare feet. In the village, it is *doli*-drum: *shuf-thuk shuf-thukka*. It is the sound the goats of the moon make pulling their master's old cart across the lip of the sea. The little boy sits in the crook of the branch and slaps the beat on his thighs and laughs. He feels its pulse in the webs between his fingers and in the joints of his knees. In the next tree he can see the empty sockets of his ancestors' eyes, two deep wells in the dark forest.

"I am coming," calls the priest.

Puffing steadily, the old man pulls himself to his feet on a branch beneath Ppeprek, so that his eyes are level with the boy's. From his sack he pulls a length of cloth, which he proceeds to wrap around Ppeprek's head, starting with the eyes and entwining first the tight black curls of hair, the bulge of forehead, and then winding it back down over his soft face. He ties a knot below Ppeprek's nose while the boy giggles and tries not to lose his balance in the tree.

"Hold still," says the priest.

He reaches again into his bag and this time brings forth a leaf, folded into a small package. He unwraps it to reveal two small balls of wax.

"You will tell me," he says to Ppeprek, "when you know."

Ppeprek nods and squirms. Tk'kanu pushes the little balls into the boy's ears. The sound of the drum inside Ppeprek's chest swells and fills his head. He thinks, I have the ocean inside me. The ocean with the sun gripped in its fingers. I will listen to the sound of the ocean in me opening its greedy fists and letting go the sun, and I will know.

From where he stands Tk'kanu can see the stone-coloured waters of the sea lightening with the coming dawn. He can see the secret spot between the ocean's thighs, where it will birth the sun. Ppeprek has selected a fine tree – taller than its neighbours, with sturdy branches mounting almost to the top. In this spot, if all goes well, the bones of Ppeprek's father, Pelerek, will rest until the end, safe from the scavenging cats and a small step toward the throne of god. A fitting resting-place, Tk'kanu believes. If on the other hand Ppeprek should fail, Pelerek's shell will be buried in the worm-eaten soil to feed the jungle – to feed, perhaps, the very tree in which they are waiting. Tk'kanu looks around him, and sees the bones in the branches, the ancient faces watching him. And the moss and creepers that caress the old skulls. All around him are the arms of the weak holding up the bones of the strong toward heaven.

The priest draws from his bag a pinch of dried seeds, and pops them into his mouth. The taste is bitter and secret, the blood of trees. Tk'kanu feels his heart slow. The jungle peels away on all sides of him. The last handful of stars falls from the sky like ashes. He hears a joyous music coming from deep within him. He sees the crown of the old god in his mind's eye: a bright line like a golden stitch between sea and sky. Tk'kanu fancies he can see the curve of the old man's head rising from the water. In his mind he is counting the drum. The numbers are sounds in the jungle. The sky is brightening. Ppeprek is standing, blind and deaf, reaching his hands toward the sea and smiling broadly. The first rays of sunrise illuminate his young face.

"It is time," he says. "The sun is rising."

And Tk'kanu's spirit returns to him in an instant, bearing gifts, he feels his feet have sprouted wings, he loves, he sweeps the small boy into his thin arms and crushes the little body to his chest.

When they stumble into the village, the midday drums have finished. Along the perimeter the children are chasing through
the foliage, beating one another with sticks and laughing and
collecting nuts in their shirts to bring back to the women who
will grind them with blunt stones into a thick paste. The men
are passing from hut to hut, huddled in close conversation,
smoking their small wooden pipes. Inside the shelters Ppeprek
imagines his name being tested by the bearded lips, imagines
hooded eyes peering from behind the leather flaps.

In his mother's hut, the attending ladies are gathered in a
circle, preparing the drum. Mumbawe, his mother, has removed
the skin from his father's carcass in a single piece. She has used
the old knife, the stone one that has been in the village as long
as Old Onnon, but which is still sharper than the foolish metal
daggers Oloro and the others receive in trade from the strangers
on the fringes of the jungle.

Standing in the doorway, Ppeprek remembers a time in the
past. His father tossing him high in the air over the river, allow-
ing him to drop like rain into the water, the old man making
time with palms on broad thighs to see how long Ppeprek can
stay under. Then tickling him under his arm, tracing a line from
pit to hipbone. Here is where they will open me when my spirit
has gone to the wood. His finger is blunt like a walking stick, the
horned nail leaving a white trail behind it, a path on Ppeprek's
dark skin leading toward the future. And along here, he says,
dragging the claw down Ppeprek's leg, then up the inside of his
little thigh. And here. He slaps the tiny penis. Ppeprek squeals,
horrified and ticklish. This will never happen to his father. But
Ppeprek has seen the big drum, his grandfather's hide with the
tattoo from his wrinkled shoulder now spread spiderlike across
the timepiece. He fancies he can hear the ancient's growl in the
drum's low rumble when his father's broad thumbs spin out the
evening beat. Then down the other leg, says Pelerek, unzipping
Ppeprek's flesh with his thumbnail. And the same on top. Now
he illustrates on his own body, running this imaginary blade
from armpit along the thick trunk of his arm, around the fingers,
back up over the biceps and shoulder, along that dark, corded
neck and over the top of his specked black-and-white head.

Then the same down the other shoulder, the other arm. So only this is left uncut, he says, indicating the ebony strip along his right torso, down the side of his leg: heavily muscled, shiny with sea water and sweat, ribs beneath his big arm like hills and valleys. Do you see? Ppeprek loving his father, wanting to be ticked again, or thrown in the water. He can hold his breath now, he's a big boy. But his father's gaze is tangled in the tree. He is listening to his rhythm, or watching the future. Watching the place where Ppeprek is now, and looking through the eyes of his son at the fat women hunched over his mortal remains with their stone knife, bone needles, gossip. Then, Ppeprek, they will unfold me, like a blanket, and underneath will be this drum in my chest, and my bones which you must honour, and all the stink and meat that is the necessary evil of this world. And you will make a new drum. Do you see?

Those fingers, strong and thick as cane trees. In the end, withered and cracked open, anticipating the knife. But still tapping with their perfect rhythm, still marking the time even as it ran out. Now the fingers are boneless. Hanging from a line across the low hut, they flutter in the hot air from the fire. Mumbawe will slit them into thin strips and use them as twine to bind the skin to its wood frame. After the fat has been stripped off and burned, and the bones purified in the fire, and the heart dried into a wizened stone. The hide will be stretched around the wooden hoop Ppeprek prepared with his father's guidance. The weather will dry it and draw it taut, make it sonorous. It will be a year before Ppeprek hears its first sound. If it is well made, it will speak with his father's voice.

"Scratch, you devil," barks an old lady who has spotted him hovering among the animal skins in the door. "You shouldn't be here." Her voice is harsh but her face is jovial. She is carrying a basket filled with offal toward the fire. Mumbawe looks up for a moment from her bloody hands; she is not angry, only tired.

"Go away, Ppeprek," she says. "This is not a place for children."

"I'm not a child," says Ppeprek. "I've been on a watch. I brought up the sun. I'm Tk'kanu's apprentice."

The attending ladies are silent. Mumbawe turns back to the hide, kneading it with her strong hands and then scraping it with a rough shell.

"I expect I shall be moving to the priest's hut," says Ppeprek.

"Go away, now, boy," says Mumbawe. She does not look up.

Back at the still pool he finds Olbek and the other apprentices lying on the jungle floor like sleepy leopards. Olbek is smoking a pipe and laughing at something someone has said. The sound is disrespectful. These bad boys have been swimming in the pool and have muddied its waters. Still, Ppeprek stands and watches them shyly. Olbek notices the boy standing in the tall ferns, and flings a stone at him without bothering to rise.

"Away, *chono*," he says lazily. "This is a man's place."

"I am," Ppeprek says. "I brought out the sun this morning." Somebody laughs. Olbek spits into the pond with a disgusted look.

"I mean a man, *chono*, not some day-old apprentice's helper three drum beats away from his mother's tit." The older boy suddenly springs to his feet. He is much taller than Ppeprek, and stout. He curls his arm before Ppeprek's face and flexes his biceps. It makes a round lump like a *bolo*-nut. "Feel that," he says. Ppeprek gingerly slaps the muscle. It feels like a ball of clay, half dry from the sun. "Your arms are little sticks, boy. A man's arms are made of stone. Do you smoke?"

"Yes," Ppeprek lies.

"I don't see your pipe. Perhaps you left it in your mother's hut, with your other toys."

The apprentices laugh, and Ppeprek flushes. Olbek draws deeply from his own small pipe. He is an older apprentice, but still too young to smoke. He must have stolen the vessel.

"At least I am not a thief," Ppeprek ventures.

Olbek folds his arms and considers, puffing thoughtfully. "A feisty one," he pronounces after a moment. "Sit down with us, *chono*, and I will tell you the story of how I got this pipe. And perhaps you will learn to appreciate the difference between a man and a smart-aleck little boy.

"This was in the dry season during the Sly Moon, when the old man's face is all but hidden in the heavens," Olbek begins.

"The still pool had dwindled to little more than a puddle, and the river had slowed to a trickle. The hunting was poor – the healthy animals had departed to more fertile climates – all that were left were those too weak to follow their herds, and the cats were at war over even these diseased few. The hunter's apprentices were sent farther and farther into the east to search for evidence of game. We were not to pursue anything – it was too far for a single man to bring anything back – only to search for spoor, and report to the master hunters so that they might not waste their energies in infertile territory.

"Most of the others had followed the usual path of migration for the *chalen* – the great herd left a trail even a simpleton could track, and apprentices were in great spirits, viewing their mission as an easy holiday away from their masters, sneaking skins of liquor and pinches of smokeroot from their betters for consumption on the trail.

"You see, little *chono*, this is the way that boys think.

"I did not follow the most obvious trail. This particular dry season had lasted longer than any other – I had listened to Old Oloro imploring the sun to release its hold on the earth, and I had listened to the council in which your father, Ppeprek, voiced the opinion that the hunt would not be successful. I decided I could be of no use if I joined the bigger group, and instead proceeded toward the southeast.

"For several days I moved in that direction, and was disappointed. I saw no spoor, no track – not even from the cats, which indicated that there was unlikely to be any large game in the vicinity. Furthermore, I had lost the sound of the drum from the village after the first day, and had no timekeeper's apprentice to accompany me, as did the larger party that went north. With only the sun to indicate the time, I grew disoriented. I did not know how to ration my preserves, how long to march. My nerves were restless. The jungle was extremely quiet, as though all other living creatures had fled or died. I was ready to give up and circle back to the north in hopes of joining the others when I came upon an unusual track.

"It was an indentation like the hoof of a *chala*, but sunk deep into the jungle floor, indicating it to be a heavy beast. I say like

a *chala*'s hoof because it was the same general size and place-
ment – there were four limbs, the front pair seven hands from
the rear. What was unusual was the shape of the print – perfectly
curved, like the arc of a doorway, with no split and no claw. It
looked as though a priest had carved these indentations in the
ground with his marking-stick. But there was no question they
were the track of a beast.

"I decided to follow them – they were not difficult to detect,
even in the dark. They smelled faintly of blood. I soon discovered
that more than one such animal had passed this way – perhaps
as many as four, walking in a line. But not a herd. Maybe a
harem, I thought, like the packs of screaming cats that travel
together in small groups, and attack as one.

"By the moisture of the depressed earth, I could determine
that the tracks were not old, and that indeed the creatures,
whatever they were, were not moving quickly. I don't know
how long I followed the trail – I had no way of knowing. The
moon was kind to me, and I continued long after the sun had
died. I continued until I heard voices."

Olbek pauses to relight his pipe, and a nervous murmur runs
through the boys. "Voices!" exclaims Avarek. "What were they
saying?"

"There is no way to know. They were not human voices –
they were gibberish. It hurt my ears to listen to them. Also,
there were other sounds – I can't describe. Like the village
drums, and the keening of women, mixed together. It was very
faint, almost a dream. But it was not a dream.

"Looking ahead, I glimpsed the light of a fire, and my first
thought was that the sounds were coming from the flame. But
as I grew closer, I could make out shapes huddled around the
light. Dark shapes, in the form of men, but not men, clustered
around an ordinary fire."

"Black devils," Lembek hisses. Olbek stares at him, then
nods soberly.

"The strange voices were coming from the figures. But the
other sound seemed to be in the air itself. There was no
drummer keeping the time, and no woman. Just the three shapes
and the fire. I crept closer. There was hardly any breeze, but I

made sure to stay downwind. The devils gave off a powerful stench. I stayed low to the ground, and kept to the shadows, and was able to make my way to the very edge of the ring of light thrown from the fire. I saw their faces."

"What did they look like?" asks one of the boys. Olbek seems to consider for a moment.

"They were pale like the bellies of fish, and covered in hair. The tops of their heads were wrapped in black cloth, as were the rest of their bodies. It was hard to detect their shape beneath the coverings – I determined that they were like men, but with enormous black wings."

"Wings?" Avarek squeaks. "Could they fly?"

"I didn't see. The wings hung down from their shoulders and were tucked among the folds of black cloth. I watched them for what seemed to be a long time. I saw that one of them was smoking a pipe, just like an ordinary man. He was smaller, this one, and moved nervously. He had an ornament around his neck, two sticks crossed, which he could not stop touching with his white fingers.

"After some time the fire had dwindled, and the devils began to prepare for sleep. One of them brought forth a black box, with a sort of a funnel sprouting out the top, and I learned that it was from this that the ghostly drum-sounds issued. The devil touched the box, and the sounds stopped. The three of them got down upon their knees and chanted together in their strange tongue. Then they lay down on the ground and folded their wings about them, and went to sleep.

"I have no way of knowing how long I waited. The fire had died to a few embers, and the moon had disappeared from the sky. But the stars were still out. I felt as though a season had passed!

"I began to creep around the perimeter of the little camp. I could smell animal scent, different from the stench of the black devils, and it made me hungry. A little distance from my hiding place near the fire, I discovered its source. Three large beasts, bigger than *chalen*, stood tethered with strips of leather to a *banja* tree. I froze and tested the wind, then slowly moved into the shadows again. I needn't have bothered. The animals were the most foolish creatures I have ever seen. I was able to approach close enough to touch them, and they showed no concern. I could have butchered them at that moment, but I feared waking the devils. Also, I had no way of bringing the meat back to the village.

"Instead I made my way back to the smouldering fire. One of the devils had begun to snore like an old man, and this slowed my heart somewhat. To this point it had been pounding like the feasting drum! There is no shame in admitting it. The sleep-sounds of this black devil helped me to recover my wits.

"I had with me a bow and a quiver, a sling, some rope for trapping, a knife, some small stones. Nothing for large game, and nothing for a stealthy kill. I was afraid that if I simply slit their throats, the death rattle of the first would wake the others.

"The devils had made camp in a small clearing scattered here and there with large stones. I picked up one of these and carded it toward the sleeping creatures. I was particularly drawn to the one who had been smoking, as he seemed more frail than the others. I waited until the snoring demon made one of his sounds – the fiend was as loud as a thunderstorm! – and then lifted the stone above me, and brought it down on the other's head. It made a sound like a *bolo*-nut cracking. I poised to flee. But neither of the others stirred. The snoring continued without disruption. I checked to see that the devil was slain. Certainly he wasn't moving, and when I rolled the rock to the side I saw that his brains had been dashed out.

"I was beginning to lose my fear of these creatures – they seemed foolish and impotent to me. For this reason, I didn't move on to the others, but began to rummage through the layers of black cloth, searching for the pipe I had seen. It was tucked inside a fold of cloth, next to his chest. I pulled it out and inspected it, then stowed it in my sack. I discovered that the devils were not, in fact, black, but that beneath their clothes – there was a ridiculous amount of clothing – their entire bodies were pale, like their faces, and sprouting with little dark hairs like an ape. For a brief moment, I suspected that they were not devils at all, but instead some primitive kind of man.

"It was then that I discovered the creature was not dead after all."

Again Olbek pauses to fuss with his pipe, which refuses to stay lit. The air is curiously still and nobody makes a sound. Ppeprek can feel his ancestors running their bony fingers through his hair.

"Its heart was still beating," Olbek resumes. "It was a queer sound, like the clacking of sticks, but more regular than even the master drums in the village. It was coming from his body. I was filled with terror, but did not move. Very slowly, I pressed my ear to his chest. There could be no doubt. I felt a lump there, tangled in his clothes. With a trembling hand, I reached inside the cloth, and pulled out his heart!

"It was perfectly unnatural – the shape of a ripple of water, and the colour of gold. Its front was inscribed with the markings of a priest. It continued to beat in my palm as I stared at it – I could feel it quivering and vibrating in an unholy fashion. I felt sick. I couldn't let it go. I held the man's beating heart in my fist and struggled not to throw up.

"I realized, of course, that these were enchanted men – that what I held was the talisman of some powerful magician that had animated and perhaps enslaved the heart of the malformed animal-man lying at my feet.

"Finally I flung the disgusting thing to the ground. It cracked open, and for a moment I saw a tiny village inside – circles of circles intertwined like dancing children, and moving under their own power. I cried out and stomped the thing with my heel. It shattered, and cut my foot.

"My cry awoke the other devils. They were now stirring, gibbering in their evil tongue, rising to their feet, their black wings curling around them.

"I yelled again and leapt right over the fire, running as fast as ever I have in my life into the jungle. I didn't notice my bleeding foot until I was far away. It was sheer accident that I ran in the correct direction. I imagined those enchanted beings flying over the trees behind me, seeking revenge. Worse, I imagined the headless one, the one I thought I had slain, with his hideous heart dangling about his neck, following behind me.

"Eventually I reached the mud-bed that, in happier times, was the river, and that brought me to my senses. I stopped to catch my breath. I washed my foot in the trickle of water that remained, drank, determined my position. The sun was rising and it pointed the way home. I rummaged in my sack to inspect my rations, for I was very hungry now that the panic had left me.

"I realized I still had the demon's pipe. Inside the bag."

Olbek draws deeply, and blows a cloud of smoke at Ppeprek's face.

Later – after the celebrations are over, after Pelerek's bones have been purified and his offal consumed in the fire, and after Mumbawe and her attendants have stopped their keening and have cleaned the ashes and grease from their faces, and after the men have staggered back to their huts, eyes half-lidded and hands wandering, grinning foolishly, arms draped over the shoulders of their wives, and after Tk'kanu has taken up the mourning rhythm on the night drum that he will play without alteration for three days – Ppeprek lies awake in the dark in his new home and thinks about the black devils. He is a little bit drunk from the beer skins passed from hand to hand in the funeral circle. The dark in this hut is different from the familiar blackness of his mother's. He can't see the walls, but he feels their foreign shape carving up the space around him. It distorts the sound of Tk'kanu's drums. The sleeping noises of the other apprentices move in the blackness like animals.

Tk'kanu has been kind to him – leading him from the last embers of the pyre to his small bunk in the timekeeper's hut, kissing his head before he lay down to sleep. Ppeprek told him Olbek's story. The holy man smiled at him.

"Are you afraid these devils will swoop down from the skies and carry you away, *ojo*?" Ppeprek looked at the high bones in the old face, the three remaining teeth in Tk'kanu's smile. The priest touched the curls on his forehead.

"There are no devils, Ppeprek," he said. "Only men, and women. Different kinds of men and women."

But in the darkness Ppeprek sees the dull shine of Olbek's black pipe – the strange sounds in the hut around him and in the jungle are the sounds of black cloth rustling and leather wings beating the air, or the sound of an unnatural heart beating.

When at last he falls asleep, Ppeprek has a curious dream. He will remember this dream through all the years to come: through the best years as an apprentice when the village is still the village and the whole world, and the voice of Pelerek pours through his skinny body with all the naturalness of falling water, and the men and women are in love and the children play at war in small ways and the drum is like the sound of thunder or the sea; and during the frightening time when the new people come for the first time to the council with their faithless gifts and sly talk, without wings but with pale faces, and sleep in the huts and chatter at one another, their harsh voices masking the sounds of the machines strapped to their arms; and at Mumbawe's last moment, when she lies dying, shame-faced and bewildered at her grandchildren's disrespectful looks and strange clothing, their unfamiliar talk, when she pulls Ppeprek's dappled head to her mouth and kisses him dryly, and speaks a word which he no longer understands; and throughout the longest, hardest time, as Ppeprek's childhood friends leave the village and trade their knowledge and crafts for the new machines, the small drums and other charms that will infiltrate Ppeprek's community slowly and inevitably; and when Ppeprek himself leaves his home and his drum and brings only the incessant beat of the jungle and the ghost of his father's voice with him inside his head – through all this burden of time he will carry the memory of this dream with him like a flame.

In it, he is standing at the still pool, watching his reflection. There has been a storm. The jungle is moving and whispering to itself with the wind. Ppeprek is watching the drops from the old *banja* tree, which is twined with vines and covered in moss. In the pool, he sees that he is a man. His arms are thick, his hair is tufted with white. A drop falls and ripples spread across the surface of the water, and Ppeprek can see the village beneath its clear surface, whirling like a marvellous animal. It unfolds itself before him like his father's skin, he can see its tiny figures and their intricate, complicated interactions. Here is Lembek, no longer fat but skeletal, beating the mourning drum. And Oloro, making love to his wife on the banks of the river, and Avarek lying in his hut with a blanket pulled up to his chin.

The sound of the village drum is faint and small, the clacking of sticks. Lembek plays them with a dreadful regularity. Ppeprek watches the funeral fires consuming the bones of Tk'kanu, watches the faces of women covered in ash, listens to the beat of the drum coming from beneath the still waters of the pond, and wonders: Where am I? The smoke from the fire curls into the waters of the still pool like black wings.

To his left he can see the past. Here is Pelerek holding little Ppeprek high over his head, plunging him into the sea, and Mumbawe singing and pressing baby Ppeprek to her breast. Here is Tk'kanu, a young man, beating a strange drum the colour of gold and shaped like a ripple of water, with markings on it like the tracks of an animal. And Ppeprek looks from past to future. In the air is the keening of the women, as it is funeral day. He sees Olbek sitting on the ground, his ear pressed to a black box, a flower growing from the box, a sound coming from the flower, smiling at Ppeprek and blowing smoke from his broad nose. He sees Tk'kanu and the other elders speaking to men wrapped in bundles of cloth. He sees women with ash on their faces, and beneath the ash, skin the colour of fishbellies. Where am I? Am I at home? In mother's hut? Her naked body lies on the floor, unseamed and burning, her hands bloody, buried in her belly. She tells him to go away. She says this is no place for children. He tries to speak to her but the sound of the drums is too loud. Where is he? He is walking in the empty village. The village is burning. On the face of the jungle, the flames cast the silhouette of wings, rustling somewhere behind him. He must find his drum, before it burns. He walks to the timekeeper's hut, where Lembek is standing in strange clothes, ashes covering his face. He is no longer playing, but the sound of sticks clacking is deafening. Ppeprek walks into the timekeeper's hut. He sees his own drum, dried now and well used, covered with dust, hanging in its place of honour by the fire stones. He takes it down and rushes out into the village. The dirt lanes are filled with people wrapped in dark cloth. Their faces are hidden to him. They push him in the wrong direction. He doesn't want to go. He must find his drum. He had it just a moment ago. But he lost it. They are taking it to the pyre. He must hurry, but the crowd is over-whelming. He cannot push forward, and there is so little time.

And while this is happening, he is telling it to old Lembek, the master drummer, somewhere far in the future. They are smoking their pipes, two old men, in an unfamiliar place. He tells Lembek about the crowds pushing him back and the strange colour of their hands and the smell of smokeroot in the air. How the crowd suddenly parts, and he can see the black devils dancing about the bonfire with his drum, and singing in the voices of women. But Ppeprek can't remember what happens next.

"What happens to the drum?" he asks Lembek.

The other man sighs heavily.

"I was never a very good timekeeper," he says sadly. "So I gave it away."

"But I can hear you playing!" Ppeprek protests. And he can: the sound of the village drum is all around him, a perfect beat, a beat like the heart of the world, and Ppeprek feels he can reach out and seize it – is seizing it, is reaching into Lembek's chest and catching hold of this perfect rhythm, this terrible clacking, and he takes the spirit of time in his hand and looks at it while the village burns around him and the black devils descend from a night sky.

It is perfectly golden and shaped like a ripple of water.

HEATHER O'NEILL

Little Suitcase

My mother's younger brother David came back from Romania. He came back with his hair all tangled at the ends in the shapes of hearts, the seat of his pants worn right out, and filled with wild stories about ladies named Rose and Amore. The room got messy around him. He washed his hair in the kitchen sink. The handle of his brush had a red silk scarf tied to it. He had a blue army bag that had a patch of Snoopy on it. He was the only person I knew who had travelled. My mother had been to Spain once. Our road trips were when my mom was running away from my dad. I remember her hair tangled up in the windshields, but a lot of things are impossible.

Now Mom played guitar. She wrote songs about Montreal. She liked snow and the light-bulb cross. She wore a blue T-shirt that said OUT. She had goggle sunglasses. She was good-looking and articulate, but she didn't have what it took to be happy. She sat in the car with groceries counting the change like she had made a terrible mistake.

David had lived with real gypsies. They had wanted to adopt him. He had photographs of them, their heads wrapped in scarves and their arms in the air, trying to get the sun to reflect off their tambourines. The way they looked at the camera, they loved him. He had maybe left his heart there in the greasy forests of Europe because he kept looking for things to be the way they were there. My favourite photograph of the gypsies said June on the back, so that is what I called her. She was so beautiful with her hair parted in the middle and her long nose and her lips like you had to be a singer to kiss her. Her earrings made out of pennies and her shirt a long V-neck down to her breasts. "She is the monarch butterfly of ladies," said David. She had a baby hanging onto her like a brooch. I loved that picture because I had started to feel that it was ugly to look after children lately.

My uncle fell in love with me because he thought I was like a gypsy child playing with the radio dials, trying to balance plates on my head at the same time. He came over in his truck and asked if I wanted to go square dancing. I put my little legs up on the dashboard, letting my dress beat all over the place in the wind. We drove and it was summer and it was lovely and the wind gave me wanderlust too like an apron full of flowers. The heat of the seat made me feel like there were bugs on my thighs so that I kept jerking and kicking my feet up at the front window. I had fancy thoughts about dancing in my head, my toes pressed against the glass sunset. I danced with a lamp at home, the heat of the light bulb kissing my cheek. We drove so long I had to get out of the car and puke once. We drove so long my thoughts started being spare change. We drove so long it was nighttime and it was getting too late for anyone my age to be up so I wouldn't be able to have a dance partner.

There were holes in my shoes and the tongues hung out, threaded like busted basketball nets. My uncle said he had met a woman. She had curly black hair and hung in the door like the cover of a folk album. She wasn't a gypsy. She was a Jew named Marla who had run away from New York City. Her accent was like coffee and a broken window with pretty girls behind it. She loved my uncle. She looked at his hips. He had his pants tied loose with a scarf for a belt way below his belly button so that she could see it. I never had to think about growing up. I stood with my little suitcase at my feet. I loved that little suitcase with its yellow and purple flowers on a polyester cover. I opened it. I wished my mother had remembered the other things that I loved. There were no toys. I sat on the little bed in the living room. A baby bed, with a white blanket and a foam mattress. Someone had drawn Mickey Mouse with a marker on the headboard a long time ago.

I ate a huge bowl of ice cream for breakfast and crawled up on the kitchen table. David pulled the record-player speakers from the living room and balanced them in the dish rack and I danced. My brain was a peephole, looking at myself in a pretty way. My ankles held on to the table as if they were rocking bedposts, and my hands held the ends of my skirt like cups. I would feel like I was a pal with the rest of the world. Just like a kid beggar, who when he is asking for change is really begging for love. And his heart is still as clean as an Andrews sister.

The school was far from where we lived and the truck broke down. The school bus stop was down such a long road that I lost a sense of time. David and I hitchhiked to school. "Wild Petunia Eyes," he called me. "I saw your eyes in Romania. Over there they would draw your eyes on a truck and pull it around with puppets." I knew every bad word from Dad. They were like tattoos. They were on the telephone wire of my memory like crows. But David and I walked hand in hand down the highway speaking gently. We never stuck our thumbs out for the first cars. That would have been unlucky. We were gypsies and gypsies were never in a hurry. David liked talking to the drivers with me on his knee and the window wide open, the wind making an unkindness of ravens out of my eyelashes. He would say that I was his daughter. We used to have the same blue eyes. We used to tell people that we traded them back and forth. He would have his chin up on my forehead like a totem pole. We would usually get to school around noon. One time I had gum stuck in my hair and my uncle said just to leave it there and to tuck it behind my ear. One time I came with a tin can with a minnow in it that we had caught on the way. It swam on my desk all day just like a pretty bullet. The teacher asked me how come I didn't know the Pledge of Allegiance by heart. I told her I had never arrived at school early enough to learn it. My school bag was more of a purse with a rainbow on it. There usually wasn't a lunch there. Once there was a dog-eared postcard of John Lennon that said, "Marla, Keep wild crazy Brooklyn baby." This girl at school gave me Oreo cookies. The teacher brought me an orange.

There were terrible holes all up my stockings one Saturday.

It wasn't that cold but it had been raining and I didn't own any pants. David said that when you are as small as I was holes are cute. He showed me a picture book of 1940s dancing girls. He said that they all had holes in their stockings. He said that gypsies have holes on everything that they wear. David knew about a formidable number of things. Some people just have pressed flowers in the pages of their minds. We were going for a drive in Marla's car. I fell asleep in the front seat folded up like a Kleenex box. I loved falling asleep in a car because when I woke up we would be wherever we were going after only two seconds. When I woke up this time David had picked up a girl. She had long blonde hair. She had a blue shirt with forget-me-nots drawn with a Bic pen. She was smiling. She was playing with my hair.

Marla left David because of the blonde girl. She ran away like the circus. I watched her from the window upstairs with my toes pressed hard against the wall. All she had to take with her was a silkscreen bag with a Degas painting of ballet dancers and a car that was almost a gold colour whose roof was covered with fallen leaves the shapes of eyes. She was a true spirit because she didn't need to pack anything. There were some plates on the bed table with blue birds, their wings spread out wide on either side. I threw them out the window for her to take with her. They broke and Marla cried.

The house we lived in had been moved from North Carolina after the Civil War. I don't know why. There was nothing special about it. The porch was messed up like a see-through container of straws. Rain fell through the roof all over the house. At night I could hear the ghosts. They rattled doorknobs or a plate of macaroni moved across the table. I was afraid of the dark but I was never afraid of the ghosts. They seemed so ordinary and they minded their own business. They crossed their legs, scratched at their nylons, and chewed on their nail polish, fantasizing about the mistakes they made in the city. They tried to feel sexy because they couldn't see their reflections any more. They turned on the radio. They sat on the toilet bowl and contemplated the lyrics of songs they couldn't figure out exactly. Some ghosts moved out if you quit smoking. The ghosts who came back from Vietnam smoked butts from ashtrays. After living there six months, I pretended David and Marla were my mom and dad. Sometimes I felt alone. I felt like I was a little ghost too. When it was raining through the roof and the humidity curled my hair above my ears I liked to believe I was dead from the 1920s.

David borrowed a car that rattled and we drove into Richmond. We slept in a hotel on the outskirts of the city. I slept in a single bed with David. The wallpaper was striped like pyjamas but we slept in our clothes. In the room next door there was a lot of noise. The people were moaning. I tied my hair on top of my head with a pipe cleaner. I had asked David if there was anything to eat and he had given me some quarters for the vending machine. I bought a Coke and then I couldn't go to sleep. I pretended I was sleepwalking in my sundress with frills like a circular apple peel. I walked to the lobby. Outside through the glass front door I could see a whore. She was dressed in yellow and she had huge lips and her high heels made it so that her bust was jutting right out. You could tell she was enjoying the moon. It was a lonely night in any part of this town. The man in the lobby told me that the whores who come out of the mental asylum turn their tricks here. If they had any common sense they would go some place busier. She is like Christmas lights in the summertime. Everybody is a little out of place in the night-time. The crickets are screaming something terrible. Cheap, cheap, cheap.

I headed to the hotel bathroom. I hadn't taken a bath in a long time. Hot water scared me. It made me feel like I was being buried in a television. But my hair was starting to feel funny. Thick and the shade of green sunglasses near my scalp. I didn't know what happened to you if you didn't wash for such a period of time. It just seemed like everybody washed. There were little pink roses painted all over the bathroom walls. The pipes had a sound that a needle makes when it gets to the end of a record. I had all the songs it had played in my head. I sang, "Bonga, bonga, bonga, I don't wanna leave the Conga, no, no, no, no, no . . ." to the roses on the wall like they were little girls in an audience. I was starting to like this hotel and thinking about us spending our whole lives there. I picked a porno magazine up off the toilet basin. I brought it under the bath water and stared at the girls like they were mermaids. If I sat quietly and didn't splash I could hear a man's voice from upstairs talking about prison.

I liked the train tracks. They looked like a shoelace that had untied itself for miles and miles. David would take me down there so that I could look at the bums. There was a lovely little shantytown with an American flag out front. I didn't know how to pledge allegiance to this flag either. There was broken glass that night like a tide brought in. And glossy magazine pictures of more mermaids were floating around too.

This hippie, Quentin, who smelt like piss all the way to the back of your throat, lived there. He had tall boots and grey lips. David said he went to college with him. David liked the bums too, I knew. He liked to talk to them because they had nothing to lose so they would be apt to say psychic things. Sometimes David brought his camera. He took pictures of me too. The living room was covered with pictures of me with his girlfriends, pictures of me with bums, pictures of me dancing, pictures of me lying in grass, pictures of me reading, pictures of me sleeping. I guessed it was great to be loved that much.

David was having a beer while creepy Quentin played his fiddle. It was skinny like a leg but it sounded like a dancer. David sang: "Jesus, Jesus, Jesus. The girl from Laredo is bothering me. I'll never trade my wandering ways for that perfect girl from Laredo again." I played with my porcelain doll, tying her little shoes. I made her do some erotic things with her hands that I saw in the magazine but then I felt bad that I had polluted her. I kissed her on the forehead and we went to look for the white rocks I collected. Sometimes I spotted a syringe like a shrimp between them. David gave me a swig of beer and this trembling from the tracks went right up my legs, making me feel like I had to pee and my head turned into glass marble at the same time. I fell over, breaking off my doll's hand. Quentin said me falling over like that was a bad omen. It meant that our lives weren't going to stay like they were much longer.

There was this way the moon had of glowing like a clean sheet. Every time I blinked, a new star came out so fast. At seven you can't remember much of your past. I couldn't remember

what my real dad looked like any more. It had only been a year
since I saw him. David carried me home on his shoulders. My
doll sat on his head. My pockets were heavy with rocks. They
came down like donkey's ears around his head. David handed me
an Oreo cookie from his pocket. I pulled the sides apart and
made them have a conversation.

"You are so pretty, I would never leave you."

"Will you be my little mama?"

"Yes, why not?"

"You are the colour of a cast-iron pan."

"And you are the colour of the black night."

"Your eyes are like two balloons let go up in the night."

"Oh thank you, sweetheart."

"Thank you, sweetheart."

David grinned and the straw he was chewing on pointed up
at the setting sun that was as pink as Lolita's pyjamas. David
said when he put me to bed, "You are my duffel bag of dreams.
Have fun in Australia." Every night he said a different place.

SUSAN RENDELL

In the Chambers of the Sea

The air on the ward is hot and dry, and tastes like sand. Not that I have ever tasted sand, at least not since I was a child in a soft, sandy country, far from here.

In the cruel days of August, when the city became an asphalt oven, my mother and my sister and I would go off to the pretty little beaches, the domestic beaches of my childhood country. We would lie on the backs of their tame dunes and scuff along in the deep bone-white sand that was farthest from the sea, bending now and then to retrieve the half-buried remnants of dead sea babies: solemn little periwinkle cases, tiny bumps of limpet shells, stiff pieces of pink starfish. And bits of mother-of-pearl from the big mussel shells, which my sister and I pretended were solidified mermaid pee.

My favourites were the sand dollars. Every sand dollar, from the largest to the smallest, had a perfect flower etched on it, and I used to imagine that God's wife spent the long summer days making them in her shop in Heaven. At night She came down and tucked them, one by one, into the soft brown sand just under the lip of the sea, for me to find. (Like stars, sand dollars make it easy for a child to believe in God: look, there is a pattern, and another, and another. He must be!)

I took dozens of sand dollars home every summer. But after a few days they would start to rot, and by the end of the week they would have been consigned by my mother to the big aluminum garbage can. This made me bitter, as bitter as a child is able to be; I felt betrayed. I didn't know then that the sand dollars had been alive when I picked them from the sea, and that the flowers of the sea will not, cannot, take root in a suburban backyard.

The air in the hospital burns our eyes and flakes our skin. No one wears their contact lenses any more, and bottles of skin cream are handed around like whiskey at an Irish wake. The air is so dry because they nailed all the windows shut two weeks after I got here, when a young man jumped to his death from one of the other floors. He landed on a ledge outside my room, about a yard or so up from it. It was early in the morning, just before daybreak. Two nurses ran into my room and nearly ripped the blinds down from the window. "Sweet Jesus," said one to the other. "Can you see it?" And then they turned around. I was sitting up, groggy with sleeping-pill sleep, but already aching for a cigarette. "You'll have to get up, my duck," said the red-haired one. "We'll open up the smoking room for you." I asked what was going on, but they wouldn't tell me. I didn't really care anyway; the smoking room was to be opened, and I could sit and look out its east-facing window and watch the sun come up, if it was going to.

While I smoked I leafed through old copies of *Reader's Digest* and waited to be allowed back into my room. (It Pays to Increase Your Word Power; in the Beginning was the Word, and the Word was God. But what was the Word: Was it *Love*? *Om*? Was it *Good-bye*?)

Early that afternoon they summoned us to a grief therapy session. It was conducted by some nurses and a specialist in grief, a large woman in a suit; her hair was also wearing a suit, and her eyes were buttoned up tight. She introduced herself and then told us that a man, a young man, had "suicided." He had jumped from the seventh floor, she said, and had landed, dying on impact, on the ledge projecting from the west side of our ward ("Western wind, when will thou blow,/ The small rain down can rain?/ Christ, if my love were in my arms/ And I in my bed again!"). The grief lady talked about the need for us to come to terms with the "terrible thing." I recited the Leigh Hunt's poem "Rondeau" over and over in my head while she talked. "Jenny kissed me when me met," Jenny kissed me, Jenny kissed me.

The grief lady said we should share our thoughts and feelings, and "vent if you need to." We patients are always being encouraged to "vent"; indeed, we are ordered to vent, at least biweekly. This process of venting is as intricate as a minuet: it must be done in front of a group, it must be done one person at a time, it must never contain anger or sarcasm or be directed at another person in the group, and, ideally, it should involve a copious amount of tears. To vent, to cry, to take a sea against an armful of troubles; to vent, perchance to heal; beat, beat, beat against thy cold grey breast, o patient; vomit up the sorrow that nourishes the worm of depression, flush it away with tears, idle tears. Weep, weep, weep; it seems odd to me that the air in here is as dry as it is.

When it was my turn, I said that at least the boy was at peace now, and that perhaps we should think of that and be glad for him. The doctor was waiting for me when I got back to my room. The nurses had told on me: Death was the enemy here, and I was a traitor. "You should not say such things," said the doctor angrily. "What about his family, and all the people who must suffer now because he has done this thing? And how do you know that he is at peace?" "How do you know he is not," I said. "What do you know, actually and really?"

The doctor reminds me of Toad of Toad Hall in *The Wind in the Willows*, only he is not as much fun. He doesn't like me. In the beginning, when he flicked out his thick tongue for my responses to his probing, I kept putting words on it that he couldn't digest. These days, I don't give him anything at all. He has told my husband that I won't listen to him, that I am stubborn. Now that I am eating three times a day, Dr. Toad mostly leaves me to his medical clerk, although he would be happier if I would cry in public, just once. Or even in private, as long as it was reported and noted on my chart.

Once, Dr. Toad's clerk asked me what my pain was like. I told her that I would rather go through childbirth every day than have this pain. But the pain is not in your body, it is in your mind, she said; no, I said, you are wrong, it is in every cell of my body, it bites at every nerve ending, it is immortal and omnipresent and omniscient and omnipotent. That was last month, though, before the pills kicked in. I can live in my body now, if I want to. It's a nice, safe, dead shell.

We heard later that the boy who jumped would have died within a day or two anyway. He was too young and impatient to wait, I guess, so he made the great leap into the arms of the Dark Angel. I imagined It carrying him out of his defeated body, up, up through the autumn fog, past the gulls that look like the silvery ghosts of birds and cry like ghosts, too; they sound so plaintive and eerie and anguished, although I can't hear them any more since they nailed the windows shut. But where did Death take him, I wonder. Somewhere? Anywhere? Nowhere?

There is a girl in here who sounds like a gull sometimes; she is fifteen, and she is here because she took a lot of LSD all at once. Last night I heard her keening in her room, like a gull with a broken wing. It made my stomach churn, but it is no good going in to her, because she doesn't know you are there when she is like that. One afternoon in the smoking room I saw her get up and claw at the air. She went up on her toes like a dancer *en pointe* – was jerked up, almost – and her head fell back, and she made a terrible noise in her throat. One of the other patients went for the nurse, and two of them came and led her away. She is never left alone, not even when she uses the bathroom. Her name is Deirdre, and she is elegantly slim and strong like a dancer, and shy and rude by turns, like most fifteen-year-olds. Unlike most fifteen-year-olds, she wants to die.

They tell me I am here because I said to my husband, quite calmly, that I intended to commit suicide. I don't remember saying that, but he wouldn't make it up. He has never made anything up in his life.

Before my husband could get me to the hospital, he had to coax me out from under our dining room table. Apparently, I had been sitting under it for an entire night and day, propped up against one of the four great carved mahogany legs, rocking myself and moaning. I hadn't eaten for five days, my husband said, although I don't remember. I don't remember, I just don't remember; I remember the things I should not remember, and I leave unremembered the things I should remember. And there is no health in me.

I read Deirdre's palm the other night. It was difficult, because no one is allowed to touch her except her mother. Deirdre's mother reminds me of our old arthritic Lab, Mickey. Like him, she is short and dark and round and worn at the edges, and moves stiffly. Her anxious dog's eyes watch her daughter in the same way Mickey used to watch my husband and me when we went where he could no longer follow, such as into the North Atlantic at Salmon Cove. ("It's okay, Mickey," we would yell above the noise of the breakers, but he never believed us.) Deirdre's mother is waiting for her daughter to return from the sea of madness, waiting for the waves to throw up her real daughter, all bright and shining like Aphrodite on her shell in Botticelli's painting. But the nurses whisper and shake their heads when Deirdre passes, a bad augury.

The other night Deirdre's mother got Deirdre to hold her right hand out so I could divine her future; it moved slightly back and forth in the dim, aquatic light of the smoking room like a frond of the ferny seaweed you find in tide pools, and it was hard to make out the lines. She is so young, after all; even the major lines – the heart, the head, the line of life – are faint at her age, and Deirdre has fine skin. I never read my daughter's palm. I thought it would be too soon; her hands were only the size of sand dollars.

Deirdre's head line indicates that she may stay mad. But at least Deirdre's mother will always be able to touch her daughter's soft brown hair and hold her long, thin hand, and breathe in her essence. I do not pity her.

My closest friends in here are Mary and Lenora. Love is everything to Lenora; she must have it washing over her like a wave constantly; it is air to her, the gills of her heart are drying up for lack of it. I feel as though I am in the presence of a beached dolphin when I am with Lenora. I run my fingers over her back like rain until they ache, and then I let her lie in my arms and I try to brush some life into the brittle strands of her bleached-out hair. No one ever comes to see Lenora except her son, and he looks like he just stepped out of the shower when he leaves here; she soaks him with her tears.

Mary is tiny and wiry and somewhere around seventy, I think. I won't ask her how old she is because she takes great pains never to be seen without lipstick on, although it looks queer in her old oyster-shell face. She is the only person I remember clearly during my first week here, except for my husband and one of the night nurses. Mary sat with me a lot, without talking or expecting me to talk. Most people don't know how to do that.

Before he left me that first night, my husband took off the T-shirt he had on under his sweater and put it on me as a life jacket against the torrent of pain that was drawing me under. I went to sleep with his smell in my nostrils, a sweet, strong, acrid smell, a smell more intimate than my own smell. I love my husband, even though we are chalk and cheese. Because we are chalk and cheese.

Mary lost her husband last year. For forty years, she and Frank never spent a day apart, she told me. They were a lot alike, she said, and from the way she talks about him, I can tell that they swam through life together perfectly synchronized until he died. Her children are still close by, but all of them work, including the girls, and they all live in small houses, and none of them have enough time, or room, for their mother. But they are all good children, Mary says, and think the world of her, especially Francine, the youngest. That's just the way it is nowadays, Mary says; they've got to think of their youngsters first, after all.

When Frank died, Mary moved into a senior citizens' complex. Although she had her own apartment, they wouldn't let her have a dog, or even a cat, and if her children or grandchildren came to visit they had to leave by midnight: there was a strict rule against overnight visitors. One day Mary fell and broke her shoulder. When she got back from the hospital she found it hard to cook and clean, and she ended up in the hospital again, this time on the psychiatric ward. "I don't know what I am doing here," Mary said to me. "They says I told Francine I was going to do away with myself, but I can't remember saying it. Anyway, if I did, she should have had the sense to keep it to herself."

The nurse who put me to bed the first night I was here was a man. I had never had a male nurse before, but then I'd only been in the hospital twice in my life, at sixteen to have my tonsils out and at thirty-one to have a baby out. I read a lot of Sylvia Plath when I was pregnant with my daughter, because you can read her when you are happy. When they put sweet, bloody, blue and red Jenny on my stomach right after she was born, I thought of the opening line of "Morning Song," which is "Love set you going like a fat gold watch."

When I first looked into Jenny's eyes, I was startled, then awed; I saw an ancient one looking out at me, the oldest thing I had ever seen. Later, after she had been washed off and swaddled, her eyes had the unfocused gaze associated with infants. My sister is a doctor, so I asked her about it. "Yeah," she said, "I know what you mean. They look right at you, and their eyes are like that creature's in *Star Wars* – Yoda, right?"

I read "Morning Song" again recently. It is in the *Norton Anthology*, which my husband's niece brought in to me. The end of the poem goes like this:

> *All night your moth-breath*
> *Flickers among the flat pink roses. I wake to listen:*
> *A far sea moves in my ear.*

The male nurse was very kind; he was short and stout and had a guppy's mouth and friendly eyes. He asked me a lot of questions, but I only remember one of them, which was whether I was having my period. I didn't answer right away. "I have to ask," he said, apologetically. "We've had cases where the nurses checked a female patient at night and they noticed some blood on the sheets, and they assumed it was menstrual blood, when in actual fact the patient had cut their wrists." No, I said, I wasn't on my period, but all of a sudden I felt like screaming at him. Screaming what's wrong with you, surely to God you must know the difference between the blood of the womb and the blood of the heart, between strong, thick, sullen menstrual blood with its sea smell and fresh, thin, bright arterial blood spraying from a shocked heart. But I didn't say anything; what did it matter?

Two years ago, my mother died of breast cancer at seventy-seven. Last year, my seven-year-old daughter drowned. Seven,

seven, seven, seventy times seven, unto the seventh generation. Sometimes I think God is math and math is God.

My husband teaches math and physics at a high school. I learned about Fibonacci's numbers from him, and about atoms and quarks. Quark really rhymes with *lark*, or *snark*, although most people give it the sound of *quartz*. (We used to call our daughter the Boojum, from Lewis Carroll's poem "The Hunting of the Snark.") Besides the *Norton Anthology*, I am reading Stephen Hawking's *A Brief History of Time*. The physicists now say that the smallest element in the universe is the superstring. If you could blow up an atom to be the size of the universe, one superstring would be the size of a tree. Superstrings loop around the eleven dimensions of the universe, holding it together like a cat's cradle. I wonder, who is holding the cat's cradle? Someone? Everyone? No One?

They don't care what I read in here, because, besides Stephen Hawking, I read only poetry and fiction. Poetry can't hurt you because it is not true. They like to see me read; to them, it means that I am getting better. I couldn't read at all when I first came in, or for months before: the words hurt like knives, they were all so sharp, even, especially *love*, *child*, *sea*.

My daughter Jenny died on a hot day in August. Jenny never liked August; every August within her child's memory (three of them, in fact) one of the family cats had been killed. I never saw this as synchronistic myself, only coincidental. We've always had too many cats, up to five at one time. The vet said to keep them indoors; I could not keep them indoors, especially the older ones. What would their lives have been? August is the first harvest month. My daughter was harvested in August by the Grim Reaper.

We were at our summer place in Salmon Cove when Jenny drowned. Salmon Cove gets its name from the salmon river that runs through its middle. Jenny used to swim in the part of the river that is by the beach; the water there is only up to her shoulders. Was up to her shoulders. Her little brown shoulders; her little brown face with its blue eyes like two flames. What I want to know is how do you like your blue-eyed girl, Mister Death.

In August, the water in the river is almost like bath water.

Jenny was a good swimmer, a natural swimmer, a baby porpoise. Even so, we never let her out of our sight when we were by the water. But she got up early that morning, and went off by herself with old Mickey while her father and I were still sleeping. She had never done that before. And she must have gone to wade in the sea, and she waded out too far, and the undertow got her. The Under Toad. What I want to know is how did you like your blue-eyed girl, Mister Under Toad.

We waited and waited for Jenny to come back. The physicists are right about time; it is relative. I have been here for two months, but it has not been anywhere near as long as the two weeks we waited for Jenny. One of the women here, Cass, told me about a vision she had in which she saw, among other things (for instance, the Face of the Saviour), what a human life is. Cass says it is like an atom in God's body, and each of our lives is less than a second long in God's time. (Cass scares me; but then, poor Cass scares herself.)

They finally found Jenny's body out by the Terrified Rocks. The Terrified Rocks are about ten yards off the beach at Salmon Cove. There are three of them, three megaliths with coarse grass growing on top in which the terns make their nests; they look like Easter Island statues with toupees. Jenny must have been taken way out at first, and then somehow she found her way back to the Cove, like the salmon that swim up its river in the spring. My husband didn't want me to go with him to identify the body, but I went anyway. I had to know. I thought she would be blue and bloated, but this is not the case with bodies that have been in the sea. If she had drowned in fresh water, the pathologist said, she would have swollen up, but salt water has an affinity with our own fluids; there is an osmotic effect. My daughter had suffered a sea change, but her eyes were not coral: she had no eyes. For a long time after, I thought of them lying like twin sapphires on the bottom of the ocean. Later, I learned about the sea lice. (Sometimes, I wish that the Under Toad had kept her.)

Last night I fell asleep in the moonlight. The blinds in my room open even if the windows do not, and the moonlight was right on my pillow at bedtime. The moon was close to full last night; I think they call that a gibbous moon. *Gibbous* is such an ugly word; it has always sounded to me like *gibbet*, and I think of white dead bodies hanging in the moonlight like rotten melons. Or how Jenny might have looked if she had drowned in the river instead of the sea.

I dreamt that Jenny and I were riding bicycles on the dirt road that used to run by my grandmother's house in the country I grew up in. My mother was waving to us from the veranda; she was in her early forties, dark and pretty, around the age she had been when I was Jenny's age. (My mother married late because all the healthy young men were away at war when she was young.) Jenny and I were going to the little store over the hill from my grandmother's to buy ice cream, but when we got there we decided to get candy hearts for my mother instead. Mine was large and mauve and made of gelatin; Jenny's was smaller, harder, and bright crimson.

When we got back to the place where my grandmother's house should have been, there was a steep hill with a huge bronze lion at the top there instead. "Let's go see," said Jenny, and she and I climbed the hill and sat on the lion's paws. I looked back down; we were high, high up and it had become night all of a sudden, and I was afraid. I have always been terrified of heights, and somewhat afraid of the dark. "What if we fall?" I said to Jenny, and I lay down on my stomach along the length of the cold legs of the great lion, shivering. "We can't," she said, laughing. "Let's go sit on his back." So we climbed up over the lion's face, up over its curly brazen mane and onto its back. We sat down together, and I held on to Jenny from behind, and I buried my face in her child's neck, fragrant as sweet grass.

When I looked up again I saw the biggest church I had ever seen, bigger than the biggest football stadium: its spire touched the moon. It reminded me of our Anglican Cathedral, although it was not neo-Gothic, or any recognizable type of church architecture (it could have been all of them combined, or none of them). The church was made of some kind of iridescent stone, like labradorite. The sight of it filled me with dread and longing at the same time. There was a light around its vast door frame, and I knew that if I were to go in, there would be some sort of celebration going on. And then I heard the sound of galloping hooves, and

I looked up. A herd of wild horses was coming toward Jenny and me; they were small but shaggy and fierce-looking; there were hundreds of them, yet they moved as one. Jenny pulled away from me, and got up and ran toward them. They were only yards from us by then, and I saw that they were quite mad – they were rearing up like huge breakers about to dash against rocks; their eyes were rolling, showing the whites, and huge flecks of sweat, like sea foam, flew from their streaming flanks. I screamed at her: "Jenny, come back – they'll kill you!" "No they won't," she said, turning around and looking at me with Yoda's eyes. "They can only hurt you if you *think* they can." And then the lion turned his big, bronze head around, and he was laughing, and I started to laugh, too, and the lion switched his tail gently against my daughter's legs, propelling her into the midst of the horses, and I heard her shriek with pleasure, and then she was gone. And I woke up.

Moonlight was in my eyes and it was all glowing and liquid like moonlight dancing on the sea; it was the whale's path, the swan's road, and in its silver wash phosphorescent sparkles shimmered all blue and gold; it was alive and full of itself. Somehow it seemed to me that I had always known that that was how moonlight really was, not pale and thin and sad, not just the sunlight's ghost, but thick and rich and molten, a live and joyful thing in itself. And I lay there and I let it wash over my face – it felt so good, I felt it go right through my skin, right down into my heart – and I heard voices in the distance, the voices of men and women and children, voices rising and falling in a light, happy cadence, and I thought that perhaps my husband had been unable to sleep, and had gone in to the den to watch television. And then a bright light shone suddenly in my eyes; it was the night nurse's flashlight, and she was asking my why I was awake, and if I needed something to help me sleep. I looked away from her concerned face, and up: the moon was a speck in the top left-hand corner of the window, high and far and tiny; it had gone from my pillow hours ago.

And a line came to me from the Bible, I think, or maybe a hymn, or perhaps the Anglican liturgy: "And the sea shall give up its dead." I started to cry then; satisfied, the nurse went to get me a pill. But I didn't take it, after.

This morning the sun has managed to poke a couple of skinny yellow digits through the slats of the blinds; it is stoking the pewter frame of Jenny's school picture. Mary was by earlier. She is going home next week, home to Francine's house. Apparently, Francine found a bit of space somewhere for her little mother to curl up in. Mary will have to keep taking antidepressants, though, and she's not too thrilled about that, being someone who would rather suffer a headache than take a pill. But that's the way it has to be, says Mary.

On Radio One, Sass Jordan is singing about time and rivers and how all you want to do is hold her, but what you try to grab evades your touch, her voice twining around the sun's fingers like rings of lapis lazuli. In her Grade 2 picture, Jenny is smiling.

I have a feeling I might be going home soon.

ANNABEL LYON

Fishes

Paul likes the aquarium. We hang there a lot. Well, not a lot but we go there sometimes. I tell my high-school friends, he's fun to hang with but you have to be prepared to go at his speed. I tell my friends, he's very mellow.

"Cool," they say. "We love your brother. He's so cool."

I can tell you what he looks like, neat little eyes and ears, warm clumsy fingers, little white nubs of teeth. The way he grins without knowing it, rubs his head. He wears a red baseball cap and a Bulls jersey. He's the big brother but I'm taller. Sure, anyone can tell you what they look like, people like him.

On Pender Street we transfer to the Stanley Park bus, which will take us to the aquarium. Paul's so stubborn. He makes us sit right up front. I fix my bracelets, kick my raw pink heels out of my sandals, smooth my nice jeans. I take the cap off his head and turn it around, but he puts it back. He doesn't like to wear it that way. We do this quite a lot.

You take him for once, was what she said. I'm tired today. How can you hate the aquarium? It's just fish.

I just don't like them looking at me, I said. I don't like being alone with them. I don't like being down at their level.

So symbolic, she said. Fucking get over it.

So we get there and all he wants to do is watch the killer whales. After twenty minutes of standing in the muggy beige cloudlight watching the big black meat flump and float he explodes: "They're not *doing* anything." He doesn't understand why the trainers aren't out there feeding them all the time. "Why aren't they *doing* anything?"

"They're probably bored, Paul," I say, looking at my Swatch. Get this over with. "Let's go inside, okay?"

He says, "No."

"Just for a little while?"

"No."

At this point I'm still feeling tolerant. After all, I grew up with him and I know how it is. "Okay, Paul," I say, and we stand there some more.

I watch this Asian boy with cheekbones unwrap a green popsicle. But he goes down those stairs to the underwater viewing room and when he opens the door I catch a chill glimpse of pure blue.

I say, "We can always come back out and check on them later." I'm shaking a little.

He wavers. I know better than to push at this point. "No, that's okay," he says generously. "We can stay here."

"Sure?"

"Yeah."

We watch the whales go round and round.

Start pushing. "Why don't we check out the belugas?"

"You can if you want to."

Look darkly and think thunderously. Control, I tell myself. Let it be. Deep breath. "Which one is the male?"

He starts chatting about their dorsals. He's memorized the trainer's spiel. A helium-voiced little gum bunny goes by with her responsible parents and a stroller-bound sibling. "Ma," she says, staring at Paul.

Catch her eye, so cool, raise those eyebrows. Doesn't work, she's too young.

"Ma?"

Catch her eye again. Flare the nostrils and narrow the eyes like I'm going to haul off and clock her if she gets within range. Forest green parent grabs her by the scruff of the neck and whips her away backwards, staring at me and Paul. "Over here, honey," he says. "Let's go see baby beluga like on your tape. Sing: baaaby beluuuga."

Paul's head moves like he just woke up. His face follows the noise like radar. "Let's go see the belugas."

I mean, you know? "Wait, Paul, there's the trainer. He's going to feed the – well the – belugas." *Such* shit.

"Let's go," says Paul.

While we're watching the demonstration one of the belugas spitsquirts and I say, "Fu – udge," which makes Paul go crinkly with laughing, which makes everyone smile, even the whale. Like it's my fault he's got that cute Down's monkey face.

Glare at everyone. Loudly: "Come on, Paul. Let's kidnap a toddler and see if it can swim. Let's feed it to the alligators."

"Stupid, they're caymans," he says.

"Mr. Know-it-all, for Chrissake. Can we please get going?"

"Ma," she says, and I catch her eye again and she steps backwards onto the sibling.

"Kirsten, you are annoying me, what do you *want*," says the purple parent. Make a fist as I pass and let the kid see it.

"Where's the baby," she says instead, "the baby beluga?"

Do not say, It died, stupid. This upsets Paul.

"Let's go inside and see the fishes," he says. Sidelong look. This is our thing, our thing we do.

"Fish," I say.

He looks at his feet, smiles. "Fishes."

"Do you go to a restaurant and ask for fishes and chip?"

"Fish and chips," he says.

"So, fish."

"Fishes."

"What about Dr. Seuss? One fish two fish. See? Fish."

"Fishes."

"I'm going to give you a dictionary for Christmas, you Mr. Fish you."

Laughing: "Fishes."

"Mr. Fish."

"Miss Fishes."

"Pass, please."

While I root in Paul's fanny pack for our day passes, Paul stares at the pretty ticket seller. She wears a teal polo shirt and cap with the aquarium logo. She has breasts and a big fast food smile. I give her our stubs and touch his arm and then he's back with me again.

"Come on, Paul, let's go see the little sharks." All right, so, it's manageable in here, the fish are smaller, the tanks are smaller, you can step away, but no, wait, no, I forgot she said don't let him see the sharks, it gives him nightmares after that movie where the shark ate the guy's leg. Of course he's just acting. No, I don't know where all that blood comes from or how they make his knee look like that but I promise it's fake. I promise. I don't *know*, Paul. Well, shut your eyes then. Just don't look.

"Is that the shark tank?"

"No, Paul, no, love, those are – cod." Don't give me that look, he's my brother and I'll lie if I want to. I suppose you'd call yourself a teacher, you with your beard and your clipboard, well he has special needs and avoiding the shark tank is one of them. "Let's go to the Amazon gallery and find the sloth."

He rubs his head.

"Of course you want to. Sloths are cool. Let's check it out, okay, Paul? Yeah? It'll be fun. Paul?"

"Okay."

On the way we pass the fossilized fish they found in Africa some place, four feet of fat, black, grinning petrification. I decide to say, "Looks like my math teacher."

A woman looks at Paul and double takes and stops. "That fish is ten thousand years old," she says to me. (Psssst, that fish is ten thousand years old, pass it on.) When I don't translate she leans forward like she's going to take a bite out of him and says loudly: "That's a very . . . old . . . fish."

"It's prehistoric, duh," says Paul. "It's a coelacanth."

Suddenly I see a sweet-looking blond boy my age at the octopus and then I have to go to the bathroom so badly. I tell Paul, "Stay here, right?"

He says, "What*ever*."

After I come out of the cubicle I wash my hands and tissue off my lipstick and do it again. I use a pink that is close to my own colour and complements my light skin. I like to freshen it pretty often. I put my hair up and take it down, can't decide. In my pouch are clips and clasps in my favoured woods – cherries,

browns, and blacks. I'm in high school but I read decent magazines and I know what's good.

But I come back out and he's gone.

All the fish are hanging around watching. Little blond
bubbles, little flicks of colour in all that water. All their faces, big
and small. *Somewhere right now some of them can see him but
you can't. Scared?*

Prehistoric fish tank, shark tank, foyer, turnstile, lineup,
back out through the glass doors, beluga tank, killer whale tank,
bottom of the killer whale tank, oh, please, not that place, *but
maybe they can see him down there, are you really trying or just
pretending?* Deep breath. Steps in the concrete down, down
through the thick doors and into black cold salt stink, the only
light the blue windows where the whales hang higher than I
stand and the surface is a dirty bright skin above, but he is
neither here nor anywhere and I leave running before my mind
goes out like the last time, when she had to carry me up and out.
How can you hate the aquarium?

It's the difference between oxygen and air.

Upstairs outside deep breath calm down retrace. Killer whale
tank beluga tank glass doors lineup turnstile foyer shark tank
prehistoric fish tank oh this is bad.

Break down. Go to Information. Can't find my brother wandered off red cap brown hair black pants pardon? How old? He's
got – well look, twenty, but –

"– oh I see," she says, "that's no problem, we'll just make a
little announcement." Shoves out a yellow hotdog microphone
on a black plastic string. "Would you like to do it? Seeing as he'll
know your voice?"

Still shaking. "God, no."

God, no echoes through the aquarium and they look at me,
some laughing, some frowning. "Oops," she says, "must've
pressed the button. Let's try that again."

"*We have a missing individual named Paul, a young man
black hair brown pants your sister is looking for you, please
come to Information by the gift shop* we'll just give him a
minute or so before we call security, does he do this a lot? Oh
you look – would you like to sit down?"

She reads to him every day. She says, "Comb your goddamn hair, Paul," and he says, "Goddamn okay," and we laugh. Once she punished me for smoking and Paul called me stupid and I said, "I know." Then he gave me a hug and she hugged both us of together because I was crying for guilt, for shame.

But there he's coming across the deck above the whale tanks with the stroller family. They're all staring at me, including the baby, and moving in a unit with my brother in the middle, like they're on wheels. They look like aliens bringing him back from the planet Zadar. They roll up and stop in front of me. They say, "We found him." They say, "We remembered him from the belugas."

He looks intact. Black jersey red cap brown hair black pants. He and the gum bunny hold pink ice creams.

They say, "We found him by the otters."

"I was looking for the sloth," he says.

Watch raindrops softly dimple his pink ice cream. "Well, thank you," I say. "I'm very grateful."

They leave, bye. "Are you all right?" I ask.

He says, "For sure." He raises the pink ice cream to lick and sees my face and lowers it again.

Quietly: "So what do you want to do now?"

The Amazon gallery is misty hot and smells green. Find the sloth. "Look, Paul," I say vivaciously, because it's very hot and I will lose my temper soon. "There he is."

"Yeah, yeah," Paul says. "This is boring. Can we go look at the whales now?"

"Let's find the ibis first. They're beautiful scarlet birds. Let's look at the tomato frogs. Let's –" But you know he always comes back to the whales in the end. That's just how it is. "Sure we can see the whales. Like that'll be so interesting, Paul. Like I came all the way out here to stand in the rain and watch the whales do zero. Really fascinating."

Paul understands sarcasm. He grew up with it. "Well, I don't care," he says.

"About what," I say.

"About," he says, "about."

He will cry soon, he does that.

"Oh, fine," I say, to stop it happening. "Whale time. Whatever. I guess you want to go downstairs?"

What are you afraid of? They're just goddamn fish. Go give him a nice day.

"I want to stay with you," he says.

Sometimes she chills on the sofa, watching the late night movie with the lights off, smoking her cigarettes in the television blue, arm around Paul – already a man, asleep on her shoulder in his Bulls jersey. When the movie ends she pats his shoulder with her free hand and says, "Son. Wake up, son."

Outside it's windy and everyone else is heading in. Stand by the railing because it's too wet to sit down. Watch the dolphin flip like a pancake and smack the water. Stand in silence watching the big black creatures and I ought to apologize but instead I shake my bracelets and hand him a tissue and say, "Use it."

KEVIN ARMSTRONG

The Cane Field

Rehana did not see Rajiv's land until the burial. The sun was high and powerful, and Rehana's father, three days dead, lay in a cardboard coffin beside her in the back of a hired pickup. The wind whipped against her shroud, and finally she removed it, her long hair trailing behind like a ship's wake. Cane fields stretched between the coast road and sea but she caught glimpses of water. The truck slowed and turned inland up a hard dirt track. In the distance, the yellow-greens of Viti Levu's mountains undulated under cloud, then dropped behind the close hills fringing Rajiv's home like the fingers of a cupped hand.

Rajiv was waiting outside his strange brick and wooden house and led them to the back of his property. The hole was very deep and very black, the heap of soil beside the grave dark as coffee grounds. There was no breeze, and when the truck rolled to a stop an overpowering stench roiled over Rehana from the box. She set her jaw and was about to step down from the truck when her legs faltered. She had no recollection of Rajiv carrying her to the house, but when she woke, the sun was near setting, its weak rays slanting low-angled and orange through the shadeless window. Body rigid, Rehana took in the white walls, the tired furniture, the quiet surrounding her. And that *smell*, the dark musk of male from the lumpy pillow, from the thin sheets pulled up to her neck. She slid a hand under her panties, checked between her legs. When the wooden door of the bedroom creaked slowly open she was on her feet, the scissors from the dresser-top clenched in hand.

"Mother?" asked a child's voice.

Forbidden to attend the burial, Ardi sat amongst the boxes in the cramped shop apartment. The room felt empty with her mother gone, her grandfather gone forever. With him dead, the place hated them like the rest of Tavua, the women in the street, the girls who pulled her hair then ran, their faces twisted. With no breeze the air was hot above the store; outside even the cars sounded angry. Ardi was almost glad to hear the landlord's steps, to hear another voice, but she loathed his crack-skinned hands, his yellow smile like a dog snarling. When the door-chain pulled taut against him, his smile slipped. Ardi watched him through the door-crack, his gravel voice rising with anger. Long minutes after he left, more footsteps climbed the staircase, but not the landlord's, or Rajiv's. A man Ardi had never seen called to her, told her to come because Mother was sick. She hesitated, then rose and stuffed some clothes into a bag. *Grandfather*. She could still smell him but the pictures were packed. Nowhere to go but with strangers.

Cruising back along the coast road, the driver asked how Ardi knew Rajiv. All she said was: "He shops at our store."

Ardi could not remember just when she had first seen Rajiv. The man was so quiet and huge it seemed he had always been there placing money in Grandfather's wrinkled hand, throwing the two fifty-pound bags – one rice, one flour, always – on his wide shoulders as though they were jackets too warm for the weather. Like the rest of him, the giant's face was big. His eyes however, were small, dark, and a bit too far apart. His nose was large, but blunted, as was the round, hairless chin. Aside from the carefully clipped moustache, the whole face had a peculiar quality of softness to it. To Ardi he just looked peaceful.

By the time the truck reached the cane field, the grave was filled. Rajiv stepped from the house, paid the driver, then took the small bag of clothes Ardi carried and led her inside. He boiled water on the hot plate for tea, and as Rehana slept, Ardi told him all she knew. What the landlord had said about the store's back rent, how he had claimed the remaining goods for his own to make up the difference, how they could not afford a real burial for Grandfather. That night Ardi lay curled up beside her still sleeping mother. The next day Rajiv returned with Ardi's key to the store apartment and loaded their few belongings into another hired truck. He also took two bags of rice and two of flour, leaving money in the now empty register.

When Rehana finally woke and learned what had happened she was furious.

"Ardi, you never tell a man everything. Never! Do you hear me? Rama knows what he has in mind for us! Did you see all his knives? He'll probably rape me and eat you! You cannot trust them! Any of them. Do you understand?"

Ardi nodded her head, but she did not look scared enough for Rehana's liking.

That second night, mother and daughter slept again in Rajiv's bed, their boxes piled up against the door. Rehana was awake early the next morning but Rajiv was nowhere to be found, a flat pillow and blanket on the floor the only sign of him.

She woke Ardi, cooked them some roti with her father's flour.

"You do not leave this room, understand me? As soon as I go, push the boxes against the door. And don't come out until you hear my voice. There's homework to keep you busy. I'll be back as soon as I can, promise."

Rehana closed the bedroom door behind her, waited for the sound of boxes being stacked, then hurried from the house. Rehana did not like leaving her, but the thought of Ardi seeing her beg for help was unbearable. On both sides of the track the cane rose up, a silent, impenetrable wall. The tall stalks swayed the faintest bit in the hot breeze as she strode the long way to the road.

The bus took twenty minutes to arrive, and as she settled into her seat Rehana realized she had never spent a night outside Tavua before. She was anxious to return to town, but as the bus pulled in, the market, the sun-bleached streets looked different to her, harsher. The shadows in alleys and corners had a cobwebbed darkness to them, and the faded store signs and façades seemed to reflect too much light. She normally enjoyed the looks: the narrow-eyed recognition of the town's women, their outrage as she stared brazenly back at their men. Even the black-eyed lust from the corner-boys had its charm, but not today. Everything was angular, including the landlords. They knew of her, and made no effort to hide their scorn. If they were women they refused her outright; if men, they cast yellowed stares over her and grinned with rotting teeth. And for the first time, their condescension touched her, bruised her assurance like skin. Worn and fragile, she retreated to the familiarity of her father's store only to find newsprint-covered windows and a new lock.

The late afternoon sun hovered over the ocean as Rehana stepped back off the bus. The walk over the hill to Rajiv's house was long and shaming. She was not sure who she hated more: the townsfolk for shunning her, or Rajiv for taking her in. And then there was Ardi, her fault, her half-breed curse. Rehana clenched her newspaper under one arm and toiled uphill. At its crest she froze in her tracks. Below, the field stretched away like a hill-shored sea and Ardi moved across its surface as though swimming, her torso gliding through green. She saw her mother and waved, floated over, impossibly tall and fluid, but when Rajiv stepped from the cane with the girl perched on his wide shoulders, Rehana's amazement flashed to anger.

"Get down from there! You put her down right now! Go on, get down!"

Rajiv's face betrayed nothing as he lifted Ardi gently back down to the beaten dust of the track, watched Rehana grab her daughter by the arm and march her wordlessly back to the house. Nor did he speak when he returned to find Rehana screwing the thick steel clasp of the lock into the doorjamb of his bedroom. He sat and ate the roti and rice she prepared, and smiled when she spurred Ardi into the bedroom and locked the door.

Rehana slipped her bus transfer into the purse on her lap. Only a month old, the purse's zipper had already broken, the vinyl handle ready to part any minute. Her cigarettes were at its bottom with the advertisement. She cupped both hands around her plastic lighter, let the cigarette's grey heat warm her lungs. The ad was marked with sweat, its thin paper fluttering between her fingers in the breeze through the bus window.

AUSTRALIAN GOLDMINER
SEEKS INDIAN WIFE
successful 36-year-old w/m seeking wife
(20 or younger) to share new three-bedroom
Melbourne house. Interviews 9 to 3, Buré #12
Vataviti Resort, Tavua

After pulling into the Tavua depot, Rehana's bus waited ten minutes before continuing on toward Ba. Across from the depot, the market's paved square was crosshatched with painted lines to cordon off one vendor from the next. Thin poles had been erected from which blue and orange tarpaulins shaded bushy-haired Fijian women lolling in cotton dresses amongst taro and dirt-encrusted yams. In sudden darkness beneath the low, corrugated roof, men shoved past one another like beetles through deadwood, sold their few wizened peppers and worm-holed lettuce heads.

Beyond the market, the bustle of Tavua's streets. Indians still ran the towns; the bakery and butcher's, the clothing and camera stores. The tinny sound of sitars plinked through blown stereo speakers. Plywood sheeting was nailed over a smashed display window, shards glinting in the gutter. Wiry, moustached young men, furtive and edgy in dark corners, exhaled smoke that rose past cracked walls and hand-painted OUT OF BUSINESS signs.

Rehana did not get off the bus. She sat on the torn vinyl seat sweating beneath her deep green *sawakamese*.

"Peanuts, *sahibdah*?"

Outside the bus window, an Indian girl of thirteen. She wore a dusty school uniform and lifted a brown paper bag of nuts toward Rehana hopefully.

"Why aren't you in class?" Rehana demanded.

The girl dropped her gaze and moved farther along the bus. "Peanuts? Peanuts, *sahib*? Only fifty cents."

Rehana scanned the depot. There were children everywhere, twice the number as before, both Fijian and Indian, all selling small bags of nuts, or cigarettes in three's, or foot-long lengths of sugar cane to be tooth-stripped and chewed. This is what life has come to, Rehana thought.

The driver slid back behind the wheel and turned the ignition. Tavuans filed onto the bus. When an Indian woman in a sky-blue sari stepped aboard, Rehana averted her eyes, pretended not to notice. Five stops later Rehana got off, and though the woman could not possibly have guessed her errand, Rehana felt dirty, as though coated by the black exhaust from the disappearing bus.

Vataviti Resort was almost entirely hidden by palms on the flank of a west-facing hillside. A low budget hostel, registration was the bottom floor of a two-storey main house, and beside the dorm rooms several smaller, pandanus-walled burés surrounded an empty pool. Rehana checked the buré number on the ad again as she moved up the paved driveway. She was just before the door when it swung open and a teenage girl and her mother stepped out. Wordlessly Rehana took in the girl's gold-embroidered sari, the coils of gold bangles, earring and nose ring with its fine chain gliding across her cheek to her earlobe, the blood red *tiki* between her finely plucked brows. The girl did not look at her, nor did the mother a half-step behind. They were past her, gone, and the door frame was filled by the wide bulk of the Australian.

His bathrobe was beige but lustrous, and his gold watch gleamed as he lounged on the love seat, Rehana in the wicker chair across the small coffee table. He had been to Fiji before, the Australian explained, and found the Indian temperament to his liking. The women were well schooled in housekeeping, and they knew how to please a man.

Rehana admired the view out the double doors to the porch as his gaze traced over her.

"Did you bring a picture of her?"

"No, but Ardi is very beautiful," said Rehana quietly.

"Takes after her mother, I reckon. Do you have a husband?"

Rehana blushed and looked away again. A small fridge hummed in the corner of the room.

The Australian leaned across the coffee table. "Choosing a wife is a bloody tough decision, I'll have to sample the goods, you understand. To know if she's the right one."

He must have noticed her shudder, because the Australian leaned back in the love seat and smiled. "You know, if she had citizenship, you could apply for immigrant status within the year."

Rehana said nothing. Even as he led her to the door with instructions when to return, she could only nod faintly. On her way back down to the road it was as though she were not a part of her body, but floating dizzily just above it.

Amidst the still cane, Rajiv was an image in motion. The swing of his upper body, the smooth interchange between cutting and clearing hands was a meditation, without end or beginning. No normal sound could have torn him from his trance.

Rajiv had long come to ignore the barbs of human laughter. But this laughter was more vibration than sound; it trembled down the cane leaves, grew through their twisted roots, and sang up his machete as though it were an antenna. He froze, felt the field quiver even as the breeze flowed overland with the first faint rumblings of the trucks. He straightened and watched them creep over the low-slung hills, studied their bulk as they shook and rattled off the track across the severed cane stalks toward him. The trucks had come to his field twice that day already. As the dozen men jumped from the trailers, Rajiv noticed A.J. himself had accompanied them.

A.J. Lowatu climbed down from the cab of the lead truck with the slow assurance of a man who could move fast when he wanted to. As he ambled toward Rajiv his men fanned across the cut-zone and began gathering the severed cane into bunches.

"Christ, Raj. You been dickin around agin. Thought yid be through the lot of it by now." A twitch of a smile as he spoke. No man could match Rajiv's pace. Two couldn't, and both knew it. What Rajiv did not know was that, through his landlord's boasting, his feats of endurance had become legendary around local grog bowls.

You know that hermit out Tavua way? Cut two hectares in a week!

A.J. reckoned his bragging was innocent enough. And there was little chance of Rajiv finding out, given he so seldom saw other people.

"Just gave Ardi a ride in from the road. She's a beauty, same as her mum. How old is she, fourdeen, fifdeen?"

Rajiv shifted his stance, but said nothing.

They watched silently as A.J.'s workers slung the tightly wrapped bundles to their shoulders and fed them into the trucks. The men worked quickly. With cane, the longer between cutting and crushing, the less the crop's yield. After a time Rajiv glanced at A.J., not so much wondering why he had come but when the man would tell him.

There were no wolves in Fiji, but A.J. looked like one all the same. Though he bore his father's dark Melanesian skin, A.J.'s straight silver hair was thick enough that one comb-stroke held all day, and under similarly thick brows his hard eyes were part amusement, part calculation. He spoke English with a perfect Kiwi accent, the legacy of an ex-pat mother and years on New Zealand rugby fields. His fifty-year-old frame had lost little in form or function from his playing days, and at six feet, five inches he was one of the few Tavuans not dwarfed by Rajiv's size. Besides, A.J.'s wealth gave him another few inches.

All native Fijians inherit land, but since returning from New Zealand A.J.'s influence had grown a hundredfold. Besides cane farming, he had a hand in housing developments, hostels, and he had led one of the most successful parliamentary campaigns in Fiji's last election. *'Yes' to Coalition: an all-Indian vote is a wasted vote*, he preached to urban Indians. *The Alliance Party is a defunct colonial legacy. Social programs to benefit the poor. Native chiefs forced to distribute wealth and land more fairly, and more equality for Indo-Fijians. Inquiries into the Alliance's corrupt past. This vote is not about race, but about class and good government.*

In the evenings A.J. drove miles inland, his pickup loaded with TV, VCR, and petrol generator. He would arrive at some Fijian village, give a brief speech, pop in a tape of the World Rugby Union finals, crawl into the back of his truck and go to sleep. He did this so often he could wake before the end of the game with enough time to yawn, comb his hair, give another quick speech, and drive off to the next village.

He won his riding by a landslide. But six months ago he had watched Colonel Sitiveni Rabuka march into parliament with ten gas-masked soldiers to march out the new Coalition prime minister at gunpoint. Now A.J. was back to watching his crew. They were nearly finished gathering Rajiv's crop when he began to speak: "I have this aunt: Fijian, from my dad's side. She was a nurse, but people go to her for different reasons, now. They say she kin see things." He looked sidelong at his tenant. "She was telling me this dream she had, about a cane field with hills around it. One second the cane was standin, the next it was all cut down."

The sun dropped lower, the sky a soft orange beyond the rim of hills.

"Was that all she said?" asked Rajiv quietly.

A.J. paused. "She said the cane was bleeding."

The faintest nod from Rajiv's dark head, then the throaty churn of a truck's ignition.

A.J. stood with him a moment longer. "Give my best to your woman." He stumbled over the cane roots toward the trucks.

From the hilltop, Rehana watched as A.J.'s trucks rattled down the pocked track to the road. She had avoided the track, using instead the narrow footpath separating the edge of Rajiv's field from the next. Long strides carried her up along the spine of the linked hills behind the house, the field, past everything but baked grass, shrubbery, and the breeze flowing inland. Once at her lookout she had faced westward, head shielded by her *dupatta* against the glaring sun. Not thinking about Ardi, or the Australian, Rajiv, or her father buried below. Not thinking. The trucks' harsh ignitions snapped her peace, dragged her down to earth as they rumbled off toward the coast road. She heard their gears shift as they pulled out, heading southwest toward the Ba sugar refinery. She could see clouds of vapour lifting from its distant stacks, and the hazed blue sweep of sea beyond them. Everything looked softer from a distance.

She rose, brushed the dead grass from her thighs, and started down the hillside toward the house. Her descent sped the sunset; light dropped behind the hilltop and she was in shadow, the cane towering overhead. A gust of wind followed her down, rattling the hard stalks. Rehana quickened her pace. She longed for the noise of traffic: sharp, comprehensible. The snake-slip of cane leaves against each other sounded too much like murmurs: they played tricks with the mind. Melbourne looked like a beautiful city; she had found a tourist brochure to show Ardi that night. When the cane whispered again she broke into a run.

Rajiv entered and there was Ardi, so small with the curly hair. Rehana was not home because it felt soft inside. The house was hot with the fried smell of roti, his father's house built under the hanging root tree. Still strange things around, their brown chairs, kitchen table, and couch that he still bumped into at night. So small her hands. Rajiv was never so small; even when they died he'd been big and maybe that was why. Strong so he could live, keep the field, fight off that cousin who wanted it, Rajiv had been lonely but glad to see him run off bleeding from the flat of his knife; his place, mother's father's place, it was Ardi's place now. Land was yours when you buried yours in it. If she listened close she'd never be lonely. There was no cruelty in the field. Cane knew no past but soil.

Rajiv leaned his cane knives just inside the door. He had ten of them, sharpened them each night for the next day's chore. He stooped under the door jamb and smiled as Ardi turned to him from the hot plate.

"Mother isn't home and I need some yams."

Rajiv nodded, reached and pulled the chain for the naked light bulb above her, then moved past the bedroom and through the back door.

Just outside, the garden was nearly as big as the house. One tilled corner was bordered by the round cement cistern, and the broad leaves from the yam stems fanned out across most of the garden's width. Rajiv lifted the shovel leaning beside the door and drove the spade into the ground, pried upward, then drove the blade in again. He stooped, and sifted the cool soil until his fingers found the fat, firm bulk of a yam. The roots gave some resistance, but his biceps twitched and he tore them free. He lay the yam gently beside the hole and severed the roots and stalk with the shovel blade, placed them back into the hole and buried them. When he turned to re-enter the house, Rehana blocked the rear doorway, her slim body tense, backlit by the stark kitchen light.

He waited.

"I must talk to Ardi about something important tonight. I want you out of the house after supper."

A brief pause, then he nodded. She stepped aside and let him in.

Rajiv watched Ardi's small fingers curl around her fork as she ate, her smooth cinnamon skin, the shell-pink of clean nails. Her mother gave regular inspections of her teeth, ears, hands, but Ardi's hair caused the most difficulty. Fanned across her narrow back, her thick curls snagged every piece of windborne jetsam that passed. They kept it coiled with a ribbon, but at least every other day Ardi was by the cistern lathering, rinsing her thick hair clean. Given the drought of recent months, Rajiv worried about the water she was using, but said nothing.

They ate in silence around the small table, and, when finished, Rajiv rose and carried his empty plate over to the newly bleached sink. He had given Rehana money to buy what she needed, but bleach was the only thing she had purchased. Bleach and soap for Ardi's hair. From the small shelf above the sink Rajiv took down the worn sharpening stone, picked up his cane-knives, and stepped out the back door.

The night was clear and, without town lights to interfere, the stars cast a faint luminescence over the house and stalks of the field. Rajiv stooped beside the cistern, lifted and filled a small steel bucket a quarter of the way. He straightened and looked around, suddenly uncertain. Usually he sharpened on the back stoop, but she wanted him farther away than that. He stepped carefully around the garden and into the cane, following the path there more by feel than sight. When he found his parents' grave, he set his knives and bucket down and propped himself against the headstone.

They were like breezes; in the field, voices always sounded like breezes at first. He cocked his head, waited for the words to sharpen.

"... *body is not holy ... something to bargain with ... one thing we have ... stolen from me ... this man likes you ... anything you want ... a nice, rich man ... you will do every ... except that ... don't let him touch your ...*"

He took a breath and waited, but heard nothing else. Finally he hefted a cane-knife, splashed water onto the grinding stone, and drew the blade firmly across the fine grit.

The sun had not yet climbed the hills as Rehana applied mascara to Ardi's lashes. She required very little makeup: a bit of rouge on her fine cheekbones, a touch of fixative to keep her eyebrows combed. The red lipstick was set off nicely by the scarlet *tiki* between her brows. Just the hair now, thought Rehana. Washed already, Ardi's curls were far more manageable when wet, and the oil glued them flat to her head under a square of pinned silk. Reaching from behind her, Rehana tucked and folded the red-orange sari around her daughter's hips.

"My mother married your grandfather in this sari. It will bring you luck."

Ardi said nothing, just lifted and dropped her arms as directed. A curious numbness had stolen over her, even as she examined her mother's intent face.

"Why don't you marry Rajiv?"

Rehana froze, then laughed sharply. "Don't be silly, girl. What has Rajiv to offer? A shack in a field with nothing but rice and yams to eat, that's what! Besides, the land belongs to A.J.! With the Colonel in power farmers are already being thrown off the land. The blacks take what they want, and soon enough Rajiv will find himself on the street, mark my words." Her hands twisted the silk in upon itself. "And don't let his silence fool you, either! He wants something, sure as the nose on his face! The men here are bad men, and this is a bad place. This Australian is a gentleman, and from Melbourne. Soon you will have your own house, your own car, and many wealthy friends." Rehana made another slight adjustment in the sari.

For a moment, Ardi wanted to tell her. How she was happier here amidst the quiet growth of the cane, but all she said was: "Grandfather is here."

Rehana's face darkened. "Grandfather is *dead*. He *can't help* us any more." Then, with difficulty she reined herself in, even smiled slightly. "You are a clever girl, Ardi. You are better than this place. It may seem hard to understand, but not many get this chance. You know how much I have sacrificed for you: you must do this one thing. It is worth it, daughter, believe me." Her voice was gentle as she forced the gold bangles around Ardi's wrists.

Rehana sat nearest the bus window so the wind would not rustle Ardi's hair. Her mother squeezed her hand reassuringly, but Ardi hardly noticed. She did not feel well. Her stomach had a sickening buzz inside, and even the faintest wafts of exhaust from passing trucks made her dizzy. The traffic slowed near Tavua, and passengers at the front began craning their necks out the bus windows for a better view. Cars and trucks were parked on both sides of the road. A crowd of mostly Indian men were on one side of a culvert bridge, some with scraps of plywood nailed to makeshift handles, their signs' hastily painted lettering still wet and dripping. There was a large pile of scrap metal and wood by the edge of the crowd, and the men were listening to a wiry Indian in a white-collared shirt standing on the hood of an old station wagon stripped of all but its tires. Resentment poured through his bullhorn; the words rose off the crowd with an odour sour enough to make Ardi gag. The bus had just crawled past when, in answer to the bullhorn's fervid cries, the men began pushing the wreck toward the bridge.

Rehana turned to her daughter and nodded toward the throng. "That is why we must go."

People milled around the depot. Out front of the market the sidewalk was thick with bodies. Rusty cars filled the streets with exhaust, but no one seemed to be going anywhere, nor did they want to. Something was close at hand. Ten minutes later their bus pulled free from the congestion that spilled over from the opposite lane, finally jerking to a halt out front of Vataviti.

Ardi dragged herself up the drive to the buré. Her mother's arm stayed fixed around her shoulders, fingers tight on the fleshy part of her arm. *Remember what I told you*, Rehana's eyes warned as she knocked firmly on the buré door. Palm trees and frangipani bushes pressed closely around them. Like the jungle, but different.

Ardi knew the unseemliness of looking a suitor in the eye, but as the door swung inward, she could not help a brief flicker. The Australian was not a tall man, but he was big. Thick wrists, a rounded middle under the beige terry cloth bathrobe. His face was wide and sunburnt, and beneath a thin blond moustache his smile displayed perfect teeth. As Rehana guided her inside, Ardi yearned to ask if he had bought them.

The buré porch was bright with sunlight. The pool lay just beneath it, and standing at the railing Ardi's numbness was replaced by a sudden urge to swim, to just leap right over the edge.

"They are filling the pool later today. It's been empty since I got here." The Australian's voice did not fit his build. Thin, reedy: only the accent made it interesting. Ardi studied his frame, the round, knobbed knees and heavy feet, the coils of grey-blond hair framed in the V of his robe lapels. He and Rehana both sat down on the plastic deck chairs.

"What's her name?"

"Ardi," said Rehana primly.

"And how old is she?"

"Sixteen," her mother lied.

"She is very pretty. That's a lovely sari, Ardi."

Rehana's eye caught hers, narrowed.

"Thank you, *sahib*," said Ardi quietly.

"Can she cook?"

Rehana leaned forward in her chair. "Oh yes, sir. Very well, and she is a very good student. Ardi learns everything quickly."

The Australian nodded, smiled faintly to himself. "Have you been to Australia, Ardi?"

She shook her head.

"It's much bigger than Fiji. And lovely. You'll like it a lot. I've a nice house in Melbourne to live in when I'm not down the bloody mines. There's some pictures inside if you'd like to see them." He stood, and held out one thick red hand.

Strange how blue veins looked on white people, Ardi thought, as his fingers closed around her own.

Rajiv had watched them from the cane, Rehana a step behind the girl to make certain the sari did not drag. A strange tightness grew in his chest as they moved slowly past. He did not stop to wonder what caused this. *She looks like flame*, was his only thought before retreating to the oiled motion of cutting. Yet the girl's image persisted, the sound of her small voice echoing within the arc of his swinging blade.

The sun had climbed its highest when Rajiv straightened and studied the swath of flattened cane behind him. He was slower today. The weight of this realization settled into his tired limbs. Rajiv licked some of the clear sugar water off his knife blade, then jerked the steel back. The liquid was warm but salty, as though sown with seawater. He frowned and slashed the knife down through another stalk. Faint laughter quivered through the ground as he examined the severed shaft, watched as thick white fluid dripped over the roots underfoot.

That is how A.J. found him, motionless, as though rooted to the soil. Only when A.J. slammed the door of the pickup did Rajiv turn and watch his landlord move hurriedly toward him.

"Best stop cutting, Raj. The refinery's closed. They're striking. Had the wife on the phone all morning to warn people but forgot you didn't have one. Got here fast as I could, but some bloody protest blocked off the road through Tavua."

"For how long?"

"The strike? Don't know. Have to see how the Colonel deals with it." A.J. paused, gave Rajiv a careful look. "The girl here?"

Rajiv shook his head.

A.J. frowned. "I own a hostel on the other side of town. Live in the top floor of the main house. Thought I saw the woman go into one of the burés. That's what reminded me of you, actually. The girl wearing a sari, an orange one?"

A slight nod from Rajiv.

A.J. turned, swore under his breath, then brought his gaze

back to fix on Rajiv's brown eyes. "Look, when she gits back you tell her to steer clear of there. That Aussie's bin here before, and she should keep the girl away from 'im, understand?" He shook his head. "I've got to go, Raj. I'll be back to let you know what's happening at the mill." He swore again as he strode off toward the pickup.

Rajiv watched A.J.'s three-point turn, the back tires kicking up dirt as he tore off toward the coast.

Like lambs. Wrapped up like bloody Christmas presents. If only he could work out some deal where he could keep their gold. Goldminer, *Christ*: the perfect touch for their freedom dream. The Australian rolled, checked his watch on the bedside table. Three more appointments but the next not for an hour yet.

He watched the girl slip the petticoat back over her slim brown legs. He reckoned she'd been easy enough to unwrap. All except for the kerchief over her hair. He had gone to remove it and damn if she hadn't slapped his hand away. No matter; silk on the pillow had its charm. If anything, that's what he'd remember about this one. He rose and pulled on his bathrobe, checked his watch again. Time enough. Walking over to the girl, he helped her draw the *choli* over her shoulders, kissed her covered head lightly, then turned and opened the door.

Outside, the mother stood at the porch, hand on throat, waiting. She'd want a smile, then, and he gave her one: faint, non-committal. He watched her face fall, took a step toward her.

"Lovely young thing. Very well behaved. You've raised her bloody well." He smiled again, placed his hand on her shoulder. "But I'll be honest; I've met many young girls, all of them nice." He paused, his eyes drifting, hand creeping to her neck. "They don't have mums like you, though." He dropped his hand. "Go help her dress. I'll be in in a bit. Maybe *you* can show me why I should take her to Melbourne."

There was no traffic along Tavua's main strip. The soldiers were nowhere in sight, but their presence remained. Vendors abandoned the depot, and the few people on the street spoke softly, kept to the sidewalk. The shops not closed already turned stereos down or off, because some attention they did not need.

Mother and daughter sat together, said nothing as their bus bounced over the steel culvert of the bridge. The wrecked car was gone. All that remained of the roadblock was some broken plywood and scraps of corrugated iron on which locals converged, bearing pieces antlike toward home because there were always holes that needed mending. The few pools of blood were covered with dust.

The bus pulled down the coast road, and Rehana welcomed the breeze through the window. Neither she nor Ardi noticed A.J.'s truck roar past in the other lane. They were two stones in a river, numb as the world flowed past. When the bus shuddered to a halt, the driver had to turn and shout to them. They began the long trek up the dirt track. Again Rehana followed a step behind Ardi, and caught her when she stumbled, her daughter's face sickly white. *I wish it were sunset*, was all Rehana could think. The sun was too high, promised too many hours before dark, coolness, sleep. The house's shade was such a relief she almost wept when they entered.

He watched them from his chair, his sweat scent blooming in the small room. When Rehana noticed him motionless at the table she gave a start.

"What are you doing here? Why aren't you in the field?"

Ardi looked away as Rajiv's wide-set eyes settled on her.

"No cutting today. A strike."

"So you just thought you'd sit here and wait and scare us half to death? What kind of a man are you? Why don't you take a walk or something? We need to bathe. Yes, go for a walk. Go on, go!" Rehana took an angry step toward him.

For another moment he studied them, then, eyes fixed on Rehana's, he rose slowly from the chair and moved outside.

The first thing to go was the kerchief. Ardi did not want her mother to help, and said so.

Rehana ignored her. "There is no need to be like that. I know it was hard, but it is over now. You are okay." Her deft hands unwound the sari, folding the silk as she went.

Ardi slipped off her petticoat. The wad of toilet paper was still between her legs, stuck fast to the matted curls. *Like my hair*, she thought, pulling the paper gently away.

Rehana wrapped a threadbare towel around her daughter's middle, tucking the ends together over her small breasts.

"You are a good girl, Ardi. Look at you." Her mother turned her to face the small mirror on the dresser. "You are beautiful. You will make a wonderful wife. Now go bathe. You will feel much better, I promise." She kissed her softly on the head.

Ardi moved out of the bedroom and through the back door to the cistern, a cake of soap in her hand. Compared to the sun's heat, the water was cold as she slowly tipped the bucket over her head, her nipples taut. Her vagina stung with the soap, and only after many rinses did the oil wash from her hair, still curly, even after this. Behind the house there was nothing to see but the close hills and cane. Ardi let the towel drop, felt the sun warm her as she stood, shaking.

The bedroom was empty when Rehana returned from her bath. She closed the door behind her, unwrapped the towel, and rubbed her black hair dry. If she thought hard enough, she could no longer feel him. Rehana caught a glimpse of herself in the small mirror above the dresser, and moved closer to examine her face. Her lip was swollen where she'd bit down, but the bleeding had stopped. Taking a step backward, she admired the curve of her throat. *You cannot break me*, she thought. Rehana was halfway across the room before her image was too small for her to see.

Scissors.

The dresser-top was bare and Rehana flew from the room. Ardi lay curled into a ball at the foot of the bleached sink. *Blood? No, strands* dark over the floor and when she screamed Ardi leapt away and out the back. Rehana fell to her knees, gathered the hair to her. When the light from the front doorway was blocked by Rajiv's huge frame she climbed to her feet, arms outstretched, strands stuck to her legs, her breasts, screaming: "*Is this what you want? Is this it?*"

Footprints in the garden. Rajiv followed Ardi's path into the cane. His pace quickened when her trail met his other older one, then halted before the small clearing. Her head rested on their gravestone, a towel drawn over her like a blanket. He stepped slowly toward her, for the first time hating his size, how he frightened them. She did not move, even as he lifted and held her, so light in his arms.

"Tell me."

The Australian closed the buré door behind the last mother and daughter, then checked his watch. 8:45. He did not usually make appointments so late, but they had come all the way from Nadi. Besides, this was his last day here thanks to A.J. Stupid cunt had barged in like a water buffalo, wanted him gone in the morning. A bit late for a crisis of conscience, he'd told him.

The Australian opened the sweating bar fridge, took out a bottle, and moved through his porch doors to the railing. A palm-mounted spotlight shone into the dark blue hole of the pool. A.J. had begun filling it that afternoon, and the deep end already had four feet of water, ripples bright as cane-blades in the light. Across the road, the ocean was only a hundred yards distant. The Australian breathed in the damp salt air, and smelled the tinge of something else, like dirt-laced sweat.

Rajiv had been walking a long time, but how long, he did not know. Hard steel in hand, he knew only that there had been daylight, then the sun slipped and fell, then overhead, darkness spread like an oil spill. Beneath stars, the night was burning. Farmers had lit the cane roots; flame encircled Tavua like the fires of an enemy camp. But the people were drawn by the sirens. Outside the tavern, a victim was cut but breathing, the stabber drunk and raging as he was shoved into the rusting squad car. Skirting the echoing street, Rajiv witnessed none of this. No one saw him pass.

Along the road there was no wind or whispers but Rajiv heard cane dying, lying wasted. As he slipped among the burés, salt air was smoky from fires; they were torching roots to turn under, burning to grow. Ash fell in flakes past the spotlight onto the pool water and an Indian woman watched from a buré porch, her arms crossed like a harness. When the door swung open behind, she turned, then held the young girl who joined her. Rajiv waited for them to go, for the Australian to appear. Too late for them, too late for him. Some men were good for soil, nothing else.

HEATHER BIRRELL

The Present Perfect

In Montreal, people walk on rooftops. Fiona has seen them, strolling casually around brick chimneys and bubble skylights and steel vents curved like periscopes. When she first moved to the city in July she would often sit on her small balcony with its zigzag of staircases above and below, and peer out over the roofs, following the small figures as they moved across the sky, some bending to fix and check, check and fix, others simply stopping to stand, hands cupped over their eyes, as they scanned the horizon. Sometimes she was certain they were looking at her, and she would lift her hand and wave, a quick but insistent flutter, as if they had arranged to meet, and were waiting, searchingly, on opposite street corners.

No one had ever waved back, and this, somehow, was a comfort to Fiona, an affirmation that the roofwalkers' presence had less to do with an aimlessness of spirit than a spiritual purpose not available to her.

Fiona had left her home in Toronto because, in the space of four weeks, her boyfriend of six years had left her, her cat had died, and her parents had blithely sold the family home and migrated to Florida, dragging their new hand luggage and waving their hands behind them like flightless birds. When Henry called her from work with his "big news," Fiona assumed it had something to do with his job as a pharmacist – a promotion or a transfer maybe – or something about one of the new queen-sized mattresses they had their eye on at Sleep World, a domestic

84

detail she could absorb and modify, then lob back at him, with a spin. She was used to this back-and-forthing, she enjoyed it, she didn't know anything else. So that when he told her he was leaving she felt less shocked or indignant than weightless, without context. He was leaving, he said, because he had to know, he had to find out what was out there, in the world, but more importantly, within himself.

Within yourself? What did it mean to look within yourself? And what could you ever hope to find there, beneath the layers, without the help of someone who had lived beside you, amongst your gestures and debris? But these were all questions Fiona thought of later, after Henry had boarded the plane, after her cat Mimi had staggered home, her face bleeding and broken. They were questions that surfaced fully formed in her mind, like sea monsters – palpable, if fantastic and fleeting.

Within weeks of that first phone call, Henry had sold or given away all of the furniture they agreed was his to sell, in a series of well-attended yard sales. Fiona called in sick but refused to help with the sales, instead choosing to oversee the exchanges from an upstairs window, where she sat like a trapped insect, her face butting against the screen. Henry was stupidly magnanimous in his transactions, letting certain items go for a pittance to men and women dressed in too much black and denim and silver, offering cryptic advice to eager-looking students, and actually apologizing for the condition of Fiona's favourite wingback chair. He made two neat piles of the contents of the kitchen cupboards, divided the remaining curry powder into two small jars, and carefully placed a stubby end of ginger root on the top of Fiona's pile where it sat, looking like a swollen chicken foot, the final ingredient in a voodooish concoction.

Fiona's mother was convinced Henry was having an affair. "There's no other reasonable explanation, Fi, it has to be a woman," she said, and cupped the back of Fiona's head against her shoulder. Fiona was crying for the first time since the break-up, long convulsive sobs that felt like sneezing or coming; that same amount of sadness and relief. They were sitting in the stark strangeness of the living room Fiona had known as a child, on two upside-down milk crates.

Fiona's parents had also sold off most of their furniture, with much less psychological difficulty, she thought, than was acceptable. It seemed they had simply shrugged off the accoutrements of their past, or shed it as if it were an old itchy skin. Fiona's mother was giving her the big blue couch treatment (without the couch); the head rub and back of the throat noises that meant safety, that meant *There, there.* The last time she had been forced like this into the warm crook of her mother's neck, she had been sixteen, her womb scraped clean in a clean white office.

She loved her mother for her suggestion, as much as she knew it could not be true. There was something reassuringly horrifying about the idea of Henry with another woman; she could imagine herself accusing him, brandishing a lipsticked shirt, screaming. But she knew Henry was not having an affair, and this is what scared her most. She knew that what had happened to Henry had overtaken him in the middle of the day, in broad daylight, perhaps while he was looking out the window, or labelling an antibiotic. It was a transgression much more serious than any sexual betrayal, a smooth and bloodless denial of the life he had led thus far.

After the initial shock of the announcement had passed, Fiona had asked him what he was going to do. "India," he said, "I'm going to India to find my path." Fiona was only prevented from outright guffawing by the intensity of his tone. Henry had never mentioned his lack of path before, had in fact never even doubted the decisions he made in his life. It had always been Fiona who was unsure, unsettled by the cloud of options that hovered around every step she took toward career, toward family. "Easy does it," Henry would say, when she came home in tears from the advertising agency where she had worked for the past three and a half years. He would run the tips of his fingers over her back until her breathing slowed and the webs of thought reined themselves in. "Bloom where you're planted," her mother said, when she called in a panic, a series of what-ifs spilling from her mouth. And Fiona had. She had taken the man and the job and been happy. She bloomed where she was planted.

Fiona's father was brusque, dismissive, and superstitious. "I always knew there was something funny about that guy," he said, peeling at the plaster over the fireplace. These were the kind of comments that used to infuriate Fiona with their vague banality and absolute conviction, but today she found her father's loyalty far more comforting than her mother's rationalizations. There was nothing rational about having your heart ambushed. It was too much like something you'd watch on the evening news, shaking your head, glad you had the option of changing the channel. Fiona's mother was looking for cause and effect, a logical sequence, while her father understood that sometimes events don't follow, people can go crooked, the world go awry.

The day she arrived in Montreal she had buzzed at the first brownstone apartment she saw, encouraged by the red and white "A Louer" sign in the window. Fiona had chosen Montreal because she knew the rents were reasonable, and because, from the few times she had visited, it seemed to her a comfortable place to be heartbroken. The crowds there didn't seem to get on with it the same way they did in Toronto, and no one was looking to settle. She liked the idea that, on the country's national holiday, everyone packed up their belongings and moved. Here, instead of digging in their heels, people kicked them up. Instead of becoming resigned, Montrealers relocated and redecorated.

The concierge of the building was friendly and slightly fatherly; he assured her that she had chosen a good neighbourhood and that the men in black coats and black hats walking the streets were not hostile. "They wouldn't touch you if you dragged them behind a bush," he said, and rotated his index fingers near his temples, making what Fiona thought to be, at the time, the sign for coo-coo, but later understood, ashamedly, to be an imitation of the single ringlets of the Chassidic Jew. Later she would come to depend on the stern, knee-socked presence of the men in black – their stride so purposeful and unflinching – but at the time she had simply nodded and smiled. The apartment he showed her was large for the price, although oddly laid out, with hallways that bulged suddenly into rooms, like the body of a boa constrictor after a feeding. There was a cat lying on the windowsill. "Shoo," said the concierge, and pushed it down. "It belongs to the neighbour."

"What part of town are we in? I mean, what's this neighbourhood called?"

Fiona was looking out the window at the laundromat across the street, from which two boys with orange and green mohawks were emerging, smoking cigarettes and laughing. They stopped to talk to a young couple in dreadlocks. The dreadlocked man had a baby strapped to his chest. The woman was carrying a straw bag full of groceries.

"This," the concierge stopped and pointed to his feet, "this is Mile-End. The whole area . . ." Now he waved his arms expansively, "is the Plateau, the flat part after the Mountain. It's very popular with the artists and the young people."

Ah, yes. The Land of Mile-End, on the Plateau. After the Mountain. This was not Canada, or even Quebec, it was the land of Narnia, Fiona thought, as the concierge led her to still another Kingdom of Spare Oom.

She asked to pay month-to-month and the concierge agreed, somewhat reluctantly, his long eyebrow hairs skimming his eyelids. Now she supposed she could have signed for a year without consequence, but she still liked the feeling of impermanence it gave her to know that there were no sign-on-the-dotted-line documents to bind her, that she could find her way up to the roof one day, take one last look at the glittering cross at the top of Mount Royal, the hopeful treetops and garbage-littered laneways, and leave as she had come, with one small suitcase and a snack for the train.

In French, Fiona remembered, instead of saying "I miss you," you say "Tu me manques," or, "You are missing from me." This is what she practised saying to an imaginary Henry in her mirror. She thought it was probably important to say these words with a pout, or a bit of a pucker, and sometimes she perched an old army green beret on her head for added authenticity. But out on the street she felt anything but authentic. She noticed that the women in her neighbourhood had a sort of gritty beauty about them she couldn't quite place. Sometimes she thought it was because they sweated more profusely, or bathed less, and didn't care. Other times, she thought it had to do with the fact that they wore lipstick to buy groceries (defiant shades of mulberry and ruby), and left their lips daringly bare when they went out to dine. But mostly she felt inauthentic, she surmised, because she was without Henry.

She joined the local library and checked out books called *India: Its People*, *India: Its Natural Resources*, *India: Its Cuisine*, and *India: It's the Place To Be!* Sometimes she dreamed of Henry weaving his way along the streets of Bombay, pushing through crowds, his eyes flitting from one set of facial features to another. And suddenly she too, Fiona, was in the dream, in the crowd, her eyes also searching, waiting for Henry to lock onto her gaze. Waiting for Henry to understand that, after all, Fiona was that part of himself he had been missing. Inevitably, her parents made an appearance, their faces tanned and paradoxically wrinkle-free, in the crowd of dark-skinned strangers. They wore white cotton shirts and unfettered smiles, and they had their arms linked in a kind of loose love knot.

She hadn't expected to get a job as soon as she did. She wore her best suit to the interview and made mental lists of her strengths and weaknesses on the way to the language school on the metro. Dependable; good-humoured; enthusiastic and creative teacher. Hard worker. Punctual. The manual she had at home said that your "weaknesses" should be ruses; humble admissions of qualities your employer might actually consider strengths. "I sometimes become overly involved in my work," she whispered while sorting through her handbag.

Actually, Fiona had very little experience with teaching. She had once led a storytime group at a daycare she worked at in high school, and a twitchy social conscience, combined with a charismatically left-leaning university roommate, had convinced her to tutor a young offender as part of a literacy program her second year. Other than that, her only experience with a second language had been at the ad agency, where her boss, sometimes, by virtue of Fiona's high school French, asked her to try her hand at translating copy.

Fortunately, the interview turned out to be less of a test than a recruitment; ten eager candidates crowded around a conference table while an equally eager "pedagogical adviser" tried to convince them of their suitability for the position.

Within two weeks, Fiona had four contracts, teaching at various corporations around the city. The agency sent her to places with names like Laval or LaSalle, rhymy places that belonged in jump rope songs. One of her contracts was in Île des Soeurs, or Nun's Island, a small settlement of low-rise office buildings and fresh-looking housing. The island had one strip mall, complete with a small wooden bridge that curved over a fake stream and made a satisfyingly hollow hoof-y sound when Fiona walked on it to get to the washrooms. There was a special express bus she had to take to get to the island that zoomed over the water on a wide strip of highway.

This was Fiona's favourite part of the journey – she felt a certain solidarity with her fellow commuters as they sat looking out over the St. Lawrence to either side, their bags clutched in their laps. She imagined they were feeling, like her, the excitement and risk of this particular ride. Fiona had never been much for history, but she thought she felt something of the arrogance and terrible naïveté of Jacques Cartier bubbling in her breast as the cold sea air rushed in through the sliding window beside her ear. This was not a voyage in increments! This bus would not stop until it got to the other side!

The groups she taught were small, and the students were, for the most part, happy to get away from their desks for an afternoon or two. They wandered in clutching company coffee cups, or novelty mugs that had been left in the cupboard that read "World's Best Dad" or "Pobody's Nerfect" or "Black coffee drinkers make better lovers and I have the mug to prove it." Fiona had once tried translating them, awkwardly with very mixed results from her students, who seemed to think she might be making fun of them.

"The present perfect," Fiona told her classes, "doesn't really have an equivalent in French. It begins at a point in the past, and continues up to the present, and possibly into the future. It might seem to you that because it is perfect, it's finished, an event completed, but it's not." Fiona drew a timeline on the white shiny board using an orange Magic Marker. The present she marked in the middle with a scribbly dot. She hesitated before drawing another dot slightly to the left of the first one. This was the past. Then she drew an arrow in green Magic Marker from the second dot to the first dot, from the past to the present. "We might say, for example, I have eaten many bananas. In other words, up to this point, I have eaten bananas, and it's entirely possible that I may continue eating bananas in the future. We just don't know." She drew another arrow from the present into the empty line of the future, then turned to look at the class, her face open and inviting as a peeled banana.

Fiona was sitting at the breakfast table one morning in early August, trying to read the newspaper, when she saw a man outside her window. Her building was two storeys higher than the one next door, so that her balcony was level with the neighbouring flat-topped roof. The concierge had informed her proudly when she asked that he was also responsible for the smaller building and that there was a famous musician living in one of the larger, more expensive units. She had, on several occasions, noticed beer bottles, and the soggy end of a blanket strewn across the roof. Once there had been a pigeon nesting and cooing in a woman's high-heeled boot. Still, it surprised her, to look up at another human, at eye-level, so close. She was sipping her coffee slowly gnawing at a bagel and still considering a return to bed, when the man began pacing back and forth, peering into the windows of the apartments adjacent to hers. She stood up, tugged at the bottom of her oversized T-shirt. Who was this man? Could it be the famous musician, and, if so, why was he casing the joint? Should she confront him? She stepped onto the balcony, careful not to let the T-shirt ride up over her thighs. The man hurried over, and Fiona noticed he wore a heavy tool belt strapped around his blue-jeaned hips. Fiona had always liked tool belts for their swaggering air of usefulness. She gave a half-smile of invitation.

"Bonjour Madame, vous habitez ce logement-la?" She sighed. It was difficult to remain coy in a second language.

"Oui, comment est-ce que je peux vous aider?" It always seemed to her there were too many pronouns in French, or too little difference between what was plural and what was polite. She raised her eyebrows questioningly, apologetically. The man stared at her.

"You speak English?" He kicked at the edge of the roof, his thumbs hooked through his belt loops.

"Yeah." Defeated.

"I was wondering if I could buy some water off you. I'm trying to fix the air conditioning unit and I can't hook it up from here. I mean, I could give you ten bucks."

Fiona wasn't quite sure what he wanted her to do. She stared at his tool belt. "Okay."

The man pulled a hose up from behind him. It was slightly thicker than a garden hose, although it looked to be made of the same malleable rubber.

"If you could just grab a hold of this when I throw it over, I think you should be able to attach it to your sink."

Fiona nodded and stretched out her hand.

"Actually, you better just get out of the way. I don't want to hit you."

"Oh. All right." Fiona moved inside. The hose flew through the air between the buildings like a snake possessed and landed on her balcony with a clank, the metal spout caught for a second between the rails. She picked it up gingerly and walked over to the sink. The spout was too big, it slipped off the faucet when she tried to screw it on.

"It's too big," she called out to the man.

"Damn," he said, and stamped his work-booted foot. "I'll see if I have a washer." He reached into his bag and pulled out a tiny silver ring. "Here," he gestured and drew back his hand.

He was going to throw it at her! This small, shiny, useful thing! She watched it sail through the air and stretched out her hand to catch it. The washer spun and arced, the sun glinting off its bevelled sides. The man was also watching, scratching his head and frowning at her.

She missed.

The washer spiralled down quickly and landed somewhere in the narrow strip of grass between the buildings. The man huffed and threw his arms in the air.

"Great. Now I have to go all the way downstairs to get a new one. If I have another one, that is." He glared at her and stomped away.

Fiona watched his retreating back and bum, denim-clad and strong. "I have missed the washer. I have missed an opportunity," she said to the neighbour's cat, who had somehow found his way into her apartment again. The cat followed her into the bedroom and lay down on her computer keyboard. "It's true that sometimes there is really not much difference between the simple past and the present perfect," she explained to him when he looked at her. "Sometimes it is more of a change in nuance than a big change in sense. It's the expectation that the action may be repeated, or, conversely, may not be repeated for a specific reason that makes the present perfect unique." The cat blinked twice, then closed its eyes.

"Your father thinks you should come visit us, Fi. I told him you were busy with your new life – that you weren't interested in hangin' around us old people, but he thinks a vacation is a good idea. So I promised him I would mention it to you anyway. How are you? Did you get my e-mail? It's the first time I've ever used the Internet – it's very cool."

Fiona was sitting on the futon, the neighbour's cat in her lap, a pile of workbooks on the floor next to her lamp. She had been planning on doing a little marking in bed, with the help of a glass of cheap Chilean wine from the dépanneur, when the phone rang.

"Actually, I wouldn't mind a little Florida sunshine, but I'll probably wait till the weather gets worse here." She looked out the window to Mount Royal in the distance, where the trees were still leafy and green, stalwart in the face of the rambling city that surrounded them. She imagined her parents in the shade of a broad-leafed palm tree, their lives tethered behind them like giant air balloons that had borne them up and over, to this place, this sunny beach, these lapping, lukewarm waters. "Are you guys okay? Do you like the condo?" Fiona shoved the cat away and lay down, shrugging the phone to her ear.

"The condo's great, but your dad's going nuts with nothing to fix. You know how he is with relaxation time. Hey, honey, have you heard from Henry at all?" Her mother's question was like her wardrobe, pre-planned masquerading as casual. Fiona lied.

"Mmm, hmm, I got a postcard, he seems to be doing really well. I guess I'll hear from him when he gets back. I think he really just needed this time on his own."

"You're probably right. Well, we love you and miss you, here, down south. Keep on keepin' on, eh, Fi? You just gotta bloom . . ."

"Where you're planted. I know, mom. Say hello to dad for me."

Fiona hung up the phone. The cat was asleep at her feet, making small engine noises. She rubbed its head until it began to purr.

"Le chat ronronne," she said, and felt her tongue vibrating at the back of her throat.

Fiona was careful to start all of her classes with conversation, casually. Sometimes she talked about a current event, sometimes she took an odd or surprising fact from the back page of the *Globe and Mail*, the "Social Studies" feature. When the day was slow, the air stale, and she could see an eerie, computer-induced glow reflected in the eyes of her students, she revealed too much trying to lure them in, provided details of her relationship with her ex she supposed were probably best left unsaid.

"The present perfect may also be used to denote a repeated action in the past. For instance – Henry and I have eaten at that Thai restaurant many times; the coconut milk stirfry is really quite delicious . . . Or – I have tried to get in touch with Henry several times this week through his mother, but she seems to know as little as, if not less than, I do about her son's whereabouts."

Fiona began having an affair with one of her students. He was shy and tall; an attractive, stooping combination, and he seemed to think she had cracked the code to the English language, that it was not something she grew up in, like a fish in water, but instead a series of secrets imparted to her by a mysterious superior. She did little to dispossess him of this notion.

Later, she would wonder why more ESL teachers were not involved romantically with their students. It would occur to her that the makeshift set of symbols and gestures, the drawn-out syllables, the exaggerated charade – all of these attempts to be understood – were so very like the secret languages created and inhabited by lovers.

Henry had always told her that what he loved about her, about them, was how well they fit; the easy rocking of their lovemaking, their bodies twined together in sleep. With André it was different, halting. He was lanky; his limbs hung off the sides of her bed. He was all splayed parts and complicated angles. Sex involved a constant and very physical reordering. After they had negotiated themselves to climax, André would fold himself up and begin his bilingual inventory of Fiona's body.

"Les lèvres; lips. Le cou; neck. Les épaules; shoulders. La clavicule; collarbone. Les seins . . ." Fiona used to believe it was important, especially for women, to avoid perceiving one's body in parts. She had often told Henry she hoped he stressed the importance of holistic healing when he dealt with his customers. "I only have about five minutes, Fi, and these are seniors we're talking about here." Henry had been practical that way.

But when André parcelled her out the way he did, Fiona had to admit to a certain thrill, a floaty feeling at the top of her head. It was the same feeling she got sometimes at the hairdresser's, as the stylist separated and snipped, his eyes fixed on a new Fiona in the mirror, a parallel-universe Fiona, a woman Fiona could never hope to know. She supposed this was objectification.

André was from France; he had been transferred to Quebec by his software company, a large multinational whose head offices were in Chicago. Once he had mastered English he was hoping to move to the American office, but in the meantime he was happy to cook for Fiona in his small flat.

"The Québécois, they want to be their own country in the truest, bluest sense, non?" he asked her, while ladling vichyssoise into her shallow soup bowl.

"Mmm, hmm," Fiona replied, holding the soup in her mouth for longer than necessary and noticing the complicated place setting. At home, she used a fork for everything except soup and cereal. She couldn't understand how André had so quickly acquired such a complete set of cutlery. When she had arrived at his apartment that evening, there were three sleek forks, a stolid-looking knife, and a pair of spoons winking up at her from the table.

André sat down, shook his napkin between her and the soup.

"Well, yes, but they still want to maintain some links to Canada." She scraped the bottom of her soup bowl and put her spoon down, carefully, beside its mate. "That was amazing."

"Ah. So they are trying to kill two dead horses with one stone." He placed a plate of coq au vin in front of her. She began to cut it tentatively, marvelling at the weight of the knife in her hand. André looked at her as though he might have asked a question.

"Not exactly." She poured him some more wine, took a bite of chicken, rolled the sauces around on her tongue. He was still looking at her, waving the napkin in inquisitive arcs. "It's birds, or else just one dead horse," she began to explain, but André just smiled at her and rushed off into the kitchen to check on the crème brûlée.

One day, after an afternoon of paperwork at the language school, Fiona came home to a message from Henry on the machine. She was listening to it intently when the line beeped once, then twice quickly, the code for long distance, for high priority, for do not delay! She imagined it was probably her mother's weekly checkup call and considered ignoring it, something she found almost impossible to do, despite the fact she knew the call would be rerouted to the answering machine.

"Fiona?"

It was Henry. Henry on hold and Henry on the line. "How are you, Henry, are you okay?"

"I'm fine. I'm visiting this ashram near Hyderabad and I've been taking these posture workshops." Henry was slightly

breathless, and the long-distance line made his phrasing tele-
graphic. Declarative. Important-sounding.

"It's absolutely incredible. We do these sun salutations every
morning and practise selflessness. It's great – you should really
try yoga, Fiona – it's wonderfully freeing."

Fiona had tried yoga once, when she was going through a particularly hard time at work, although it had not been at Henry's
urging. She went to the classes faithfully, twice a week for three
weeks, but then she missed one for some reason – a flu bug? a
meeting? – and hadn't gone back. Now the only thing she
remembered about them was the way the instructor used to add
syllables to words, stretch them out in order to guide the class,
soothingly, through the exercises. Ex-hah-ah-la-tion. Trans-feh-
ehr. In-hah-ah-la-tion.

"So, when are you planning to come home, Henry?" She tried
to stretch out the sounds, to keep the pleading out of her voice.

"Oh, I don't think I am – at least not for a long while – I'm
trying not to plan at all, y'see. I met this guy from New Mexico
– we're thinking of travelling up through the Himalayas. He
knows someone in Katmandu, and I've always wanted to see
Tibet . . . Anyway, just thought I'd call and let you know I'm
okay . . ."

Let her know he was okay? Fiona held the phone away from
her ear, so that Henry's voice was still audible, but unintelligi-
ble; a news broadcast in a language not her own. What was most
irksome to Fiona was that, in some crevice of her heart, she
knew that Henry loved her, still, from across the wide and weird
expanse of world. But what she could not fathom was this voice
she held in her hand like something mistakenly shoplifted, this
Henry, but not-Henry. She brought the phone back up to her ear.

"Yeah, I'm glad you did, but I actually have to go. I have
someone on the other line. But take good care of yourself and
everything."

"Oh, that's exactly what I'm doing. Finally, taking care of
myself."

Fiona hung up the phone and sat down on the floor. The only
other time she had heard Henry so high, so fast-talking, was the

night he had misfilled a prescription and had had to devise a plan to get the drugs back, before the patient took them, and without revealing that he had made a mistake. Then, she had attributed his flushed cheeks and frantic pacing to a worry bordering on panic, but now she wondered if he had not been thriving on the crisis. What was it that she had missed, and how could she have missed it? Was love believing in someone or something so completely that it swallowed you, and you lived quite happily, never knowing you were in the belly of the thing until suddenly you were disgorged, unprepared, into an unfamiliar world? Or maybe not so suddenly. . . . Maybe, like some thick cloud, all that atmospheric affection gradually, secretly, seeped away.

Some days Fiona believed she had somehow, subliminally, forced Henry into his voyage of discovery and out of their relationship. She was not unaware of the power of the aside, the muffled comment, the unconscious clench (of teeth, of fists, or of less obvious parts of the anatomy). She knew that, if she squinted her mind's eye hard enough, she could come up with, if not concrete reasons, at least diaphanous premises for his leaving. Still, she had watched her parents squirm their way through such miscommunications and emerge, if not exactly butterflylike, at least with some measure of grace from the temporary cocoons they had built for themselves.

There was only one incident that stood out in her mind as a possible catalyst for Henry's behaviour. It was an argument, more of a discussion, really, they had had one evening over a story Henry had read in the paper on his way home in the subway.

"You should read this article," he said, after she had kissed him hello at the door. He was flicking at the page and shaking his head. "It's so incredibly sad." And the story was sad. A Japanese exchange student studying in the States had been killed two nights earlier because of an unfortunate misunderstanding. He had been invited to a Hallowe'en party and had gamely disguised himself – as Frankenstein or a superhero, Henry imagined. The story didn't say. Somehow, unwittingly, the student arrived at the wrong address, and the man who answered the door felt compelled to defend his home. He waved a gun at the student and yelled "Freeze!" But the student did not freeze. Instead of reaching for the sky he had extended his hands out toward the gunman, in a gesture of pleading or prayer, or, perhaps, a half-hearted attempt at humour. A trick-or-treat in the face of terror. The parents of the student, in their grief and incomprehension, were certain their son had misheard the gunman. "I think he must have thought the American said Please," they were quoted as saying.

"It's terrible, isn't it?" Henry had asked, watching her closely. "That we can so easily mistake someone's intentions – I mean Freeze – Please. It's just bizarre."

It seemed to Fiona that Henry had missed the point. Didn't it have more to do with cultural differences, with the right to bear arms, with the rights of the individual versus the safety of the collective? And when had the Americans ever said please?

"Henry," she said, "when have the Americans ever said please?"

Henry stared at her, and seemed about to say something either witty or retributive, then shook his head, close-mouthed and disappointed. She had let him down somehow, had ignored the wet puppy-dog gleam in his eyes. He had thrown something long and loose and ropelike in her direction; a noose or a life-buoy, and she had pretended not to see it. At the time, Fiona had felt a small bitter nugget of satisfaction lodge in her throat, but now – picturing his collapsed expression – she felt only a puzzled regret.

André took Fiona for ice cream and she told him about Henry – the phone calls, the ashrams. He listened without speaking throughout her account, squeezed her hand at all the hard parts. It was times like this Fiona understood that what she really wanted from André was not passion, or even compassion, but a sort of tender complicity; the knowledge that if she were ever arrested, the police would be on the lookout for a sidekick. Maybe it was all anybody ever wanted – someone to drive the getaway car. André asked her what kind of ice cream she was eating. "It's vanilla, with chunks of walnuts and stuff, with chocolate fudge swirls."

"Squirrels?" he said, and gave her a wary look.

"Oui," she replied, "les écureuils dans la crème glacée." Her accent was bad, and it made him smile.

"For all intensive purpose," he said, and looked into her eyes, "you should be forgetting about this guy. What you need is someone to put some springs in your feet."

Sometimes, on those hurtling bus rides across the St. Lawrence, Fiona thought she could feel her entire life around her; as if she could actually sense the whole of it, in the atmosphere, in the sky and sea to either side of the concrete bridge. It occurred to her that her birth and death were not really that far apart, and she often imagined these momentous events detachedly, as if she were watching a well-made documentary. Her death she less saw than intuited, in flashes of light on the water, or the lurching of the bus as it changed lanes. It was discomfiting, to feel one's own death, but it was not frightening. It made her think of Henry and his searching, and most times it made her feel used up and a bit empty – épuisée. But what seemed more revelatory to Fiona, although she supposed they were less far-fetched, were the dream trances in which she was introduced to her beginnings. Fiona, who had never been able to remember her childhood (a fact that had prompted her to remark jokingly to friends that this was either because it was incredibly traumatic or incredibly uneventful), this same Fiona could see her head crowning through her mother's vagina, scraggly and red; could feel the soft grapefruit of it in the doctor's large palm, and could sense a cry straining in her lungs, like a breath, only more emphatic.

Fiona sat on her balcony one day in early September, staring out across the hydro wires and TV antennae to the red and gold-tipped trees at the top of the mountain and thought to herself that she did not feel lonely. "I do not feel lonely," she said to the neighbour cat, who was eating what looked like the remains of some old poutine on the balcony next to hers. "I have not felt lonely for some time now." She thought that she missed Henry a little, in the same way she sometimes ached thinking of a view she had been forced to leave behind, or the way her feet used to carry her, instinctively to the nearest bus stop, and afterwards she could not recall exactly how she got there. But she did not feel lonely. She was shading her eyes, straining to see the time on the clock tower three streets over, when she saw the concierge on the neighbouring roof. He was poking around with what looked like a broom handle, prodding at the tennis balls and empty Coke cans that had landed next to the miraculous mounds of grass that grew out of the gravel. She watched him for a moment, then shouted a hello, feeling a bit embarrassed and voyeuristic at not having identified herself at the first sight of him. He turned and smiled at her.

"You know, the woman who used to live here, she would grow moss up here, then use it in her artwork. It was quite beautiful, really. You do artwork?" He walked over to the edge of the roof, closer to Fiona's balcony.

"No. Well, sort of." Lately she had taken to doodling on napkins and the backs of photocopies – swirls and spirals – small vortexes that went on forever. "I have the rent for you, I can give it to you when you come down." Fiona gestured toward the fire escape.

"No, no, no, you can give it to me here." The concierge pointed to the roof and then to the distance between himself and Fiona; a deep, dark elongated rectangle between the buildings. He extended his stick across the gap and grinned.

"Oh no, it's okay, I can give it to you when you come down." Fiona looked down into the gap and half-shrugged an apology. The concierge began picking up bits of leftover moss and string, in the hopes, she realized, of fashioning some sort of sticky grabber for the end of his stick. "Uh, I have Scotch tape," she said and went inside to find her chequebook. When she came out he was tying a pop can carefully onto one end of the stick.

"You can roll up the cheque and push it inside the hole," he called out excitedly without looking up. But the can was too heavy and would not stay, and eventually Fiona persuaded him to extend the stick to her side as it was, without modification. She rolled the tape and fastened the cheque to the sticky spiral. The concierge drew the stick back in toward him, slowly, like a makeshift fishing pole, and retrieved the cheque from the end. Then he began to laugh. He bent his knees slightly with each gasping inhale, then held up one finger to Fiona.

"Un moment," she whispered. It was that time of day when the sun is bent on lowering itself, a clutch of clouds at the small of its back. The air was warm and still.

"Thank you," said the concierge, and wiped a tear from his cheek with the back of his hand.

"No problem," Fiona replied, and looked out over the city. The rooftops spread to either side of her like rectangular lily pads. On the neighbouring building a pigeon was pecking and preening, and, in the distance, she thought she could make out a human silhouette against the sky. She nodded politely at the figure, then watched as the sun settled, slowly, into the dark slits between them.

VIVETTE J. KADY

Anything That Wiggles

Early that summer, my grandma dropped dead watching "The Price is Right," and the following week Aunt Lois, my mother's sister, moved in and declared we would no longer be running a breeding factory.

"This place is disgusting, Sandra. It stinks," she told my mother after she'd dragged her suitcases up to my grandma's old bedroom. "Dog poop under the kitchen table, piddle everywhere you walk. We won't even talk about the yard, which is a total disaster. And what's that piece of mouldy bread doing over by the sofa?" She placed a cool dry hand on the back of my neck. "You can't raise your daughter in a pigsty."

A few days later she counted the $450 she got from selling the last of our poodle Antoinette's puppies, then wiped her hands on her pink button-front beautician's smock and announced that the bitch would be spayed and that was that.

My mother winced and hugged her arms across her belly.

"Now don't give me that long face, Sandra," Aunt Lois said. "She's already had five litters."

But bullying our tenant, Roy Steele, into getting rid of the pigeons he kept in our backyard wouldn't be so easy.

"He'll probably die without them," my mother wailed. "Don't make him, Lois."

"He sometimes even talks like a pigeon," I added.

"Poorrrr poorrrr," my mother cooed, closing her eyes. "Poorrrr poorrrr."

"I had an agreement with your mother," Roy Steele told Aunt Lois. "I take care of the yard, and I get to keep my pigeons."

Roy's voice was soft as a puppy's belly. He stroked his beard and squinted in the sunlight. He was carrying a large plastic No Frills bag, and wearing his usual outfit: a stained grey suit jacket with patched elbows; flip-flops; a waist-length white halter-top blouse; a below-the-knee summer skirt with bunches of tiny white flowers on a background that matched his blue eyes.

"That's right," my mother nodded fiercely. "He did, Lois. Mom said he could."

Roy became my grandma's tenant soon after his wife, Bernice, died. He must have been about fifty-five or sixty. He had a spongy nose and a sweet face that crumpled when he smiled, and he kept Bernice's ashes in a dog-shaped cookie jar. My grandma used to look out the kitchen window and sigh at the sight of Roy cooing to his pigeons. "Grief," she'd say.

"You've got to be joking," Aunt Lois said. "Look at the state of this yard."

"Lawnmower's broke," Roy told her. "You get a new lawn-mower, I'll cut the grass."

When Aunt Lois said we were running a breeding factory in my grandma's house, she didn't just mean Antoinette's puppies and Roy's pigeons. She also meant me, because if my mother has any idea who my father is, she's never let on.

"Could be that schoolteacher down the road, whatsisname, McDougal," my grandma once said. "That'll explain where Angie gets her brains. And that man'll go after anything that wiggles."

Aunt Lois figured my grandma should've had my mother fixed years ago so she couldn't have any babies, because of her affliction. Aunt Lois's eyebrows lifted and her nostrils got wide when she said "affliction."

Grandma shrugged and said, "No matter – a baby brings its own love into the world."

My mother fell off a dresser onto her head when she was six months old. She does most things slowly – she talks slowly, blinks slowly, laughs five seconds after everyone else. And she has seizures.

"I get lightning storms," she once told me, "right inside my head," and for the longest time after that, whenever my mother's eyes started to flutter and it looked as if she were slipping off into one of her fits, I'd peer up her nostrils, hoping to see the bright jolts that lit up her shocked blue skull.

Aunt Lois decided she was going to quit her job at Top to Toe Beautiful! and open a beauty salon in our house. She figured the basement would be perfect, and counted the advantages on her fingers: "Separate entrance. Separate bathroom. No rent. Zero travel time to work. Location's not bad – there's a bus stop right around the corner. And I get to be my own boss. Plus, I can keep an eye on things around here."

My mother shoved a forkful of meatloaf into her mouth. Her calm brown eyes slowly blinked. "In the basement?"

"Please don't talk with your mouth full, Sandra. It might be a little dark right now, but nothing a few fluorescents and a fresh coat of paint can't fix. It maybe needs a couple pieces of drywall. We'll make it nice."

My mother chewed and swallowed before she spoke again. "But Roy lives down there. In the basement."

"Well yes, I'm aware of that. And I'm sorry about Roy. But somebody's got to work around here."

"We had an agreement, your mother and me," Roy said quietly. "Signed. I've got the lease."

He was sitting very straight in my grandma's favourite armchair, with the knotted No Frills bag on his lap. I tried to guess what he kept in it. Something bulky – maybe the jar with Bernice's ashes. He'd shown me that jar one day, down in his room – a happy-face dog with black spots and a sloppy red tongue. You opened it by twisting the head off.

"Well," Aunt Lois said, "you know, circumstances have changed."

"Hey." My mother looked up from the spot she'd been staring at on the carpet. Her face had lit up like a soft white moon. She pointed at the ceiling. "You can live upstairs, Roy."

"Upstairs." Aunt Lois's voice was flat.

My mother nodded happily. "In the attic."

Aunt Lois sighed and shook her head. "No, Sandra. There's no way he's living up there. He'd have to share our bathroom."

Roy scratched his beard. "That'll be okay."

"We're all females," Aunt Lois said.

Roy shifted back in the armchair and crossed his scabbed, hairy legs. "I don't mind."

"Well there's no kitchen up there."

"I don't like to cook. I'll take it." His blue eyes creased at the corners. "Less fifty a month."

Aunt Lois arranged for her ex-husband's cousin Tony to cover up pipes and ducts, put in some new lights, replace the stained broadloom, and patch and paint the basement.

"He's giving us a good price," she said. "And I've got nothing against Tony. He can't help it if his cousin's a loser."

Tony came and went in his blue panel van, carrying tools and drywall and cans of paint. He was big – over six feet, and heavy – but he moved around so quietly you almost forgot he was there until the hammering and drilling started. He didn't say much – "He's not exactly the sharpest knife on the block," Aunt Lois said – but that didn't stop my mother hanging around him. She kept bringing him doughnuts and Diet Pepsis.

A couple of days after Tony started on the basement, he arrived as Roy was going out to take care of his pigeons.

"Something wrong with that guy?" Tony asked.

I was holding the side door open while he carried his stuff in.

"No," I answered. "He just dresses weird."

"Yes there is," my mother said. She'd come up suddenly behind Tony and he jumped when she spoke. "Grief."

"Jeez," he said, "you scared me."

"From his wife. She died."

"Oh," Tony said.

"Bernice. She had cancer." She pushed away some hair from her eyes. "Want something to eat?"

He shook his head. "I'm okay. I just got here," he said, and ducked down the basement stairs.

School had been out for a couple of days when my grandma died. I'd been playing with Antoinette's puppies on the kitchen floor. I could hear the TV in the living room: "Travis Conway, come on down!"

"Angie!" my mother screamed.

On the TV, Bob Barker was saying, "Here come my beauties with the next item up for bids."

My grandma was in her favourite armchair, her head flung back, legs thrust forward.

"It's a new washer and dryer!"

My mother had backed away from my grandma. She stood, rigid, next to the TV. The mute blue-suited blonde woman on the TV screen curtsied and smiled as she caressed the top of the washing machine with long red fingernails. "Call 911," my mother said.

I ran to the kitchen, dialled the number, gave the emergency operator details, ran back to the living room. "He says we have to talk to her until they get here."

"Mom," my mother said. She stayed next to the TV set. "Please, Mom, don't."

"Actual retail price is $550," Bob Barker said.

Within minutes, sirens were wailing. I opened the door, and pointed to the living room. Large black-booted paramedics clumped in and swarmed around my grandma's chair.

"And it's a fabulous trip to Denmark!"

The lucky contestant was hopping and shrieking and flapping her arms. My mother rocked back and forth, her hands clawing at the sleeves of her T-shirt.

One of the paramedics took the remote from my grandma's lap and turned off the TV. My mother kept rocking. A thick humming sound pushed past her throat and tongue.

When the basement was ready, delivery men arrived with boxes of beauty supplies and an adjustable esthetician's table. We unpacked lotions and creams, cuticle sticks and cotton balls, and stacked clean folded towels on shelves. Aunt Lois hung her framed beauty school diploma on the wall. On a sheet of blank paper, she carefully wrote:

Esthetic Care by Lois
~ facials ~ manicures ~ pedicures ~
eyebrow & eyelash tinting ~
~ waxing ~ nail extensions ~
Exclusive Professional Service for a New You
Call 245-3063 for an appointment
331 Bartlett Street (side door).

She drew daisies with intertwined stems around the border of the page, then made five hundred photocopies on bright pink paper. We shoved the flyers through mail slots, tacked them up in laundromats and supermarkets, and stapled them to hydro poles. Within three days, she'd set up an appointment for her first client.

"A bikini and underarm wax," she announced triumphantly. "Now Roy had better get this yard in shape."

Half an hour before her first client was due to arrive, my mother and I were helping Aunt Lois prepare. We smoothed a crisp blue sheet over the padded beauty table; we set out some powder and Kleenex and cloth strips.

"Listen, both of you," she said, adjusting the temperature of the melting wax, "I want to make sure you understand I'm running a business here. Please don't come down while I'm busy with a client."

Blood flared across my face. "We wouldn't."

"Good. I don't mean to hurt your feelings, Sandra. But you'd scare people off if you had one of your fits down here."

"Yes," my mother said. But I knew it was an almost unbearable loss, to be excluded from the mysteries of those beautiful bottles with their sweet-scented lotions and masques; the rows of sponges and Q-tips and nail polish; those tidy towels.

Before Aunt Lois's first client could make it to the side door, she was greeted by Antoinette and Roy. Antoinette had darted past Roy when he opened the front door. She bounded up to the visitor, wagging her tail and yapping, then stood up on her hind legs, hugged her forelegs around the woman's skinny calf, and began humping it enthusiastically.

Roy nodded politely. The client gaped at him. She shook her leg, but Antoinette held fast. The poodle's tongue was licking in and out.

"Dog's taken a fancy to you," Roy said.

"Oh for Chrissakes," Aunt Lois hissed from the hallway. "Angie, go get that stupid animal!"

I ran out and scooped up Antoinette. "Bad girl!" I scolded. "Sorry," I mumbled to the woman.

Roy winked at me, bowed slightly to the woman, and walked off down the street. The woman looked stunned. She rubbed her leg absently.

Tony had fastened a brass sign to the side door: *Esthetics by Lois*. Aunt Lois smiled brightly as she opened the door. "You must be Celine," she said. "This way."

"The guy with the beard, is he one of those, whatyacallits, cross-dressers?" Celine asked as she followed Aunt Lois down the basement steps.

When the appointment was over, Aunt Lois's face was grim. "In future, when a client comes, stay out of my way," she said. "All of you. And lock up that damned dog."

"Squab," Roy said. "That's what the young ones are called. People eat them."

"Yuck," I said.

"They do, though. In fancy restaurants. Pay a lot of money for them, too. They're tasty – plump and tender."

I fake-vomited. Roy smiled. He spread grass clippings over the wood shavings that lined the pigeons' nest boxes.

What I liked best about Roy was that he never asked difficult questions. A whole morning could go by without him once asking what you learned in school, or what you planned to be when you were older, or why you didn't have friends over.

"Hello, Mabel. Hi there, Percy," he said. "Are you my beauties? Yes, you are. Poorrrr, poorrrr."

He put fresh water and pigeon pellets into tin cans. His fingernails were chewed and dirty, and covered with chipped silver nail polish. The birds inched closer, bandy-legged, their small hard heads pulsing in and out. They blinked their eyes.

"If that makes you throw up, you want to see what the parents feed the babies."

"Is it really gross?"

He opened his mouth wide and pointed down his throat. "Pigeon milk. Stuff they make inside their crops."

I pulled a disgusted face. He looked pleased.

The screen door slammed and my mother came charging toward us.

"I'm going on a date!" she yelped.

"Whoa," Roy said.

She stood red-faced and breathless. There was a bright blob of jelly at the corner of her mouth. Her smile was pure joy. "For Chinese food. Tonight, with Tony."

Tony stood in the entrance hall. He shuffled from foot to foot and smoothed his hair. He looked around at the walls, the ceiling, the baseboards, as if checking for cracks.

"I'll go see if she's ready," I said, and ran upstairs.

Roy was waiting outside the bathroom door. He rolled his eyes at me. "I think we need to send in a search party. She must've got lost. I'm dying out here. Hey, Sandra," he called out, "you planning to take much longer?"

"How bad do you need to go?" she answered.

I rapped on the door. "Hurry up, Mom. Tony's already here."

"Tell him to wait."

She emerged a few minutes later, cheeks rouged, hair sprayed, eyes lined with baby blue iridescent shadow, lips painted a thick glossy coral. She'd used a generous amount of my grandma's old perfume, and she was clutching a black satin purse with both hands. She thrust her chest out and her chin up. "Am I pretty?" she asked.

I nodded. "And you smell good."

"You look very nice, Sandra," Roy said.

"Thank you." She wiggled her shoulders, then reached inside the neck of her dress to adjust her bra strap. Roy darted into the bathroom.

Aunt Lois came upstairs. "What's taking so long?" she asked.

She inspected my mother and frowned. "Wait a minute. Angie, quick, get me a Kleenex."

She expertly wiped the excess rouge from my mother's cheeks, then held the tissue to my mother's lips. "Blot," she said.

"I don't know why we bother. None of them are worth it," she muttered as we followed my mother down the stairs. My mother turned and gave a little wave when she opened the front door. Tony's hand crept toward the rustling fabric of her dress and his fingers touched her back as she flounced out the door.

Days went by after their date, and Tony didn't call. My mother became distant, drawn into herself, as if she had curled around a secret. She sighed at magazines and the TV, or she lay on the floor patting Antoinette, who watched her with worried eyes. She sat in the yard, listlessly swatting at insects and staring at the grass. Aunt Lois offered to teach her how to give manicures, and my mother practised with orange sticks and bowls of warm fragrant water, but she still moped.

At night I'd thrash my way out of nightmares and slip into her bed. She'd wind strands of my hair around her fingers and we'd lie there, wordless, until we fell asleep, leaning into one another.

Tony finally called, on a sweltering afternoon, more than a week after their date. The air was so thick and humid you could barely breathe, and I'd put on my swimsuit so I could run through the sprinkler in the backyard. Roy and my mother were sitting on folding lawn chairs under the lilac tree, and Antoinette panted in the shade under my mother's chair. Aunt Lois came outside after her two-thirty eyelash tint.

"Have a seat," Roy said, standing up. "I'll get another chair."

"Thank you, Roy." There were wet circles under the arms of her pink smock, and she fanned her face and throat with her hands. "I've got an hour between clients. What a scorcher."

When the phone rang, my mother stood so fast she knocked over the chair, and Antoinette raced with her into the house, barking at her heels. She came back outside a few minutes later and crashed through the sprinkler spray, whooping softly, her arms pinwheeling. Antoinette circled her, yapping.

"No need to ask who that was," Roy said.

My mother stood in the centre of the spray, grinning and gasping.

"This place is a complete madhouse," Aunt Lois said.

My mother flopped down in her chair, soaking wet. "Tony's coming," she announced.

"You better change out of those wet clothes," Aunt Lois said.

"No. I'm nice and cool," my mother said.

"Go on, Sandra. You can see right through that blouse."

My mother giggled, then covered her mouth with her hand. Aunt Lois frowned.

"I was going to anyway," my mother said. "You don't always have to tell me what to do." She stood, haughtily. "When Tony comes, tell him to wait," she called over her shoulder.

Roy cleared his throat. Antoinette came over and began humping his leg.

"Antoinette, stop that!" Aunt Lois said.

Roy uncrossed his legs, bent over and patted Antoinette. She rolled onto her back, and he slipped his foot out of his sandal and scratched her belly with his toes.

I lay on a towel in the sun, my legs positioned to catch the cool shiver of water as the sprinkler passed to and fro.

"It's too hot to be watering the lawn. You'll scorch the grass," Aunt Lois said.

Roy shrugged.

"He'll break her heart, you know."

Roy shrugged again. "Maybe not."

"They're all the same. Only after one thing." She drew her mouth into a thin line.

"Well," Roy said, grinning at her, "I guess sometimes it's worth it. As I recall, that one thing can be very nice."

Aunt Lois looked at him for a moment, then laughed. "Sometimes," she said. After a while, she said, "What are you doing, wearing a jacket in this heat? There's a humidex warning and you're sitting out here in that jacket."

Roy smiled, shyly.

"Go on, take it off. You're making me hot just to look at you."

He took off the jacket. He had dark hairy armpits under the white sleeveless blouse. He smoothed his skirt over his knees, and folded his pale arms across his chest, and I suddenly decided that the skirt and blouse must have belonged to Bernice.

"Do you have children, Roy?" Aunt Lois asked.

"One. She's an artist, out on Galiano Island. She sent me a card a couple weeks ago. Made it herself." He closed his eyes for a few moments, then he opened them and said, "I better go see to my pigeons."

"Oh, sit a while. They can wait. It's too hot to move." She sniffed. "Tell me, Roy, what's so special about those birds of yours?"

He thought for a moment. "They always come back."

"They always come back?"

"They'll fly off into the wide blue sky, but they'll come back to you."

"There's a lot to be said for that, I suppose," Aunt Lois said. "Speaking of which, here's Tony."

I sat up on my towel. Tony walked over and sat down carefully in the chair next to Aunt Lois.

"Do you believe this heat?" she asked him.

"It's pretty warm," Tony said.

"There's a humidex warning."

"I heard," he said.

"You did a good job in the basement. No complaints so far."

"That's good," he said.

We all sat in silence until my mother came out. She walked up to us, slowly, in her soft yellow sundress. "Hi, Tony," she said, and smiled wide. There was something off-centre in her eyes. And then her eyelids fluttered, her mouth twitched, and I was sure I could hear the shift and crackle of the boisterous nerves inside her skull.

"Oh boy," Roy said, "she's off again," and we all rose into the heave of that steamy afternoon.

MARGRITH SCHRANER

Dream Dig

The Dream

Ulyssa Segantini can hardly believe her eyes when, upon approaching her meticulously clean kitchen counter just after midnight, she sees a fleshy, crescent-shaped *something* lying there, all by itself, in full view. Upon closer inspection she recognizes the soft, fleshy, pink rim – lobe and all – as the outer shell of her own ear. She stares at it in disbelief. Upon turning it over, she discovers telltale signs of an abscess: two spots, the size of nail holes and approximately an inch apart. The holes have been filled with white putty; they make it look as though a hinge had come off.

Ulyssa realizes at once that she won't be able to have the earshell sewn back on; the deathly whiteness of the tissue communicates this to her with finality. She has never heard of doctors resurrecting wasted, dead tissue and sewing it back onto live flesh, and this disturbs her no small amount.

Facing the mirror to the left of the counter and resolutely lifting her shoulder-length hair, she courageously inspects the left side of her head. To her surprise, there is no blood where the earshell has fallen off. There are no signs of ripping or tearing. There is simply a stump, close to the ear canal. She looks down at the earshell on the counter. The awful, dead whiteness of the tissue reminds her of a vegetable that has succumbed to the ravages of hoarfrost, making the tissue soft and breaking it down; it could be a cauliflower left in the fridge for too long. She looks back at her fleshy stump in the mirror. The small protrusion surrounding the ear canal is like a stalk and faintly reminiscent of a trumpet. It reminds her of the inner spiral of a magnificent, pink conch shell, shattered by beating waves, the truncated remnant sadly unable to issue the faint murmur of the ocean she once heard as a child.

Flesh-eating disease! The thought rises spontaneously in her mind. Far from suggesting a possible cure, this self-diagnosis only serves to confound her even more. More dreadful consequences begin to suggest themselves; ghosts of fear begin to creep in and insinuate what is likely to happen next: first one, and then another body part – fingers and toes and such – might decay, soften, and fall off. A progressive disease, as she sees it, and incurable.

Still, she must try to get to the doctor, and quickly. Rummaging in the kitchen drawer for a piece of tinfoil to wrap the earshell in, she notices with surprise that the underside of the foil is covered with silvery writing and that the silvery writing is her own letter to her mother, dated three years earlier, reporting the onset of a mysterious infection. The infection had resulted in an itch that made her scratch, first her neck, then her chin, then her cheeks. Finally the itch had mounted to a region behind her eyes.

Ulyssa realizes at once that these were the early symptoms connected to her present condition. She discards the option of using the tinfoil, puts it back in the drawer, and reaches for a shallow white soup bowl. She places the earshell in the soup bowl and puts a kettle of water on the stove to boil, thinking she should sterilize the earshell before presenting it to the doctor.

Her eyes are drawn to the postcard-sized photograph affixed to the clipboard door above the kitchen counter. The photograph seems to have been taken early in the morning, because there are neither shadows nor sunlight. "Win a week in Tuscany," reads the caption. It depicts a twelfth-century castle that has apparently been converted into modern rental apartments, situated halfway between Florence and Siena. The path approaching the castle is flanked by dark cypress trees, columnar and slender, which produce a feeling of hushed anticipation.

The Castle

No wind stirs as Ulyssa – soup bowl clutched at her waist – approaches the castle. Morning is on the verge of dawning. The castle sits on a large mound overlooking a town whose name has been chiselled into a boulder. The name is a strange mixture of hieroglyphics and Roman numerals; the odd script makes the name indecipherable and therefore unpronounceable.

A bluish-green haze lies over the middle distance and obstructs the view of nearby hills and mountains that Ulyssa instinctively knows are there. The cypress trees to her left – hundreds of feet tall and hundreds of years old – stand like sentinels, piercing the sky darkly. The road leading to the castle is extremely dusty. No rain seems to have fallen for a very long time. Beside the road, she spots the dried fruit of a conifer, a globe-shaped cone that magnetically draws her over to it. She holds the soup bowl with the earshell in her left hand and picks up the brownish grey cone with her right. The shieldlike scales guarding the seeds are rough and slightly sharp to her touch. She is familiar with the species name, *sempervirens*, meaning it lives forever. She puts the cone in the pocket of her skirt and continues to walk slowly and meditatively in the direction of the castle.

She has travelled most of the night to get here. The arched doorway of the castle is decorated with the same odd hieroglyphics she first witnessed on the boulder beside the road. The name continues to elude her. Undaunted, she pulls back the heavy wooden door and enters the castle. There are two vast stairways, one ascending and the other descending. Choosing the latter, she heads down the worn steps and finds herself in a vaulted stone hall. Behind a door that bears the image of Sekhmet, the lion-headed Goddess of Healing, there lies a large chamber that she realizes is an apothecary. The wall at the far end bears a larger than life-sized reproduction of the painted sun barge that was said to have carried dead pharaohs to the next world. Two of the remaining walls are covered with various papyri bearing conjuring health formulas, tomb inscriptions, and motifs from *The Book of the Dead of Ani*.

Ulyssa seems to be the only person in the room. Suddenly realizing how chill the air has become, her body responds by shivering. The large counter to her right is flanked by an impressive number of shelves displaying a systematic arrangement of various surgical instruments: knives, tweezers, chisels, blades, mortars, and so forth, and above these are many kinds of resins, herbal powders, oils, and ointments in tinted glass containers of varying sizes and shapes. The display is augmented by salve spoons, swabs, linen material, and bandages.

A man who looks faintly like a butcher appears behind the counter and gestures to her. She turns around to ensure that the man is addressing her and not someone else. Approaching him, she proffers the soup bowl containing the earshell. No words are exchanged. The man, dressed in the usual pharmacist's attire, graciously receives the bowl and disappears with it into the shadows of a labyrinthine stockroom.

"Ulyssa Segantini," a sepulchral voice announces several minutes later over a loudspeaker, "your order is ready for pickup."

She discovers that she has been absentmindedly gazing at her hands, as though in a trance. When she looks up she notices that the pharmacist has returned from the stockroom and is now for some reason wearing a jackal mask. He hands her a small, white delicatessen box around which some string made of knotted grass has been tied in a bow. Taking the box, she nods her appreciation. She notices that a label has been affixed to the box. The typed message says, "Illumination is the space between your ears." The word "between" is underlined in pink.

The Elevator

Ulyssa does not know how she has come to be in the elevator. During the ride, which seems to take an enormously long time, she looks at the peeling paint on the walls and the posterlike advertisements that were obviously designed to educate visitors to the castle. Her eyes are drawn to a quote attributed to Ramses II: "The past is never dead, not even is it past." Directly above it is an encyclopedia-style, full-colour depiction of a sarcophagus. The pictorial script labelling the various components of the sarcophagus is illegible; either her eyesight is dimming or the light in the elevator is too feeble to read by.

The largest of the labels, and one which she can make out by squinting, is the word *sarkophagos*, which has been playfully cut in half, with translations on either side: *sark*, or *sarx*, meaning "flesh" and *phagos*, meaning "eating."

Flesh-eating! The word reminds her of something, but she can't remember exactly what. She begins to feel caught, as if in the machinations of a confusing dream. She looks down at the small white box in her hand. Did she feel something stir inside? Did she feel something shudder? She is not sure.

Directly across from the poster with the sarcophagus is a photograph of a newborn, three days old at most, wearing a tiny knitted blue cap; the hands of the mother are visible in the picture as they hold up the infant's head in profile. The picture reveals a remarkably large left ear that she recognizes as her grandson's.

"How odd," she mutters to herself. "What is a photograph of my grandson doing here in this elevator?"

The Excavation Site

The elevator opens out onto a roof garden. The railings around the periphery of the roof are supported by stone pillars that bear stylized renditions of the calyx tubes of wild pomegranate flowers. She steps out onto a balcony-sized platform and looks out over the extensive herb garden below. Workers in dusty garments and painters' caps are digging in the garden, but for a reason she cannot fathom there seems to be an excavation of a crypt in progress.

Already a large part of the crypt has been laid bare. She looks through the tiny viewfinder of a spotting-scope that has been set up for purposes of observation: an amazing array of mummified birds, cats, and serpents have already been unearthed from the burial site and propped up in a row on a rough wooden board. The mummified creatures sway slightly in the breeze that has begun to stir. The wind carries whirls of dry soil up to where she is standing. Sneezing, she must avert her eyes for a moment.

When she looks again, the workers are taking a siesta. To her amazement, she discovers that the spotting-scope is now focused on hundreds of porcelain ears sticking out of the dirt sides of the excavation site and that the porcelain ears are glinting quite fiercely in the hot noon-hour sun.

She draws back from the spotting-scope, even more mystified. The sun has begun to set in slow motion. There is a sudden din of chirping that she recognizes as the sound of crickets. As the sun sinks below the hills, the insistent chirping is gradually reduced to a dull roar, like that of traffic on a faraway *autostrada*. This sound is succeeded by the whispered prattling of birds – or is it the buzzing of bees? She is worried, unsure. It might be the effect of tinnitus, a ringing sound in the ear that is the result of frayed nerve endings.

She senses it is time to open the small white delicatessen box. She unknots the bow and unwinds the string from around it. Hesitantly, she lifts the lid. Inside the box, lying on a bed of cypress twigs, are two ears connected as though by a fleshy hinge. The ears begin to flap tentatively, much like the wings of a butterfly, slowly, as though rousing themselves from a long sleep. They proceed to flap more insistently, then with even greater vigour. Before she can close the lid, the ear-shaped butterfly has lifted itself out of the box and is flying off over the balcony railings. She tries to seize it in flight, but falls into a swoon as she tumbles over the railing.

The Acupuncturist

Ulyssa blinks once, then twice. She stares at the photograph taped to the kitchen cupboard door. For a moment, she thinks she has seen someone fling herself from the roof of the twelfth-century castle, in pursuit of a butterfly. Now she thinks it might have been a trick played on her by her senses. She must have temporarily fallen into a daze, a reverie of some kind. Yes, that must be it.

A week earlier, she had gone to see her acupuncturist, a practitioner of Traditional Chinese Medicine. Due to her extremely fragile constitution, he had decided to refrain from sticking needles into her body and experiment instead with an alternative method that involved affixing tiny seeds to strategic spots on her ears and securing them with adhesive tape. She could then activate these acupuncture points by pressing these seeds several times in the course of a day and thereby be in control of administering her own treatments.

The acupuncturist had pointed to a large colour poster hanging on the wall of the consultation room. It depicted a very large ear. She recalls his explanation that the outer part of the ear mimicked in shape and outline the position of a child *in utero* and that the exact position of the organs could be charted accordingly. The earlobe, for instance, coincided with the head of the upside-down baby, and so on, up along the rim of the ear.

In Chinese Medicine, he had said, the ear was perceived to function as the window to the kidney.

"Large ear – large kidney – long life!" he had added.

She recalled the saying about eyes being the window to the soul and asked him if this analogy was correct.

"No, in Chinese Medicine, the eyes are the window to the liver," he had responded, laughing politely.

The Soup Bowl

Ulyssa realizes that the ringing in her ears is actually the sound of the kettle whistling on the stove. Turning off the burner and removing the kettle, she takes it over to the counter. Seconds after pouring boiling water over the earshell in the soup bowl, she realizes with horror that she has made a grave mistake.

"Oh, God – now I've cooked it!" she titters incredulously, unable to believe her own stupidly. What had possessed her? What had she been thinking of? A growing feeling of agony rises in her chest as she contemplates the finality of her actions that have resulted in the irreversible loss of a body part. She thinks that she is altogether in the wrong life, and that it is all due to too much stress. Indeed, she has probably passed on some of this stress to her daughter and even to her grandson.

Suddenly, she feels as though her moorings had been lost. She feels adrift in the New World, no longer connected to her home in Switzerland, a terribly insubstantial and flimsy shell of a human being. She must nourish her weak condition and now drinks the water in the soup bowl, absentmindedly, sipping it slowly, like a broth. The earshell bumps up against her lips several times, forcing her to push it out of the way with the tip of her tongue. She spits out a small piece of cellophane tape that has entered her mouth by mistake. A small, dark seed – vaguely globular in shape – is stuck to it.

"My God!" she thinks. "It has come to this – drinking broth made of my own ear. How horrible!"

With a sense of sad inevitability, she takes both the seed and the scalded earshell out to the backyard and, by the light of the moon, proceeds to bury them in the loose, rich soil of a potted lemon geranium. In no time at all, the seed sprouts and begins to grow into a lovely tree. The roots wrap themselves down over the rim of the pot and twist themselves into the earth and the trunk shoots like a rocket toward the night sky. Her sense of sadness is replaced by amazement and delight. Judging from the scalelike leaves growing in dense, fan-shaped sprays and the reddish-yellow bark, the tree is a descendant of the king of all cypresses, the *cupressus sempervirens*.

The following night, when she goes outside to view the marvellous cypress again, she notices that innumerable ears have sprouted from its branches and have cocked themselves in the direction of the moon, as though to better listen to the pallid glow sliding down through the night air.

HEATHER BIRRELL

Machaya

"Stay away from all the big beaches, eh, all the hoo-hah. You don't need that. Just the sand and the sun, that's enough." Misha's father was sitting at the kitchen table, his empty dinner plate pushed to one side. When he said hoo-hah he moved his arms suddenly, like a party.

"Leo, are you sure you can't come with us – the break – it would do you good." Misha's mother's voice sounded softer than usual, and as she spoke she fiddled with a Kleenex she had tucked up her sleeve.

"Sophie, you know we've been over this before. This is a crucial time, what with the new shipment coming in. It would be completely stupid for me to leave."

"Yes, yes." She ran her fingers through Misha's hair, tugged on his ears, whispered into one of them. "Alors, ce sera nous deux, seulement, *habibi*."

"You'll have to take care of your mother, eh, Misha? Hold her hand on the airplane." Misha's father looked at him, waiting. Misha nodded, then watched his father's gaze shift and reconfigure as if there was an interesting TV show playing in the next room.

But Misha had not been altogether sure of the whole idea of a vacation and what it would entail. It seemed to him there were perhaps more pitfalls involved in the process than his father was letting on; more sneaky obstacles to be overcome than were initially obvious to the untrained traveller. He thought he might like to stay home.

Misha's room is at the back of the condo; a small room with many windows, so that, in the morning, he wakes to an intense red, his eyelids made transparent by the strength of the sun. At the edge of dream there are sounds; tennis balls *donking* against the court, or *thwanging* against tautly strung rackets. And this is where he thinks, *Today, Vacation,* his red eyes still closed, and the so-very-new sensation of saltwater pulling his skin tight across his bones. He remembers, in the porousness of half-sleep, one hundred watchful shorebirds, their legs like oversized french fries, who stood guard around his bed somewhere in the night. He remembers sleep itself, the sensation of being held, gently, by his own body. When he finally, forcefully, opens his eyes, the slow red sun bursts into the white light of southern hospitality. "Y'all," says the sun, and really means it, "Y'all!"

He spends his mornings in the sand, sand stuck like sugar on the backs of his legs, sand clumping in folds in the crotch of his swim trunks, bits of grit caught with sunshine and saltwater in his scalp. He meets people on the beach: Jocelyn, a gorgeous bossy ten-year-old with sparkly nail polish on her toes, and Evan, a four-year-old whose sun-bleached hair falls in a chunk across his blank blue eyes. Misha hates Evan. Misha makes him dig the moats of the castles they scoop together, then shoves handfuls of sand back into the shallow trenches while Evan is fetching stones or shells from the edge of the ocean. He hates Evan because Evan lets him give the orders and sabotage the results, hates him for the floppiness of his manner and his slow, unblinking trust.

"I saw what you did to Evan. You're nothing but a piece of dirt under my feet." Jocelyn crosses her arms over her chubby torso, her puffy new boobs caught in the crooks of her elbows. "I'm gonna tell my mom, and she's gonna tell your mom, and then you're gonna see what you're gonna see."

Jocelyn has a way of stretching out her threats, elaborating on what would otherwise be more effective retorts. For Misha, this makes her both more attractive and slightly less intimidating. It means he has time to think while she is talking. He knows she will only turn him in if there is nothing better to do. Above him, the sun is a clean white ball high in the endless sky. The ocean laps at Jocelyn's perfect pink toes. She stares at him, then grabs her beach bag and stomps off.

Misha's mother is wading out into the ocean, on her tiptoes, her palms poised above the glitzy waves. Misha is watching her, and she knows it. She looks back at him, sprawled like a doll on the beach blanket.

"Machaya!" she shouts out. "What a life!"

Misha says the word to himself, *machaya*, and pulls a smooth green piece of glass from the sand. He holds it up to the sun, peers through it and scopes the length of the beach. He can see Jocelyn and her mother making their way down from the motel. Jocelyn is half-running, her feet crazy and uncertain in her flip-flops. He doesn't feel like dealing with her, traipsing through whatever elaborate punishment she may have concocted. He is weary of this whole vacation with its constant state of sand and sun. He misses the quietness of his playroom, the grit and dash of the schoolyard. *Snow*.

Misha's mother, now waist-deep, is already moving her arms in heart-shaped formations in the water in front of her. Jocelyn has spotted Misha and is flip-flopping purposefully in his direction. He turns away from her pushy girl's body, squints through the glass at his mother, who is still fake-swimming. Then she trips, he thinks, is caught for a second in an underwater crumple. Then, screaming. Like he has never heard before and at first does not believe, until he sees other people running toward the sound that has pierced the endless morning.

Later, after the intermittent light of the ambulance has retreated into the stew of pink balconies, magnolia blossoms, and asphalt that coats the city, and Jocelyn's mother has taken charge of him, Misha will close his eyes against the worry tattooed across her face.

"I'm going to call your dad, okay, Misha? Okay?" Misha stares at her, with her orange and yellow sarong, so strangely tied, so that the ends stick out like tiny extra hands from her hip.

"It's the shock," she whispers knowingly to Jocelyn, and leads her away by the elbow. Jocelyn peers back at him over her shoulder. *Shock*, her eyes say, *it's the shock*.

But Misha does not feel shock, a sensation he associates with suddenness and electricity. Instead what he feels is a slowness like swimming, and an unwillingness to become excited by the events of the day, which, it seems to him, have been unfolding at a safe, shimmery distance. Jocelyn's mother has draped a blanket across his shoulders, and plumped the pillows on the sofa bed to make him more comfortable. He is not tired, and he can hear rustlings and murmurs from the kitchen: a steady lowing of anxiety. He shifts the pillows around to create a small fort for his head, buries his nose in the cracks between the cushions.

Misha understands that somehow, in some way, he is guilty of something. A lack of vigilance, or a misunderstanding grown fat with its own mistaken importance. He has allowed himself to fall, artlessly, into this vacation and its trappings, and, in some small, whispered way, is responsible for the terrible way it has evolved.

When the plane first touched down in Florida, Misha had watched as people clapped and turned to each other with congratulatory smiles and brisk, happy nods. The stewardesses fussed dutifully and warned the passengers not to unbuckle their seat belts until the *bong* that accompanied the warning light had sounded. But Misha saw that his mother unbuckled anyway, sighed and filled her abdomen with air as if it were the seat belt itself and not their airborne state that had kept her movements restricted, stilted. He reached out his hand to hold her back, then changed his mind and turned to the woman next to him, who shifted from side to side, pulled a makeup bag from her carry-on, and fished out a tubular case with tiny snaps on the front. Inside was a lipstick in the sleek shape of a bullet, and a small rectangular mirror was fastened onto the case's flapping lid. The woman, whose name was Christa, Misha knew, unscrewed the lipstick lid and swivelled the stick of colour up into the stale atmosphere of the airplane's cabin. She brought the case up to her face, angled it, then pressed the lipstick along her bottom lip. Then she turned to Misha, held the tiny mirror up to his face, and passed him the tube.

"Here, you try," she said, and smiled, her darkened lips stretched to either side of her small turned-up nose.

"Okay," he said, took the lipstick, and tilted his head to see in the mirror. His mother was also sifting through her bag, stacking passports, pens, and brochures in her lap.

He finished putting on the lipstick and puckered his lips at Christa, sucking in his cheeks as he had seen his mother do. Christa laughed and puckered too.

"That's it, sweetie. Perfect." She reached across the seat and cupped his chin in her hand. "You look perfect."

Earlier in the trip there had been a meal in tiny plastic compartments – chicken and round tasteless potatoes, then sweet icinged cake for dessert. At the end of the narrow aisle next to Christa was a metal bathroom with a swift sucking toilet and a Kleenex box stuck to the wall. Misha had visited the bathroom twice, by himself, following the curved sides of the plane that surrounded him like a shining city nighttime, its long line of peepholes blinking out into the blue, seemingly solid air. He had watched as his mother slid one of the peephole's sliding panels back like an eyelid, had leaned over her to look out, and down. Below the plane, on the ground, unadulterated blobs of turquoise and hunter green nudged up against each other. Above the blobs, everywhere, always, were the odd top sides of clouds, stretched, puddled, or piled under the plane's sharp silver wings. And through it all, his mother, with her voice like an animal that lived inside of him, nuzzling and fierce. On the ground, behind him, in a newly snow-whitened city called Montreal, was his father, with his smooth blue suit, and quick hard hugs.

"You'll be all right alone?" he had asked, Misha thought, but it was less like a question than an announcement, his mouth shaping the words that would carry them through to the other side, the other country. "Remember, you'll take the St. Petersberg shuttle – it leaves every half-hour," he said, his eyes skimming over the other passengers boarding. "Looks like you've got a lot of Peppers on your flight."

"Leonard, ne soyez pas raciste." Misha's mother leaned into his father, placed her hand on the lapel of the blue suit.

"I'm not being racist, I'm being realistic. They're a buncha meshuganahs, always with the smoking and the drinking and the junk food . . ." He looked down at Misha, winked at him.

Misha winked back with both eyes, feeling stupid and pleased, which was how he always felt with his father.

"Viens, mon cherie." His mother pulled her purse up on her shoulder, then took Misha's hand and reached up to kiss her husband.

Then it had all been like a big show: the handing over of things – tickets, small pillows decorated with tiny maple leaves, scratchy blankets, empty trays, and bulging brown wastepaper bags, the view from the peepholes, Christa the friendly seat-mate, and the smiling-strict stewardesses, with their questions and pats and pinches. And now, finally, the applause, and the deep pilot voice wishing them a pleasant stay and informing them, convincingly, of the time and the weather.

"There's a dead snake on the beach. I'm going to operate on it." Misha flung out his arm in front of him, half-point, half-showmanship. "You can come if you like."

Jocelyn and Misha had been playing together for three days, their friendship half-buried like an abandoned pop bottle in the sand.

Jocelyn hurled a dismembered crab claw at him, but agreed. Evan, who was busy scrabbling in the sand castle's shallow moat, followed them, looking a little like a crab himself.

The snake was not actually a snake; it was a trailing stem of seaweed that had washed ashore, but once the fiction had been established, neither Misha nor Jocelyn felt any need to dismantle it.

"Water snakes are the most deadly of all snakes," Jocelyn pronounced, and held her arms out in a prohibitive, parentlike gesture. "First we must ensure the area is clear of any dangerous particles." She marched around the periphery of the snake site, inspecting the sand, reaching down every so often to nudge at something (a particle?) with her finger. Misha and Evan stood at a respectful distance, eyeing the snake with the reverence and caution it deserved.

Finally, Jocelyn declared the area safe, and the boys moved in to begin the job. The snake's skin sliced open easily with the edge of a seashell, although its innards were not as satisfyingly gunky as they had hoped. Misha sent Evan to fetch a bucket and spade to aid in the dissection, and reabsorbed himself in the work.

When Jocelyn was concentrating she sometimes sang a little, under her breath, tuneless.

"What is that song?" Misha asked, after they had been hacking at the snake for what felt like a long time. Jocelyn didn't hear him at first, continued picking and peeling at the snake's skin with her stubby fingernails. He leaned over her, spoke into her face like a microphone.

"Jo-ce-lyn. What is that song?"

And her eyes changed somehow, the quiet fixedness required by the task at hand replaced by something momentarily wild and zinging. She stood up, cleared her throat.

"It's James *Brown*. It's my *dad's* favourite song." She pushed the sand to either side of her with her feet to make a stage, closed her eyes, and tapped her open hand against her hip.

Then she began to sing. Her eyes snapped open and skidded over Misha and Evan to the cheering throngs she had conjured on the beach. She paused for a beat to hiss to Misha. "It's called 'I Feel Good.'"

A couple of teenagers wading in the water stopped for a moment, then turned and snickered, lording their beautiful hybrid bodies over the show. Jocelyn, undeterred, increased the volume, stomped forward semi-sexily, then threw back her head, opened her mouth to the Florida sky.

The teenagers were now laughing raucously, adding their caws to the cranky din of the seagulls. Jocelyn stopped singing, and it was like a power outage or an eclipse. Misha inched his way over on the sand, reached up to touch her elbow. She flicked his hand away angrily, shoved his shoulder out of her performance space, then turned, trembling, toward the shore.

"Fuck. You." She was crying, shaking her fist at the teenaged boy and girl, who had already begun kicking their way through the surf, untouchable.

The girl smiled apologetically at Jocelyn, then, with a delicate laxity, spoke: "This machine's out of order, fuck yourself and save a quarter." She shrugged, orbited gracefully away from the singer, the two staring boys, and the stringy seaweed.

All of this made Misha tired. How long before he could stand and sing, like Jocelyn, two young disciples snared in his glamorous wake? And how long after that before he could kick his way through the sand, his supremacy glaringly casual and far-flung?

Evan had returned dutifully to the problem of the snake, which now looked truly less like a reptile than a soggy mess of vegetation. Jocelyn crouched to poke at a silvery strand, sniffed, then stood up again.

"I'm bored. I'm gonna see if the ice cream guy's here."

Misha didn't want to leave but knew that without Jocelyn the game would devolve into something of a sham. This was the alchemy of play; a game could spring, like a god or a genie, from the ether, and dissolve just as quickly, leaving nothing but curious babblers and wrong-headed believers in its golden wake.

Evan was already scrambling after Jocelyn. Misha sat still and stubborn for a moment before following.

On the sixth night of the vacation, Misha woke before dawn, having dreamt of his father. He stumbled to the window, checked the tennis court and the pool for a sign. In the dream, his father was laughing, his head cocked to one side under the half-hearted spray of the poolside shower.

"Met any little friends?" he called out to Misha, then spat a smooth two-pronged plume of water between his teeth. The water landed with a splash on Misha's shoulder and ran, tickling, down his chest. Misha stared at his father, who grinned, then shook his head briskly, sending more tiny bits of water flying through the air. "Bon voyage, eh, Misha, bon voyage!" he called, then stepped easily from the shower, dry and dressed, his blue suit aglow in the sunlight.

After breakfast, it began to rain, the drops tippling down from the undersides of large taffy-coloured clouds. Misha wandered the apartment, which had a clean, boxy feel to it, so unlike his apartment at home with its creaking wooden floors and sloping walls. The low ceilings and sharp angles made him feel large and businesslike. He stepped outside to patrol the hallway, which was also a long strip of balcony that girded the outside of the building. The wind was strong, and for a moment,

Misha was scared at the way it whipped through the large American flag in the parking lot. The sound made him think of wrestling and choking.

Through the window next to his apartment door he could see a TV glowing like a friendly beacon. Misha knew TV, he liked TV. He leaned in close to the window, and cupped his hands around his face to cut down on the glare. The show was a funny one; he could tell by the way the people moved, as if they had important places to go but not really. Misha watched until he saw a man inside the apartment coming toward him with a cereal bowl. Then he ducked and ran back inside for his own breakfast.

"No beach today, 'tit chou," said Misha's mother, and poured herself another cup of coffee. "No beach today."

No beach, but after Misha had finished his toast, Jocelyn's mom called to invite them to the outlet mall, a glorious cluster of shops with stuff for cheap. They took the rental car, a white Ford with a whirring air conditioner and a smell like lemons and dirty pennies. On the bridge into the city the sky began to clear, sending a rainbow arcing down through the yellow-grey smog that hung over the buildings. Jocelyn pointed out the window to a salmon-coloured condominium complex with two matching kidney-shaped pools.

"Someday," she whispered loudly, "this will all be mine." Then she poked Misha in the ribs and drew her mouth into a lip-sticked pout. Misha crossed his eyes and stuck out his bottom lip until she laughed.

"Here, try this," Jocelyn said, and drew Misha's head toward her, so that their foreheads touched. "Stare into my eyes."

"No," said Misha, "gross."

"You are such a baby." She took his head again. "Now, just stare into my eyes as hard as you can."

Misha stared. Jocelyn's eyes were a flat brown colour, the irises ringed with bands of tiny green stars. As he stared, her eyes floated together, linked themselves above her nose. He blinked. Behind Jocelyn's linked eyes, out the car window, the world went rushing past, street signs and palm trees and cars just like theirs, going shopping.

"Ha! You see!" she shouted. "We're cyclops!" She shoved him away triumphantly.

"What's a cyclop?" Misha asked, and felt immediately ill-equipped.

"It's a monster? With one eye? I can't believe you've never heard about it before. It's like the song." She looked at him, waiting.

He shook his head and looked out the window.

"My one-eyed only love!" Jocelyn belted it out.

"Quiet in the back, you two," her mother called, but in a nice way.

Jocelyn swore under her breath and turned her back on Misha.

Once arrived, the mothers insisted on entering every beckoning store, where they fingered fabrics and flipped over price tags to compare. Misha's mother tried on a pair of half-price cross-trainers at the discount store but they were too small, no luck. Jocelyn tried on a pair of platform sandals with daisies glued onto the toe strap.

"You look like a hussy," said her mother, and pulled the shoes from her feet.

Misha lingered over a pair of black and white wingtips. Magic shoes. Or at least the type of shoes a magician might wear.

In a jungly beachwear store, both the mothers donned sarongs, then stood like overstuffed tropical birds, eyes squinting in appraisal, in front of the long mirrors.

"You're so slim," said Misha's mother admiringly, patting down her thighs.

"Well, you know, you don't get fat drinkin' Diet Coke and sleepin' alone." Jocelyn's mother patted at her own thighs and sucked in her cheeks. Misha watched his mother watching Jocelyn's mother, her eyes widening and narrowing in a shuttering of understanding. There were lessons to be learned at the outlet mall.

In the food court you could get fast food from any part of the world. Misha chose China because of the triangular hats the happy men in the picture were wearing. Jocelyn chose California because of the waitress' deep tan and unerring smile, and the mothers ordered sandwiches and salads from the deli, which was just plain American food. They found a booth near the centre of the court, and Jocelyn slid her bum in next to Misha's.

"Mom, after this can we go to the drugstore? Cause I really wanna try that new hair stuff to lighten my bangs. So can we?" Jocelyn reached over Misha to tug on her mother's sleeve.

"Honey, Sophie and I just want a bit of peace and quiet to chat. Why don't you and Misha go get some ice cream?" The mothers pulled money out of their wallets, and Jocelyn glared at Misha, but grabbed his hand and pulled him away.

Their first night in Florida, Misha and his mother had gone for dinner, just the two of them, like a secret club. They chose a fish place near the beach that was also a bar, but you could get pop if you didn't drink beer. The waitress' name was Suzanne and she smelled like something close to the earth and bursting. Misha's mother wasn't very hungry so Suzanne let her have the kid's portion, and she refilled Misha's pop glass for free. The grouper sandwich was delicious; the white bun giving way to the crunchiness of the batter between his teeth, and his mother looked so beautiful, with her hair pulled off her face and her green baseball T-shirt. He wished his father could see them, and this wishing, this picturing, made Misha glad – his mother, himself, and Suzanne, all bent over the menu, deciding, and his father watching them from an unimaginable distance.

At the ice cream counter, Jocelyn ordered bubble gum flavour and flirted with the scooper, a fourteen-year-old boy with an earring in his lip. Misha counted his change and came up short.

"God, you practically have to know another language to order coffee these days," Jocelyn's mother was saying, pointing to her café-au-lait as Misha approached the table. "Where I come from we call that milky coffee."

Misha's mother looked down, sipped twice at her milky coffee. "How long have you been separated from your husband?"

"Oh, we haven't seen hide nor hair of him since Jocelyn was two. Doesn't even pay his support. Had to hire a lawyer again this year to go after him. He just dumped his latest girlfriend, now she's after him too. Apparently he owes her money. And it's not that he doesn't make enough, you know – he's a salesman, and a good one. He's just a goddamn weasel is all, excuse my French." Jocelyn's mother took a bite of her danish. "What about you, Sophie, what does your husband do?"

"Oh, he owns a furniture store. Quite successful, but still just starting out, you understand." Misha's mother sat up in her chair and adjusted the sunglasses she had perched on her head.

"Sure, I know how it is."

Misha crept up behind his mother and placed his hands over one of her eyes. *Maman is a cyclops*, he thought, and cleared his throat. "Maman. Mom. I need a dollar."

Misha's mother dug in her purse without looking at him, then passed him a handful of coins, coins that seemed less shiny, but somehow more substantial, with their serious bunch of presidents, than the ones from home: the loon, the leaf, the beaver, the caribou – all of them backing the snooty queen. He jingled the coins in his palm, counted them.

Two months ago Misha and his father had driven to a small sports shop in Cote-St.-Luc where Misha's father knew the owner, Art. Misha wanted to spend his Hanukkah gelt on a new pair of skates. Art was up front when they arrived, stacking shin pads next to the counter.

"Hey, Leo, long time no see. This your son?" He pointed to Misha, a shin pad hanging from his arm like an armadillo.

Misha nodded.

"Yes, this is Misha." He nudged Misha forward. "We're looking for some hockey skates. And you, how's the family?"

Art pulled the last shin pad from the box and placed it on the top of the pile. "Oi-a-baruch! Marcia's all right now, but you should have seen her last week – she had the flu like you wouldn't believe. . . ."

Misha looked around the store. He could see the skates he wanted hanging on the wall next to a poster of Wayne Gretzky. He tugged on his father's sleeve.

"You want my money now, I suppose," his father had said, reaching for his wallet. "There, now it's your money." He tucked some bills into Misha's back pocket, and pushed him in the direction of the skates.

When Art had fetched the right size from the stockroom, Misha's father came over and kneeled in front of Misha to help him. He pulled the large stiff tongue back from the body of the skate while Misha pushed hard with his foot. What Misha remembered most was the ridge at the back of the skate: the way it felt scraping slightly against the back of his heel as his toes slid satisfyingly into place.

His father was still kneeling, his head bent so that Misha could see the hair growing above his collar on the back of his neck. He had watched his mother cut those hairs with long silver scissors, the tips of her fingers poking through the grips as she instructed his father, softly, to turn this way, move that way.

"Can I have these?" Misha nodded his head at the skates, which his father was now lacing with small insistent tugs.

"You've got to get them really tight," his father said, straightening up. He reached down and squeezed Misha's shoulder, then looked over at Art, who was busy behind the counter. "It's your money," he added, and dusted off his pants with his open hands.

"Why didn't your husband come then, Sophie? He must be able to afford it, with the store and all. Would be nice to have a man around." She made a big clown wink at Misha's mother, and patted Misha on the back.

"Oh, yes," said Misha's mother and laughed high and quick, "he's just very busy with his work. Very busy, you know how it is . . ." She sipped at her café-au-lait again.

*How it is? * Misha thought, *How is it?*

"Sure, I know, they're always busy with something, aren't they?" Jocelyn's mother laughed a laugh that wasn't really a laugh, and wiped at the corner of her lipsticked mouth.

The night before they left for Florida, after Misha had gone to bed, he had heard his mother and his father in the next room, arguing. He pushed aside his covers, walked quietly to their door, and crouched against the baseboards in the hallway, being careful not to set the doorstop coil that stuck out from the wall *thrumming* back and forth.

"Sophie, you're being so unreasonable. There is no big trick to this decision. The store needs me, that's all there is to it." Misha's father sighed like the sound of a book closing.

"This is not the sum of life – a dilemma and then a decision, a dilemma and then a decision! Why do you always think we are in control? Don't you think Misha might want you there?" her voice reminded Misha of a crow, the way its black wings beat for an instant against the air before it took flight. "You waste nothing, and these decisions you make – they mean everything. Ce n'est pas comme ca qu'on vit sa vie. Dilemma, decision, dilemma, decision . . ." She began to cry.

Misha had stood up then and brought his foot down heavily on the doorstop, so that the sound of the thick coil vibrating from side to side followed him back to his bedroom.

The condo was not far from the beach, but in the afternoons, when it was hottest, Misha's mother liked to sit by the pool, where there was more shade, and the water was clear and diluted. She asked him to sit on a deck chair while she took a shower.

"I'll be right back, okay, Mish?" She pulled a towel from her shoulder bag and spread it across the sticky white weave of the chair. Misha nodded. There was a beefy man with a white crew cut bobbing up and down in the pool. Misha liked his look, so unlike his father, or his grandfather, both small and wiry. He stared at the man.

"What's your name, son?" The man had pulled himself over to the edge of the pool and allowed his legs to float up behind him like drowned sausages.

"Misha."

"Mee-cha? Well, I'm pleased to meetcha too." The man's laugh was a rumble that caught and broke, then caught again, somewhere between his throat and his stomach.

Misha's mother had stopped and was waiting to see what Misha would try next. She didn't wait long.

"Michael is his name. Mike. It's his first time here."

"Well, Mike," said the man, "are you enjoying your stay?"

"Sure am," said Misha, which was something he had heard Jocelyn say to her mother when she asked her if she was hungry or thirsty. His own mother looked at him, surprised, but she seemed pleased, and waved at him on the way to the showers.

There was another man at the pool's gate. This one was tall and bald, and he was with a fat woman who limped a little. They sat on the edge of the pool with their feet in the water.

"Another hot one, eh, Walt?" The first man was speaking to the second man.

"Sure is, got the air conditioning cranked right up." The tall man splashed some water on his chest, then rubbed it into his arms. The woman was lowering herself into the pool, her mouth already forming bubbles. Misha watched her as she swam. She was breast-stroking around the edge, her lips barely grazing the bright translucence of the surface.

"How many you gonna do today, Margie?" It was the beefy man again.

"Oh, I guess I'll just keep going till I'm tired out." Margie splashed him a little as she passed. Misha liked these people, their big bodies and the way their words seemed to expand as they spoke them.

"Went into town yesterday for the breakfast special. Shoulda got there a bit earlier though, almost all the French toast was gone. Isn't that right, Margie?" Walt turned to Margie, who nodded into her chest and swallowed water, then coughed and swam to the side. "What about you, Rick, you make it in for the Early Bird?"

"Yeah, we were there real early. Stopped by the mall for a while afterwards. May wanted to check out the beachwear sale. It's such a pain in the butt these days – so many of the shops been bought up by the Chinks. Soon as you turn your back they're chattering away – Hi-yah this, and hon-yah that." Rick was making frightening rabbit faces as he spoke, biting down hard on his lower lip. Misha watched as he hoisted his elbows up onto the pool deck. There was a bikinied woman tattooed on his bulky shoulder.

Margie was nodding quickly at him. "It's the same thing in Philly. You go into a shop and as soon as you've got your back turned it's Yiddish this and Yiddish that . . ."

At school, back in Montreal, there was a boy called Dickweed, even though, Misha had divined, this was not his true name. There were times, he knew, when it was all right to call the boy, who was lumbering and petty, by this name, but there were other times – for instance when his mother led him by the hand from the back doors – when it was wise to remain silent. And it was the same with French. His mother spoke French, and Misha spoke French, and many people in Montreal spoke French, but at school, speaking French, being French, was a little like being Dickweed, only worse, since it could cling to you like something that stuck on your shoe and would not shake free, even outside the boundaries of the playground. And now, Misha understood, in this hot place, next to this rectangle of a pool, it was unwise to speak Yiddish, that half-imaginary language of prayer and exclamation. It was complicated but also simple how he had to behave, the words he spoke – words backed by thoughts so ineffable they were less thoughts than the elongated shadows of an impulse, the grey aftermath of intention.

Misha's mother had returned from the shower and was sitting, dripping, on the chair next to him. "On va nager bientot, okay?" she murmured, and opened her book. Misha took his mini cars from his mother's bag and went to sit closer to Walt and Rick, who were lounging in the shade of a palm tree.

"Where exactly did they say they're from?" Walt asked.

"Montreal, Canada. You know, part of that country north of Buffalo," Rick said, laughing. "But it sounds as if she's got a Spanish accent or something so I'm not so sure."

It was true. Misha was from Montreal, and so was his mother, but before that she was from France, and before that, Egypt. His father had been born, like him, in Montreal, but Misha's great-grandfather was from Russia, a land older and colder than Canada. There were reasons his mother had moved the way she did, hopping borders, straddling language. Misha knew the word: *apatride*. Without country. But in his mind the stories had melded, coalesced into something confusing or compelling, depending on the day, or the hour, so that the Egyptian sun beat down, relentless, on the bare head of a French schoolgirl, and an old man wearing a fur coat and a salt-and-pepper beard galloped by on a shaggy camel toward a snow-capped pyramid. In the midst of these fantasies Misha sometimes found himself caught in a web of anxiety not unlike the feeling he got when he heard certain fairy tales read aloud. He could sense that the family stories, too, were hiding something – a wolf, or a witch with a grudge. There were two things he knew for certain: There was always something to be afraid of, whether it be in the woods or the desert, and everyone, everywhere, came from somewhere else.

"Michael! Michael!" someone was calling. Someone he knew. He looked up from his cars. It was his mother. This mother he knew like he knew his own instinctive, fleeting thoughts.

"Michael, I think you've had enough of the sun, your shoulders are starting to burn." She began gathering up his toys, then stopped and pulled him close. "*Habibi*," she whispered.

And now his mother is in the hospital, felled by some underwater thing.

Misha hears the phone ring and thinks of his father, far away and perhaps working. Or thinking, his hand swiping at his black hair. Sometimes, after school, his mother would drop him off at *Granowsky's, Your Furniture Store*, to stay with his father while she did her errands. Misha would sit in a chair in the small office at the back of the store and listen to his father speak, slow and careful – as if he was trying to convince someone to come in from the laneway for supper – on the sleek white phone. Sometimes Misha wandered the showroom, stepped quietly into wardrobes and stayed there inhaling the black forest scent until he heard his father locking up.

The ring is loud and repeats like an important lesson, jangling and hurtling through space. He clenches his teeth, wills it to stop. Instead, from across the kilometres, he can see his father look up from whatever it is he is so intent on doing, and peer at him across the border that separates them. Peering and scowling, as if Misha himself has caused the phone to ring on both ends, to interrupt. And maybe Misha has. It is possible he has chosen incorrectly; the wrong word or gesture, a botched thought.

Behind his father, Misha thinks he can make out his mother's navy winter coat, bulky and worn, still draped over the banister where she left it. He wants to touch it, but it has become one of the signs and signals for home he now strains to remember, along with the clanging sound of his hockey stick against the metal staircase to his front door and the signature his breath used to make on the cold air.

"The hospital called. Your mother is fine, honey, just fine. She'll be able to come home tomorrow." Jocelyn's mom is bouncing on her toes excitedly, again plumping the pillows beside Misha's head.

He reaches down into his pocket, feels for the piece of green glass that is still there, smooth and waiting. Then, because it seems she expects him to do or say something, he pulls it out, holds it up to the light, and winks at her with both eyes.

Jocelyn has found a book on stingrays in the local library, which she brings to the beach two days later, a day before Misha and his mother are scheduled to return home. Evan has already left, embarrassing both Misha and Jocelyn with drooly, teary hugs. Misha's mother is *fine* behind her novel, the bandage around her instep glowing against her sun-darkened skin. Jocelyn reads to Misha like a radio announcer, punctuating each phrase with a grave downturn in voice.

"The stab from a stingray not only injects *poison*, but also cuts and tears *the flesh*, and many people that have trodden on a stingray lying in shallow water have had to have *stitches in their feet*. The effect of the poison is *immediate* and inflammation spreads around the wound almost as soon as the spine *has penetrated*."

Then she shows Misha a picture of the stingray, photographed from above, undulating and huge in the water. The creature hovers, just below the surface, unfurling in the underwater breeze like the flag of some misty undiscovered country. It looks soft and flowing, incapable of instigating the heart-stalling shrieks his mother emitted. It occurs to him she may have been faking it. He glares at her, happy and safe and reclining on her brightly patterned beach towel.

"Hey, Joss, you wanna go for a walk?" He feels tough today, invincible. Jocelyn considers him a moment, registers the combative stance, the shrewd challenge in his eye.

"Sure." She brushes some sand daintily from the backs of her thighs. "Where to?"

"Thattaway." He points toward the pier and sets off, lifting his knees slightly higher than usual as he walks. Jocelyn trails behind, holding her sun hat on her head like a southern belle.

"We could pretend we're in the desert dying of thirst, and our camel just collapsed," says Misha, thinking *hero*, thinking *rescue*.

"Nah," says Jocelyn, and that is that.

Misha can tell by the sun that it is nearing noon; soon the mothers will be tapping at their watches, mouthing *lunchtime* as they sort through their beach bags. He presses onward, but Jocelyn is so slow, with her ugly hat. Up ahead he can see a small crowd on the beach, their heads drooped down, wondering at something washed up. Behind him Jocelyn has stumbled upon an oasis, and is draped across a piece of driftwood with an abandoned teen magazine.

Misha pauses for a moment, digs his heels into the wet sand. The problem with Jocelyn is that even when she's ignoring you, she's somehow not. She nags and frays at your plans until they unravel to the point of insubstantiality.

But Misha is now nearing the attraction on the beach, and Jocelyn shows no sign of following. He counts seven grey-haired onlookers, then skirts the periphery of the group, stations himself at the edges, too far to see the centre, but close enough to hear a man's gruff, proprietary voice.

"I tell ya, they're just like the trout I used to fish up in Lake Michigan – they put up a good fight when you hook 'em, and a bigger fight when you get 'em to shore."

Misha pushes his way closer to the man, fighting his way through the veiny calves of the assembled retirees. Finally, he finds himself on the inside of the ragged circle, and, crouched unobtrusively, takes in the sight of the fisherman's catch.

It is a stingray. Smaller and meatier-looking than the one in the book, but a stingray nonetheless. And still alive, its rubbery wings flapping and slapping noisily against the edge of the ocean.

Misha closes his eyes and allows some facts to tumble around inside of him: His mother is fine. His father is in Montreal. You should stay away from the hoo-hah at the beach. There are fathers who leave. They take their bags of things and their money with presidents or snooty queens, and they leave. Water snakes are the most deadly of all snakes. The whole of the French language is actually a swear word. Shock is a made-up thing, made up by Jocelyn and her weirdo mother.

He inches around so that he can examine the tail, a long ropy extension that runs down the centre of the body. He wants to grab on to it, to heft the stingray above his head, swing it round and round like a lasso. Once, on another beach, Misha's father filled his small red plastic sand bucket to the rim with lake-water, then swung the bucket up and over. Upside down! And the water did not spill.

"It's gravity!" his father called out, to Misha's round eyes, wide above his round open mouth. "It controls the oceans. It's what keeps us from hurtling off the earth!" Then he set the bucket down, where it sat, rocking slightly, the water dribbling over the edges.

Misha reaches out toward the stingray.

"You touch that you'll be sick for a good twenny-four hours, if not longer." The fisherman is standing above him, his sneaker planted between Misha's outstretched hand and the ridged tail. Someone in the crowd is curious.

"What are you going to do with it?" It is a petite, well-packaged woman, her pastel pink T-shirt tucked and poofed lovingly into the waistband of her khaki shorts.

"Them's good eatin'. You just take some cookie cutters to the wings, I tell ya, they taste just like scallops." The fisherman grins at the woman, who backs up a little.

Misha withdraws his hand, but the impulse is still there, surging inside him like an ancient mission.

In the sky overhead a jet plane spews a fluffy white trail. Misha would like to be on that plane.

Soon it will be everything in reverse: the drive to the airport, the airplane itself, the weather, so uniform and unflappable above the clouds, suddenly transformed into something brittle and unforgiving on the ground.

Once arrived, and seated for dinner, Misha's father will examine him, then hold tightly to the edge of the dining room table, as if trying to make a point, only instead he will ask a question.

"So, son, how was it?"

And Misha will long for it: the scent of suntan lotion buzzing like an amiable insect inside his sinus cavities, the big-busted friendliness of a Florida waitress ricocheting around inside his small heart, and the temporary relief from a life that seems, suddenly, to be accumulating around and inside him without his sanction.

He will try to tell the vacation like a story, but what comes rushing forth will instead be an excited verbal miscellany, punctuated by too many *and thens* and marred by a breathlessness he cannot control.

"Mee-sha! Oh, Mee-sha!" It is Jocelyn.

Misha takes one last look at the stingray, whose wings seem to tire for a moment before they burst into strange, violent flight, sending the body up and over, so that the tail rests in the love of a wave.

"Mee-sha!" Jocelyn is getting closer, jerking her head this way and that, searching. Misha jumps out from the crowd, ambushes the helpless damsel with his stealthy adventurer ways.

"Yeah. As if." Jocelyn jumps up and down in an effort to see past the people.

"It's just a bunch of seaweed, stupid." There will be no sharing of the stingray.

"Zero times zero is how much I care," says Jocelyn, and skips ahead, then turns around and sticks out her tongue. "Race ya, big man!" Sprinting, hat in hand, all the way to the mothers. All the way home.

CRAIG BOYKO

The Gun

I decided to buy a gun. The gun that I bought was small and expensive. –You get what you pay for, assured the gunman. –And then some. I am somewhat embarrassed to say that I bought the very first gun he showed me. The gun was on a display case near the entrance of the gunstore. I pointed at it and asked the gunman very basic gunquestions. The gun that I purchased is manufactured by a guncompany called Glock. It is (the gun, not the company) a semi-automatic pistol. A "handgun." It is very nice-looking; this I cannot dispute. It seems competently, heavily put together. It is small, too, and thus convenient, portable. As any good gun should be, one supposes – depending upon one's gunneeds. I suppose in some rare cases the biggest gun is best. My gun (I soon came to think of it as "my" gun) is a nine millimetre, which is the metric measurement of the width of the bullets it dispenses, if I am not mistaken. Such compactness is, to me, breathtaking: less than a centimetre! The plastic case that my gun came in had a sequence of letters printed thereupon: GLK 17 9MM PST 10 RD FS. I believe I can decipher the "GLK" and "9MM" portions of this rubric; the rest is quite a mystery to me. If I were a "gunperson" such hieroglyphics would doubtlessly carry complex, esoteric meaning. Nonetheless, I am content with my gun. Despite its price. –Six hundred thirty dollars! I said to the gunman. My shock soon gave way (no doubt aided by the gunman's gunsavvy rhetoric) to mere faux-shock (with which I hoped to wrangle a better price). I ultimately, gladly, paid the full price. $630, I thought to myself, carrying the guncase home with me (I had decided to walk, not sure of the bus system's official gunstance), a new gunowner. $630 for such artistry, such simplicity. A gun, after all, is not the kind of thing you'd feel good about getting a deal on. Guns should not be super-saver items. Unlike other purchases, to spend a hefty sum on a gun is rewarding; its price a hallmark of quality. $630, thought I to myself: small price to pay to become a gunowner; no one can take your gunownership away from you; small price to pay!

My gun even came with a small brochure. According to my brochure (which I only skimmed through, familiar as I am with the purpose and various uses of a gun), my gun is a model #17, and has a Tenifer Matte Finish. (This sounds very fine.) Its sights, my brochure assured me (how euphonic!), are "fixed." (I do not think I would care for the alternative.) Its stock is or is of a Polymer Grip Angle sort. Its "action" is of the "double action" variety. Its barrel length (the barrel is the gunny/pointy part from which the bullets are dispensed) is a discreet four-and-one-half inches. Its entire length is a nominal seven-and-three-sixteenths. It weighs only twenty-two ounces – just over one-and-one-third pounds – a negligible 623 grams. It has a magazine loader. (The bullets come inside a disposable – or possibly reusable? – "magazine"; very handy!) The gun came with two full magazines, each of which held ten bullets apiece. It even came with a cleaning rod and brush. (The brochure stresses the importance of a clean gun for proper operation.)

I bought the gun, ashamed-to-admittedly, so quickly, without heartfelt haggling or "weighing my options," because I was afraid the gunman might ask questions to which I had no answers. I did not want my gunnaivete to be apparent. Silly, I know, to feel thus self-conscious in the presence of a mere gunman, whose job demands a certain modicum of unctuousness and pity – No, not unctuousness and pity, but . . . affability and professionalism – when dealing with gunignorant gunbuyers, like myself. Nonetheless, I mildly dreaded being asked such questions as –What do you *want* a gun for? or –What will you be primarily *using* this gun for? Which just-aforementioned questions, and many others, were soon enough asked me by my husband.

–A gun! he cried, when he one night caught me stowing it under my pillow before going to sleep. He also cried such cries as –Good Lord!, –Heavenly merciful!, –Crying out Jesus!, and –Holy Mary fatherly Christ! (My husband is of the curious unreligious sort who can only curse or swear with religious significance. With no idea how silly he sounds. I suppose that very obliviousness to silliness is, in its own way, charming.) –How long has there been a goddamned loaded, loaded? [I nodded reluctantly] loaded! Christ almighty *loaded* gun lying under your pillow at night while I sleep and dream my naive and gunless dreams with a fully real, a fully *loaded* gun lying under your, you, my very own till-death-do-us-et-cetera wife's pillow pointing probably at my head, probably pointed at my head I assume? [I shrugged unconvincingly] good mother of Christian love my *head* pointed at my very own *head* while I slept and dreamt with not a care or fear of sudden death by gunshot wound to the head in *any* of my dreams no matter how bizarre or heavily sublimated let me assure you! How long has this then been going on?

I love my husband very very much; but more on him later.

I soon took to carrying the gun with me everywhere I went.

Speaking of husband(s), the thought of the gunman comes to mind. The gunseller, gunpurveyor. What beauty he held, in the mere worldly tissues of his body, T-shirted and innocently tattooed; what makes us forever think these thoughts? His beauty augmented by the roughness of his silhouette, as though he had been cut carelessly from the pages of some glossy magazine, and the savviness of his gunknowledge. (Does "savvy" come, perhaps, from some englishification of "savoir-faire"?) Must we forever be thinking "Him? Him? *Him?*"

I soon took to carrying the gun with me; everywhere I went. At home, when alone, at my rare privatest, I had options: I could carry the gun aloft, clutched tightly in both hands, arms rigidly raised and perpendicular to the ground, tangential to the curvature of the earth. I would walk from room to room, scowl on my face, full of laser-sharp focused malice, kicking open bedroom doors, swinging the gun in plenipotentiary arcs, leaping around corners and screaming threats at spectrely interlopers: *Halt!*

Freeze! You! I could also carry the gun at my side, insouciantly, carelessly, laughing and pretending to smoke a cigarette, occasionally holding the gun up and eyeing it incuriously: –What, this old thing? Or, I holstered it in my belt, walked about peremptorily, hip-first, arms akimbo. I stirred soups and coffee with its barrel (after which I cleaned it thoroughly, guiltily). I left it in various hard-to-reach places, then pretended to find it serendipitously, five minutes later: –*There* you are, you old rascal! I scratched my inner thigh with its handle and smiled at its profile adulatorily. I whispered to it in glossolalic phrases I did not understand. I pointed it at everything, everything, and imagined outcomes, scenarios, immaculate destructions . . .

I soon took to carrying; the gun? with me, everywhere; I went.

–What on earth do you *need* a gun for? he asked me, that night, once he'd calmed down enough for ratiocination.

REASONS TO OWN A GUN:
1. To kill (another human being).
2.

I carried the gun with me to work, also. My workplace's gun-stance had never been explicitly stated to me, but I could easily imagine vague outlines of employerly attitudes. I assumed clandestinity to be my choicest method. For a time, I carried my gun in my briefcase. My briefcase has a three-number combination lock that precludes unwanted access. Three such numbers (if we count 000) allow for a total of one thousand unique combinations. Not foolproof, but certainly reassuring. Alas, opening my briefcase while at work (something that an average workday required, on average, many times) became harrowing. I soon instead fashioned an abdomen–centred holster with silvergrey duct tape and took to wearing loose–fitting sweaters and billowing blouses. Did my coworkers raise their eyebrows behind my back? Did they whisper conspiratorially: –Pregnant? again? so soon? Did I, behind their backs, point my gun at them and whisper: –bang?

To name a gun would be the bourgeoisest sentimentality. "As if that name, Shot from the deadly level of a gun, Did murder her." Shakespeare said that. Or wrote it, anyway. Romeo said it. O, Romeo!

Forever thinking "Him? instead of . . . ?"

My Life had stood – A Loaded Gun –

I love my husband dearly. Powerfully, passionately. We often think that the word "voluptuous" relates only to buxom women, but . . . My husband's name is Ken. My husband is beautiful. From my admittedly subjective point of view, that is an objective fact. Such arms on his body; such rippling thigh-muscles(!). Herculean, Adonisian limbs and teeth. He has a gym in our basement, a gym he built himself with the necessary tools and know-how; he works out daily, with an unworldly self-ardour, an unsecular body-fervour. One assumes that he does this for one. One wants to feel blessed, honoured, as if this perfect body were a benefaction. One wants to believe this ded-ication-to-self is a sublimated dedication-to-one; or, if not a dedication-to-one, then at least a dedication-to-self, not a dedi-cation-to-other. His pulchritude and elan and my love for him are without dispute. He is an apotheosis, a god in human form; he is a theophany, my personal theosophy. He is not the smartest man alive, though. He is not "wise." Neither "learned" nor "knowing." His simplicity is just so endearingly charming, though. Still, all the same, he is ignorant. He has a worldless, parochial – yet endearing! – ignorance. A profound lack of pro-fundity has my husband Ken. A panoply of sundry ignorances has he: an indiscriminate, global, rakish ignorance. I love him to death – is that the phrase? Still, though, after all, it is striking, is it not? strange it is, ironic that a man named "Ken" would have such a small one.

To name a gun would be the bourgeoisest sentimentality. The sentimentalest theatricality. The theatricalest bourgeoisie.

REASONS TO OWN A GUN:

1. To kill (another human being).
2. To protect one's kith, kin, and Ken.
3.
4.
5. So many reasons!

To a squirrel at Kyle-na-gno, Irish poet W.B. Yeats (1865–1939) once said, "Come play with me." The squirrel would not "Come play with [him]." Yeats, confused, bewildered, put-off, asked: "Why should you run / Through the shaking tree / As though I'd a gun / To strike you dead?" Well, that's Yeats for you.

Does the word "manifesto" have some etymological connection to the word "Manifest"?

In Corners – till a Day –

Speaking of husband(s), there is a man at my workplace who often works late. This can be either admirable or despicable, depending. To the employers, it must seem admirable. Unless my coworker (Randy) is charging for his overtime, which the employers might be loath to pay, but, constrained as they are by self-imposed bureaucracy, *must* pay – in which case his overworking might be seen as despicable. To me, it is admirable that he is so seemingly selflessly dedicated. However, it is despicable that he is so seemingly selflessly dedicated. It is particularly despicable when I want to leave at the end of my workday and Randy tries to make "chat" with me, which he is wont to do (if indeed he is charging overtime for this "chatting" then he is despicable), especially once everyone else has left and he sits with one leg slung casually over the northwest corner (front-left) of my desk and I am trying to appear either busy or distracted when in fact I am eager to pack up and leave for the day but since my gun is inside the centre drawer of my desk I cannot remove it or transfer it to my holster until Randy disengages, until he goes back to "work," so I am forced nightly to make inane "chat" with inane Randy. Sometimes, instead of surrendering to his mindless blanter, I take my gun out from my drawer and shoot him in the head, more or less always between the eyes since he is so close – it's not terribly difficult to make a good shot – and then he dies, blood and brains flying in a graceless arc from the back of his head, and though it's a terrible mess for the poor cleaners, at least I get to go home at a timely time.

REASONS TO OWN A GUN:
6. You can get more of what you want with a kind word and a gun than you can with just a kind word.

I built a mounting plate for my gun. With oak from a tree that I felled with my own two hands. I shaped and sanded and lacquered the wood for many patient hours. (The hours were patient, not I!) I carved it into a sort of escutcheon, with noble curves and royal points. I hung it on the wall of the "living" room, over the faux-fireplace. Then I hung my gun from it. It was appealing to the eye. It provided a certain symmetry. –One for every room! I cried. –One for every home! Still, though, I preferred to carry the gun with me. For, as Anton Chekhov had told me: "If there is a gun hanging on the wall in the first act, it must fire in the last." This seemed portentous.

Al Capone said that.

My husband, it can safely be said, was displeased with my gun-purchase. Displeased perhaps, more generally, with my whole gunideology. My apparent "guncavalierness," he might have been quoted as saying, more or less. Does his contentiousness vis-a-vis this issue stem, perhaps, in some small degree, from the fact that I have been known to, late at night, every night, when he is deeply aslumber, withdraw the gun from its "hiding" place beneath my pillow and hold it, the gun, to his head, barrel first, as one might do if one wanted to murder one's husband while he slept? Is this perhaps contributing to his discomfiture? Does he even know? It *is*, admittedly, the sequence of steps that one would take if one were attempting to murder one's husband in his sleep. To employ logic: all those who murder their husbands must take these steps; but do all those who take these steps murder their husbands? Of course not. Is my pulling of Angelique's trigger (I have named my gun Angelique Dufresne) – with her barrel pointed, at such proximity, at my husband's head – what is bothering him? Subconsciously, perhaps? Does he know? Does he waken, one glutinous eye cracked open, and watch me, only pretending to sleep? When I pull the trigger of my loaded gun, does he – No! I do not pull the trigger. What silliness.

"Aren't you afraid of him?" Robert Frost asked me. "What's that gun for?"

The Owner passed – identified –

–Why do you even *need* a gun? asked my husband. I could think of no reasons; I could think of so many reasons. So many, in fact, all of such unimpugnable quality, that I didn't know where to begin. –Think of the children! he said. I pointed out that we had no children. He said other people's children, the children of the world. –The children, I asked, –who break into your house in the middle of the night and steal your television, but ineptly, and awaken you with their fumbling and thus force you to put a bullet in their hearts, with your gun? Those children? –Yes! he said. –Think of the goddamned children!

Why would anyone shoot a squirrel?

The measured ticking of a clock in an otherwise silent room.

REASONS TO OWN A GUN:

7. An inflated sense of
8. This indescribable feeling that you're
9. So fulfilling when
10. A renewed faith in

I told Robert Frost (1874–1963), I said, I told *him*, I says to him I says: –Listen, you . . .

My husband, out of purported concern for me, talked to our priest. We do not have an "our" priest, per se, since we subscribe to no particular religion; or, depending on the day of the week, we subscribe to *all* religions. The "priest" came to our home. He wanted to talk to me. We sat in the "living" room. I poured him a tea and cognac. –This is about the gun, I said knowingly. –Yes, he said gravely. . . . A colloquy ensued. A tête-à-tête. A heated discussion, a near-altercation. His brains vs my brawn. My obstinance vs his obsequiousness. His theology vs my theophagy. His vs my. My vs his.

Q: Now listen!
A: Stop interrupting!
Q: I've had quite enough of –
A: Well and I haven't?

The simplest act of surrealism – according to French poet, essayist, and critic André Breton (1896–1966), whose creative writing is characterized by surrealist techniques such as "automatic" writing – is to walk out into the street, gun in hand, and shoot at random.

Q: If you'd calm down we'd both –
A: I'll calm down when –
Q: Will you please hear me –
A: If you weren't so impossibly –
Q: Take that back!
A: Make me!
The gun, wall-mounted, went off. Right through the priest's heart went the bullet. See? I told you: portentous.
And carried Me away –

LISA MOORE

The Way the Light Is

Mina O'Leary pulls a long silver skirt from her cupboard and holds it to her waist, one hand sweeping the folds. The fabric falls in sharp pleats, the light from the bedside lamp flashing in it like a sword fight.

How about this?

You sure have beautiful things.

It's stuff. I just like *stuff*.

The price tag still dangling from the waistband. Dried roses, petals crusty, in a vase on the vanity. I focus on the roses, but they look inert. The lack of motion in the dead roses buzzes. She picks a pair of nylons off the floor.

I'll put these on, I'd be wearing them in real life.

She takes armloads of clothes off the bed and throws them in the closet. She stretches the white duvet over the crumpled sheets.

Mina: I'm doing this mainly so you can watch me move.

Me: Put on that gold coat and give it a flap. Like the wings of the insect.

Mina: Okay, cool.

I'm making a five-minute film based on a poem by John Steffler, "The Green Insect." The poem is about the *elusive*. I want to shoot a combination of animation and live footage. I need a woman who looks like a grasshopper. A woman who will sit in a white wicker chair with her ankles drawn up near her bum, knees sticking out. A woman who doesn't get kinks in her neck. The insect doesn't have to be a woman. It could be almost anything you follow because you can't help yourself. It could be a chiffon scarf floating down Duckworth Street in the wind. I saw a beautiful Chinese film with a recurring shot of a long, almost transparent scarf tangled in some branches at dusk. But I like faces. French movies always take a long time with a face. The plot turns when a man raises an eyebrow. Bergman spends a long time on a face, but there is no plot.

What could capture the essence of this poem. No single image by itself, but a furious fluttering of images. Some children with sparklers running down the sidewalk at dusk. Bannerman Park with Christmas lights. The insect is anything there's no holding on to. And greenness. Something you ache to own.

My eight-year-old daughter in a purple bathing suit, swinging in the hammock Mina brought back from France last summer. We're in Broad Cove, my daughter reads a book, and I'm watching her from an upstairs window. She's completely absorbed in the pleasure of reading, the warmth of the sun, the long grass brushing her back with each sway of the low-slung hammock. Finally she gets up and wanders onto the dirt lane in front of the house. Her feet are bare. She's been wearing that bathing suit all summer, sleeping in it, picking blackberries that stain her teeth, leaping off a boulder into the river. Her long hair in a loose ponytail. She throws a baton. Far up in the blue sky it becomes liquid, a rope of mercury, but it comes down fast, bouncing off the pavement on its white rubber ends. There's no way to keep this moment in the present.

INTERIOR. RAMSHACKLE SUMMER HOUSE. DAY

Mina stands at a window on the second floor of a weathered saltbox. The glass is old and warped. She's watching a child in the long grass throwing a baton. A man enters and stands behind her. He's wearing swimming trunks, his body is wet. She tilts her head and he kisses her neck. He unbuttons her blouse so it falls off her shoulders. Lowers her bra strap.

Mina
She can see us.

Man
She can't. The way the light is.

Mina closes her eyes for a moment, lets the man touch her breasts. Then, tentatively, she waves to the child on the lawn. The child waves back.

I want Mina O'Leary riding the bus in St. John's in a rainstorm. She's in the back, a blur of green moving toward the door. She gets off and snaps open a green umbrella. Droplets of rain spring away from the tight silk. The airbrakes sigh, steam rises from the pavement. The umbrella tips over her head. Drops hang, jiggling, from the steel points of the umbrella's skeleton. Her face, *thinking*. Liv Ullman is always thinking, her face is young, young, young. They just talk – Bergman's actors – straight into the camera about humiliation, fear of the dark, death. Liv Ullman strikes a match and lights the lantern, a glow floods up from the wooden table to her chin. They are always on an island. There are vampires, sacrificed lambs. A crow with a giant beak. Bodies draped in white sheets lying on slabs of stone, desolate fields of snow seeping into the mud. Trudging, a lot of trudging. Then like a jewel, a flashing ruby dropped in a bucket of tar, Bergman offers a bowl of strawberries, or a child. A greenish cast over Mina O'Leary's cheeks from the streetlight through the silk umbrella.

INTERIOR. AN ABSTRACT SPACE. DAY

Mina is twenty-seven, she has dark, shiny hair that she tucks behind her ears, a severe cut that's growing out with deliberate dishevelment. When she's listening she becomes very still, captivated.

Mina
My mother was young, she was twenty-one when she had me and I was the fourth. My father was away.

Young Woman
Where was your father?

Mina
Oh, fucking around, I guess (laughs) . . . no, my father
drank and he was a musician, so that was part of it.

(She reaches for a lobster claw from a platter in front of
her, cracks it open with a hammer. She's eating the meat
with her fingers; such intent pleasure, both aloof and sen-
suous; unwittingly intimate.)

Mina
He'd get these houses for us on the outskirts of town,
isolated, and she'd have to wait for him, just wait . . .

Young Woman
To bring her food and stuff?

Mina
To get her out of there. She'd wait and wait, and he just
wouldn't come. I think she went kind of crazy. She saw
things . . .

Young Woman
What kind of things?

Mina
Scary things.

Young Woman
Like what though?

Mina
Well, like once . . .

Young Woman
No wait, don't tell me if it's too scary.

Mina
No, it's nothing, she saw a dog, that's all, a dog on the
lawn pacing back and forth, waiting to get in.

The John Steffler poem says that after the insect was trapped
it tore up history. "It ripped up reality, it flung away time and
space, / I couldn't believe the strength it had, / it unwound its
history, ran out its spring in kicks and rage, denied itself, denied
me and my ownership."

There's a dried squirt of breast milk on my computer screen. I
wipe it away with the tip of my finger and saliva, the pixels mag-
nified in the wet streak. The way my husband, Philip, talks to
our new son: Oh the saucy thing, the *saucy* thing. Philip can't
get enough of him.
Mina will be here soon, I say.
She'll eat him up, Philip says.

EXTERIOR. AN OAK-LINED ROAD IN FRANCE. DAY

Mina is in the backseat of a black Mercedes that passes
through a giant wrought-iron gate onto an oak-lined road.
The shadows of overhanging branches lace the windshield.
She rolls down the window and sticks her head and shoulders out. She's wearing a wedding dress. The veil flies out
behind, her eyes half-shut against the wind. The car passes
large stone houses, each isolated in acres of forest. Finally
the car pulls up to a circular driveway in front of a castle.
Mina gets out of the car and stands for a moment dwarfed
by the estate.

Mina, in Paris, about to miss her flight home for Christmas.
She has to find an elevator, a moving sidewalk underground,
swinging doors on the left. Forget *that*. She drags the luggage
cart outside and crosses the four-lane highway between the two
wings of the airport.

EXTERIOR. PARIS AIRPORT RUNWAY. DAY

A plane is taxiing away from Mina, who is running through a blizzard. She stops and waves her red wallet over her head. The plane stops like a sluggish animal, a crocodile, the staircase falling open like a jaw. The attendant steps out into the snow in a short-sleeved white blouse and navy skirt.

Bergman has said about writing a script, "All in all, split-second impressions that disappear as quickly as they come, forming a brightly coloured thread sticking out of the dark sack of the unconscious. If I wind up this thread carefully a complete film will emerge, brought out with pulse-beats and rhythms characteristic of just this film." I think about how so much of a good story seems to happen elsewhere, off the canvas or screen or page, in Europe, or a backwater New Brunswick town, in what is left unsaid. A word on the tip of the tongue, ungraspable. The teasing smush of a feather boa over naked breasts in a strip-tease. Mina is ten years younger than me, and is rarely jealous of her husband, Yvonique. It's New Year's Eve, a dinner party at Mina's. Her necklace has broken and she's trying to fix it.

Mina: I can't believe this. Can you believe this? I loved this necklace.

Yvonique asks the baby, Do you know what Coco Chanel says? When you walk into a room *think* champagne, *feel* champagne, *be* champagne. But of course, you will be carried into the room. The same rules apply.

He talks to the infant with an easy chat that suggests an affinity between them I can't imitate. Anything I say to the baby sounds studied or when I'm overwhelmed by the fact of him, maudlin. Yvonique rips a bottle of champagne from an ice bucket and tells us one judges the quality by the size of the bubbles (the tinier the better) and their plenitude. They must taste crisp and clean.

I think *plenitude* is one of those words that only gets spoken by someone whose native tongue isn't English. I want to say this, but I'm afraid of offending him. Yvonique becomes shy at unpredictable moments, blushing dark red, his earlobes the darkest, his gold earring seeming to brighten.

Philip says, Can you taste a bubble?
Yvonique: *Oui*. But of course.

INTERIOR. KITCHEN. NIGHT

Mina is dipping roses in a bowl of egg white, then a bowl
of sugar so they crystallize. She tears off a few frosted
petals and eats them. The rest she drops on the top of a
cake covered with cream.

> Mina
> I hadn't been seeing him very long. I just couldn't go
> through with it. I didn't want a child, I knew that. I was
> only twenty. I was afraid of being trapped. That's all I
> could think.

Yvonique reaches over the fireplace for a machete that he
unsheathes from a tooled leather case hanging by a gold braid
and tassel. He places the champagne bottle on its side with the
neck sticking over the edge of the dining table and raises the
machete over his shoulder.
Mina: He's bluffing, he doesn't know how to do that!
Yvonique brings the machete down hard on the bottle and
lifts the cleanly sliced, spurting neck so champagne gushes over
his upturned face and open mouth for a moment before he fills
the crystal glasses on the sideboard. We have finished the second
course and there is a pause.

In the kitchen Mina has thrown out Yvonique's *roue*. We hear a
spat of bitter words.
She says, But I thought you were done with it.
Philip and I sit at the table waiting for the main course. The
other guests have left the table to smoke. The baby is nursing.
We sit for a long time in the empty room.
Philip says: What colour are these walls?
Wedgewood blue, I say.
Someone in another part of the house turns on some music.

Apocalyptica – four cellists playing Metallica – so loud the ornaments on the Christmas tree vibrate. Then it's turned down and then off. The whole house is silent. Outside the city is covered in a quick, brief snowfall.

Philip says, Maybe we should order out.

Yvonique kicks the swinging door open, holding a platter of lamb studded with wizened apricots. We eat and exclaim how good it is, but afterward Yvonique seems disappointed. He says, Has nobody noticed the flavour of green tea?

The dessert arrives with a young Australian woman; a President's Choice tiramisu with a tartan ribbon around the rim.

I want to catch the dessert on fire, says Mina, all season I've been lighting desserts on fire. I ask the Australian what she does.

I can't tell you, it sounds too pretentious.

Oh, go ahead.

I'm a digital artist.

INTERIOR. DOWNTOWN CAFE. DAY

Mina is sitting in a fat armchair near the window looking out onto Water Street. She is speaking to her girlfriend. The waitress brings them lattés in tall glasses with long spoons. It's lunchtime and at first Mina's distracted by the passing lawyers and teenagers.

> Mina
> Do you know what Yvonique said, that he developed my palette. Can you believe that?

> Young Woman
> He roasts a mean duck.

> Mina
> Like I'm trailer trash. (giggles) It's true.

> Young Woman
> Me too. I'm trailer trash too.

Mina
Lay it here, sister.
(they slap hands in the air)

Young Woman
But you don't care for him?

Mina
We were both coming out of heavy relationships and we
agreed not to get emotionally involved. But the sex was
so good. So good. We just kept going like that, a month,
two months. This was Paris. Then I told him I cared if
he slept with someone else.

(We hear Mina's voice while watching her running through
a sparse birch forest. She's wearing a white cotton dress
and white sneakers, she is running very fast. Her feet
hardly touching the ground, sunlight crashing through
the overhead branches, she is just a blur.)

Mina
That's what we agreed we'd say if we found ourselves
getting emotionally involved. I care if you sleep with
someone else. And he said, *run*. Just that one word,
run. I wrote it on a piece of paper in big block letters
with a highlighter at work. RUN. I just stared at the
word. I kept it on my desk for a long time. It would turn
up under a pile of books. It was my father all over again.

After midnight on New Year's Eve the digital artist and
Yvonique got lost in the crowd on the waterfront. They fell into
a snowbank together, kissing.
Everyone did Ecstasy, Mina says, it happens.
And that doesn't bother you, I ask.
She's sucking the last bit of meat from a lobster claw.
Not *really*. She thinks for a minute, wipes her lips with the
back of her hand. I mean, if it *meant something* I guess it would

bother me. *I guess* it would bother me if it meant something. I'm not sure.

Philip and I sit with the car warming up on the parking lot of the Avalon Mall, Cuban music on the radio. I think of a tropical ravine we passed once, in a tourist bus, and a band that came out and played at a dusty bus stop at ten o'clock in the morning, an hour outside Havana. There was a corrugated roof of green plastic and the musicians wore white straw hats and white pants that looked green under the shelter. Philip bought a mango, which he peeled with a Swiss army knife. How charged the musicians were. I had licked a drop of mango juice before it dripped off Philip's chin. I think of the possibility of him kissing someone else in a snowbank, just kissing. It would bother me.

Mina tells us while we're eating that she smuggled the cheese through customs.

She says, It's illegal outside of France, unpasteurized cheese, it's a problem with the EEC. The other countries want to ban it. But the French, you can imagine how they feel. They're so passionate.

Philip lays his fork on his plate, wipes his mouth with a serviette. I put down my fork.

I say, I'm breast-feeding, you know, there could be anything in that.

Mina says, We used to give our hens lobster shells and the yolks would be bright red. Bright red yolks in a cast-iron skillet. Too bad this film isn't about a red insect.

She's fastening a necklace with a pendant of medicine-blue beach glass.

Fold your limbs like an insect, I say. Mina raises her arms to the back of her neck, elbows jutting. A green velvet dress she got married in.

Lean into the mirror and put on lipstick, I say.

I'm getting all this on video, then I capture stills on the computer, print them. Twenty-four pictures for one second of film. I'll loop the clip of the lipstick moving over her mouth. During the twenty-four frames her eyelids droop and close, and open. An amber ring on her finger fires a sparkle of light in frame twelve. A bar of sunlight moves over her nose and across one cheek. I'll colour the background with oil pastels, lime green, lemon, emerald, an ocean of grass.

Philip looks at the print I've thumbtacked to the wall over the computer. He says, Mina O'Leary could be a movie star.

You think?

She has that kind of face.

Mina says, I wrote a novel while I was in France. But I used too many words. I'd rather a novel with less words.

Shorter, you mean?

Not necessarily shorter.

What was it about?

It was about – she looks up from her beer and adjusts the collar of her jacket, a big, distant smile as if the novel is unfolding in front of her and she likes it. A Scottish swim team crowds through the door with a blast of snowy wind. Snow on their shoulders and caps. One of the team, a man with a beard full of ice and steamed glasses, interrupts Mina, begins a conversation about trade unions. The singer is doing Bruce Springsteen, snapping her fingers and tapping one foot. When she's finished she scans the audience with her hand over her eyes.

She says, I'd like my bass player to come on up, unless he's taking a leak.

She tells a filthy joke and the whole bar groans. Mina takes a notebook from her purse, writes something, tears off the page, and gives it to the Scottish swimmer, who balls it up and swallows it. She laughs and lays her hand on his cheek. The team has gathered around her and they all raise their pints and give a cheer.

I say, I'm surprised anyone would tell a joke like that.

Mina's eyes narrow.

She says, I'm not surprised at all. I've seen her tend bar at the Spur, not that I go there.

All of the joy from flirting with the swim team vanishes. She is grimly considering the singer.

Finally she says, I'm not that keen on other women.
Green things. Lantern glass, John Steffler mentions. Escapes.

INTERIOR. ABSTRACT SPACE. DAY

Mina hammers another lobster, the crackling of shells.
She's talking to her friend. Her face is full of the memory
she's describing.

> Mina
> He took me up in his arms in the middle of the night. A
> drop fell from the eave onto my forehead, and that's
> how I woke. I was about eight, too old to be carried. He
> walked over the field of snow for a long time and into
> the woods. We hadn't seen him for months maybe, or
> days, I don't know. We got to a clearing and there was an
> eclipse of the moon. It turned red. The moon was red, a
> bright red yolk.

Mina thinks Liv Ullman's face is grotesque.
She says, Her lips are so puffy, her cheeks, bone structure.
Her face bugs me. But she's beautiful too. A face can be beautiful and grotesque by turns.
The thing about beauty, says her husband, it's mostly anticipation and memory.
Somehow, when she was in France, Mina met a very rich
man who was working as a bicycle courier. He had wanted to try
out work, and he'd enjoyed it, liked winding through traffic in
black spandex, lithe and rubbery as a stick of licorice. His bike
was so light he could lift it with his pinkie. She married him and
brought him home. I met him for the first time at a party. He was
handing out tiny drinks called lemon drops that you toss over
the tongue. After three of these the black-and-white tiled floor
karate-chopped my knees. I demanded of Yvonique that we
become blood brothers. He took up a paring knife from the
counter, wet with lemon juice and pulp and cut his thumb. I cut
my thumb, felt the sting of lemon, and we staggered around the
crowded kitchen, yelling and holding each other up by our

joined thumbs. Mina helped me home, through Bannerman Park where the trees lay down on their sides and the moon shot through the air like a high bouncer, crazy zigzags. There was no hangover the next morning. It was as though the party hadn't happened. It made me think their marriage couldn't last.

INTERIOR. A COMMUNITY HALL. NIGHT

The hall is crowded for a turkey-tea. A handsome man in a cowboy hat sits alone on the stage playing a guitar and singing "Your Cheating Heart." Nobody listens.

> Man
> Thank you very much, thank you. Now I'd like to invite my daughter, Mina, up here with me for a duet we've been practising together.

An eight-year-old Mina dressed in frilly pink with a bow in her hair walks onto the stage and the room goes silent.

EXTERIOR. AIRPORT RUNWAY. DAY

Eight-year-old Mina, in the frilly pink dress and bow from before, stands on an empty runway in a blizzard. The sound of roaring planes, descending. She looks up into the storm trying to decide which way to run. We hear adult Mina speak and the roar subsides.

> Mina
> I got a phonecall while I was in Ottawa at a swimming competition. They told me there was a call. I was watching through a big glass window, girls from all over Canada, diving into the pool. The way they entered the water with hardly a splash. My aunt told me I had to come home, I had to be on the next plane. I knew he'd died somewhere, probably drunk. That I'd never see him again.

EXTERIOR. COUNTRY ROAD. DUSK

An isolated trailer on cement blocks in the middle of a field of dead grass and snow. One window is lit and we see a woman passing back and forth. A hungry dog trots across the lawn and disappears into the woods.

INTERIOR. BEDROOM. NIGHT

Mina is sniffing a line of coke on her vanity table. She then stares at herself in the mirror. There is a vase of dried roses, the petals covered with dust. She touches the petals and a green spider drops on a thread. The bedroom door bursts open behind her, and with it the noise of a loud party, laughter, techno music, her husband waves a bottle of champagne at her, and goes to the closet, grabs a tuxedo jacket, is telling her to hurry up, but we can't hear him over the noise. She watches him in the mirror behind her. He shuts the door and the room is silent. She stands and puts on a long gold satin coat with a cream lining. She flaps it once, twice. The fabric falls over the lens and the screen goes gold.

We show Mina the video of my son's birth. Her face is contorted, her fingers gripping her toes. She writhes.
Do you want us to stop?
She puts one hand over her eyes, and drags it down her face. For a moment I can see the pink of her under lids.
Keep going, she says.
The baby's head. I see my own fingers – reaching between my legs trying to pull the skin of my vagina wider. The ring of fire, a friend told me later. All the burning.
I say, It hurts, it hurts.
Philip only shot video during the contractions. During the three minutes between contractions I was joyous. I made jokes. The room was full of laughter. Keith Jarrett playing on the stereo. The way he sighs, the piano bursting loudly into the room and

dragging itself out like a big wave over stones. A training ambulance attendant was invited to watch. He stood in the dim part of the room in a uniform, his hands clasped behind his back. The baby's head emerges, the doctor lifts the cord away from the baby's shoulders. Watching the video I am amazed by the skill with which the doctor lifts the cord. Unhurried, like crowning a prince, a rite that requires a lifetime of devoted practice to perform simply.

There was a complication. The doctor's voice off camera: We have an emergency.

Everything speeds up. The baby's head is between my legs, the doctor's hand tugging the cord out of the way, and a giant gush of blood.

Philip puts the video on pause. On the still TV screen the splashing of blood stands out around the baby's neck like an Elizabethan collar.

That's it, says Philip, his first second in the world, right there.

He presses play and the baby's body comes out after the head and the blood flashes like a bull fighter's cape twisting in the air. I wanted to ask everyone to leave the room. I remember suddenly the desire to be alone. I wanted to die alone, and it seemed I would die. But I didn't want to offend the ambulance attendant by asking him to leave. He has been standing so straight, and quiet, I can barely make him out of the dark.

Everyone who reads John Steffler's poem says, Wow. Or, Pretty powerful. Everyone knows what it means to want something with such intensity you crush it in your haste to have it. I felt a terrible vertigo during those moments while the blood poured out of me. As if I were falling from a great height, and I hit the hard bed with a jolt. Philip stopped shooting then. But in the next shot on the videotape we are fine. The baby is in my arms, and I am holding the receiving blanket open, I am touching his foot.

EXTERIOR. BASILICA. NIGHT

It's midnight, New Year's Eve. People have gathered on the steps of the Basilica to watch the fireworks. I'm there with my eight-year-old and my new infant under my coat. The fireworks fall through the night like bright, spurting blood. Mina is standing beside me. Horns honk, cheering, party hats. Mina closes her eyes and the screen goes dark for a few seconds. Silence. We see an ultrasound of a fetus kicking against the dark, we see gushing champagne, then champagne bubbles falling through the night sky, the statue of the Virgin Mary in front of the Basilica with a mantle of snow, her hand moves just slightly, a benediction, Mina's husband grabs her and kisses her. The video of the birth seen previously plays in reverse, until the baby has disappeared, unwinding history.

I say to Mina: Now, try to look as if you are about to alight.

BILLIE LIVINGSTON

You're Taking All the Fun Out of It

He used to wear suits. These snappy-looking slacks-and-blazer combos in rich chocolate browns, and blacks so black they were blue. He was a snappy talker too, always had a clever comeback for the neighbours or cashiers at the supermarket. Not too clever though. I guess that's one thing I picked up watching him in those days, wondering what made him different from other witty guys in suits. A person hates to feel as though what comes out of his or her mouth is merely a set-up for what comes out of yours. When my father spoke, it was as if he were pleased you spoke first because he'd been waiting to hear you all day. And he'd say something double-ended, something that made your opening remark seem as funny and clever as his reply. That, and the voice he used, softer so you had to listen closely, a little conspiratorial. Nothing like an implied secret to make a person feel special.

Except for her. My mother never seemed to feel so special around him, that I recall anyway. Although she must have at some point. She was snappy in her own right, or perhaps snappy's not the right word. She was effervescent. That is before she got so agitated. It seemed, when I was about nine or ten, a switch flipped and her playfulness became a humming energy that she could barely contain.

She tried four or five different jobs, mostly clerical – office filing, answering phones, that sort of thing – but her mind wandered, there just wasn't enough going on at a reception desk to hold her thoughts. As I recall, she quit, officially, once, was fired twice, and once she left for lunch and never came back. At first the only thing that seemed to soothe her was driving, or rather being driven; she didn't have a licence. But she loved moving fast down highways; it seemed to give her a sense of peace that nothing else did. So, on weekends, my father would drive us out to the country and each time, as the speedometer passed the sixty-miles-per-hour mark, my mother would sigh as though she had just lowered herself into a warm bath. She would begin to smile and say things like, "Look, honey, sheepies," into the back seat at me. Playful and relaxed again, eggs became *eggies*, sheep were *sheepies*.

Problem was, my mother never seemed to see logistics in quite the same way he did, and often the country drives would have the two of them very much in their own seats staring out the window shaking their respective heads. My mother might see a small herd of horses along the highway. She would say something like, "Oh, look at them . . . sweet old things. Alan, stop the car, pull over." Trucks might be roaring past from the other direction, cars in front of us and behind. I would get excited, flinging myself half over the front seat, seconding the request, yelping for him to stop.

He'd zoom right past, though, and she would look back out the rear window with her mouth open and say, "Alan! Why didn't you stop? They're back there. Stop!"

Quietly, serenely, he'd reply, "Honey, they're on the other side of the road. There's nowhere to stop."

Then she would say something like, "Of course there is. Don't be silly. Come on, go back. You're taking all the fun out of it!"

"Go back?" he'd say and chuckle as though she had to be funning with him. He'd try to explain that he couldn't just pull over in all this traffic, there wasn't a turn-off, he needed a spot to pull off the highway.

She'd begin to sputter things like, "A spot? That was a spot. For godsake, Alan, why can't you just pull over instead of making a big production out of everything?"

My father would grip the steering wheel with one hand and start fiddling with the radio or something or maybe just rubbing at his forehead as if he were trying to get a stain off. But usually he'd take a deep breath and sigh. After all, part of my mother's effervescence was her spontaneity. She liked to just do rather than "make a big song and dance out of it." It was about here that he would try and jolly her up again, laugh and put a hand on her leg. She would most likely tisk and swat him away, look out the window, her elbow balanced on the bottom of the open window frame, touching the top with her fingertips. She might sigh again and drop her hand into the wind so she could swim her fingers through the air like fish. This is where he would get her; maybe he'd reach over again and squeeze her leg, say something like, "You better watch your hand out there, you're going to accidentally punch a cow and make some farmer awful mad."

In those days, my mother would still tuck her chin and laugh in spite of herself, call him an idiot through giggles.

She'd been working as a sort of girl Friday at a used car lot for two weeks the afternoon she showed up at school. I was in Grade 6. She walked into the classroom in her office clothes, informing the teacher that she had to take me for the rest of the day, smiling brightly, and chucking my chin as she explained that I had a dentist appointment.

"What dentist appointment?" I asked.

"Oh, I don't like to get her all upset by telling her ahead of time," she told Mrs. MacConnel. "It's easier to do it this way." My teacher nodded an "Of course" back at her.

I stared, wondering at my mother, as she smiled away, stuffing my arms into coat sleeves, pushing me along out of the classroom as if I were a toddler. "Nice to meet you," she called over her shoulder. "Thanks very much."

Once outside the school, I wanted to know what dentist appointment. "How come you never told me?"

"Oh there's no dentist appointment. I made it up. I was just tired of today and I felt like seeing you." I stared over my shoulder at the school and back at her. "Don't you ever just feel like tap dancing?" she asked me. I waited for some sort of punchline. She took my hand and we started walking. She'd been at the car lot, she said, calling people all morning from a list they'd given her. She was supposed to call each number and ask how they were making out with the used car they'd purchased at Bobby Gordon's Wheel Deals.

"Now the object of the game," she told me, "was not to find out if they really liked their car, it was just to make sure they still lived at the same address so fat old Bobby Gordon'll have a place to mail his flyers. He's starting up a carpet cleaning business. I had people on the phone screaming in my ear all morning, telling me what a horrible car he'd sold them, how it was a piece of junk and fixing it would cost more than the car did in the first place. All I could think about was tap dancing. I used to be a tap dancer, you know." I knew. She had a scrapbook she'd shown me once; there were black-and-white photographs of her when she was a kid and two newspaper clippings, one at eleven years old, the other when she was a teenager, blonde hair in a swinging ponytail, trophy in her hand. She won the district tap finals when she was eighteen years old. She met my father right about then, though, and they were married soon after she'd graduated high school.

Tap dancing became sort of silly at that point, a stunt performed by fools and people who delivered singing telegrams. So she dropped it.

My mother and I made our way over to Broadway, where she took me into The Dance Shop and had me try on four or five pairs of tap shoes until she said, "Yes, that looks like it. What do you think? Are they yours?" I tried to clack around the floor a little, dance the way I'd seen kids do on a talent show I watched Saturday mornings, but I had a bit of a nervous stomach all of a sudden, what with all this delinquency, hers and mine. In her case, though, she wouldn't have an excuse; if she didn't quit on Bobby Gordon's car lot, she'd get fired again. But still, at that moment, I couldn't help feeling like a brand new car myself, she was so pleased with my feet. She told me I should be on stage in those shoes.

When we got home, she had me put on some play-clothes and she did the same. She got me to help her move each piece of furniture out of the spare room, which, as of last year, had become her sewing room. She'd seen some celebrity on television boasting that she made all her own clothes and my mother decided she could easily make all our clothes and save us hundreds of dollars – not to mention make us into one stylish family with her knock-offs of designer outfits spotted in magazines. She made an apron.

Once the room was clear of furniture and sewing paraphernalia, she went and grabbed any tools she could find in the garage and we set to work ripping up the carpet. "You can't dance with no floor," she said.

Freeing up a corner of the rug, she had a look at the hardwood underneath declaring it to be in not-too-bad a shape, but she wanted it to glint. We'd get it resurfaced. I helped her rip free the rest and roll it up while she muttered about its colour – "Beige, why did I ever let him talk me into a beige carpet anyway? 'Nough to bore me into a coma . . ."

My father drove up just as we dragged it the last foot or two into the garage. His face dropped at the long tube of short shag being pushed against the wall. He asked what was going on. "We're making ourselves a dance studio," she told him. He looked from her to the rolled-up carpet, took a breath and closed his eyes a moment. When he opened them, he gave me a stiff sort of smile and asked if I could go make us all some tea. Then he took my mother's arm and led her into the house and upstairs. I followed quietly, hanging back a little, waiting until their bedroom door closed before I made my way to the top of the stairs.

Their words were low, his growling, exasperated, hers hissing and quick. I heard, "Marion, that carpet's . . . six months! . . . change change change . . . What are you doing?"

"Oh for godsake . . . women's prerogative . . . Would it kill you . . . ?"

"Women's what? Just because . . . doesn't mean . . . and why are you home early from work?"

". . . shysters anyway. I want to teach Audrey to tap dance. You're the one who . . . and anyway I'll use my own money."

". . . you work, it's your money but when I work it's ours . . . isn't boring just because it's not about you!"

His voice was getting closer. I snuck back down the stairs as the door opened, her voice coming clear and sharp. "Maybe not, but it's boring as hell when it's about you."

After school the next day I brought home Nancy Donner. She was in my class and wanted in on these tap lessons. My mother was thrilled to have a second student. Not only that but, "Donner? Is that your last name? Isn't that a riot, my last name used to be Donner! Wouldn't that be funny if we were related!" She told Nancy to call her Marion; she'd never liked Mrs. Adler. Was never really her.

I'd never heard her say that before. I knew Donner was her family's name but it had never occurred to me that she might miss it. She'd bought two black leotards for me that day and gave one to Nancy, saying we'd match, it would be adorable.

As we changed in my room, Nancy whispered to me at how pretty my mother was, that she was beautiful like a movie star. I yanked at my underpants trying to tuck them back under the leotard and looked at my bedroom door as though I could examine my mother on the other side. "How old is Marion anyway, she looks more like your big sister." I could feel my face screwing up at Marion. Seemed like she was just showing off now. Both of them were. "Thirty," I told her and glared at the door again.

When we came into the spare room, Marion had an old record player set up. She had scrubbed the floor and it wasn't looking too bad, not shiny exactly, but not bad. She put us in the centre of the room and stood before us, trim in her own woman-sized black leotard and tap shoes. Nancy apologized for not having proper taps; my mother told her it wasn't too important right now. Maybe we could get her some later. In the old days, they just slapped some coins on the soles of street shoes anyway, just to get the sound. The sound's what makes it come to life, she grinned at her and began her instruction with heel-toe heel-toe heel-toe. I picked the move up right away but Nancy giggled at her foot's insistence on toe-heel toe-heel. My mother came and stood beside her, demonstrating slowly. Once Nancy'd caught on, Marion stepped up the pace with a shuffle demonstration, then a double shuffle, then the grapevine. By now, Nancy was getting it all down fast and she and my mother laughed at their feet as they shuffled and snapped the floor. My feet weren't in on the joke. Marion went to the record player and set the needle down on a 45 of Sammy Davis Jr. singing "The Candy Man."

"Wait, Mom, wait for a sec, I don't get it." I could swear she sighed when she came over and showed me again, a little more slowly, the shuffle and the grapevine. Nancy appeared to be adlibbing on her own, new little grooves in the standard steps and my mother yipped and gave her a small ovation. My eyes rolled to the ceiling.

"The Candy Man" played and reset itself over and over and, by what had to be the forty-seventh time Sammy Davis asked about making a rainbow into a groovy lemon pie, Nancy and Marion were side by side, dancing up a storm, my mother singing and interjecting with, "Good girl" and "Nancy, look at you go!" I was beginning to feel like a six-month-old beige carpet and slipped out of the room telling them I needed a drink of water.

A few days later, I came home to find my mother in the kitchen, laughing and red-headed. Her hair was still long but it looked thick now and wavy and Ann-Margret red, high at the crown with a few long bangs brushed off to the side. Nancy Donner was already there as if she'd raced ahead or cut class or something. We hadn't talked much the last few days. I was sick of looking at her; everywhere I turned, there she was.

They were laughing, as usual, Nancy at the kitchen table, my mother at the counter making sandwiches. My mother grinned when she saw me and spun around, "Ta Dah!" I looked at her. "Well! What do you think? Do I look like Ann-Margret or what?"

So, it was intentional. I didn't know if I wanted Ann-Margret for a mother. Nancy's face split wide in a grin. They were waiting. Some sort of uplifting generous response was in order. "Yeah, I guess. Sort of. Why would you dye your hair anyway? I thought you wanted to keep it blonde and cut it to look like Grace Kelly."

"What would I want to do that for? The chick can't dance," she said and snapped her fingers like Sammy Davis. The two of them cackled. My mother made a face at me, mimicking the one I wore. "What are you so sour about?"

"Nothing."

She glanced at the ceiling and sighed, then, "Oh and guess what! I'm taking driving lessons. Took my first one this morning.

My instructor thinks I have a natural instinct for traffic," she gushed.

I looked from my mother to Nancy and back. "Aren't you too old to be learning to drive? Aren't you s'posed to do that when you're a teenager or something?"

"Oh piffle on that – where do you get these stodgy old man ideas, Audrey? You're as bad as your father." She was sounding a little clipped. At least she'd knocked off the gushing though. She walked over to the table and set sandwiches down for Nancy and herself. "There's another one on the counter if you want it but I'm sure you'll turn your nose up at that too."

Nancy bit into her ham and cheese and yipped through a mouthful, grabbing at a magazine lying on the table. She set her sandwich down and folded the magazine open, then turned around in her seat to show me an old picture of Ann-Margret. She swallowed as much as she could and said, "Your mom's gonna get an outfit like this and run away with Frank Sinatra!" and laughed. She had the tap shoes my mother'd bought me on her feet.

I was in the living room watching a show about a guy who swallowed an entire Volkswagen Bug piece by piece when my mother pulled up alongside the curb in the Shining Star Driver's Ed car. Watching over the back of the couch, I could see her grinning and holding up a pink sheet of paper, then laughing and shaking her head, smoothing the page down on her steering wheel. A man was in the passenger seat, his hands resting on his own steering wheel; he was too shadowed for me to make out any expression. I assumed the way she was laughing and prattling on though, he must be doing the same. After two or three minutes she got out of the car and he came out of his side, coming around the front end to hers. She left her door open, stepping out from behind it as he came close and threw open her arms. He came into her embrace and squeezed her back, his bald head smothered in her long strawberry hair. She took a couple gleeful hops as she held him. He stood back from her, smoothing his shirt front, fingers of one hand dancing to his shirt pocket, touching his pens then fluttering down to his sides. He folded his arms and unfolded them. My mother kissed the pink paper in her hands, blew him a kiss, and walked back to the house, waving over her shoulder. He watched after her with a moony sort of smile, started back to the passenger's side and then stopped, shook his head and came back toward the driver's.

I turned from the window as the front door flew open and my mother spun into the living room with another one of her ta-dahs and screamed, "I passed!" then put her arms in the air and danced to the tune of a Broadway musical, singing, "I passed I passed I passed!"

"I know. You don't have to tell the whole world, already."

She froze in mid-flounce, dropped her arms, and looked at me, face blank. Her head wobbled a little, her eyes getting watery, fixing on mine. Her hands floated up and slapped back down against her sides. She made a tiny sound as though she were about to speak, stopped, and walked out of the room.

That night and the next, I lay awake listening to the rise and fall of my mother and father's murmur in their bedroom. I couldn't catch much as far as actual conversation. It seemed as if he were holding back, never quite raising his voice, as if he were afraid that a harsh tone or any sudden movement might cause her to evaporate. I think now that maybe he was seeing something I wasn't; he was understanding that the peace she got from car rides had nothing to do with speed.

Come Saturday morning I woke up to his rap on the door. He poked his head in. "Oh, I thought your mother might be in here."

"No. What time is it?" It was ten. I felt as if I could sleep into the afternoon. My father looked of the same mind. He'd slept the sleep of the dead, he said. He had a vague memory of my mother kissing his cheek and saying something about coffee but that was ages ago, seemed like it was the middle of the night. Maybe she went to the farmer's market for fruit or something, he said, and the phone rang. He ran off to get it.

A minute later he was back in my room. "You don't know

where Nancy is, do you?" I squinted and sat up, shaking my head. He went back to the phone.

Soon he was leaning in my doorway again. "That was Nancy's mother. Their car is missing. The old one. And Nancy's not there either."

"Nancy can't drive."

"No kidding," he said. "They don't know what to think. Their daughter's not home and the car's missing."

Sunday afternoon, the police came to our house after they left the Donners'. The keys to the Donners' car were gone too. We had given it a day before we called police; maybe the two of them had gone off for a drive in the country. The Donners' car was a convertible, a fun summer drive, a joy ride. But a bag was missing too and clothes, Nancy's and my mother's. The adults argued amongst themselves as to whether these things were all related: the car, Nancy, Marion. We shouldn't assume; we shouldn't jump to conclusions.

But the police directed their questions more toward me than my father: Nancy was my friend and wives don't tell their husbands a lot. I explained that Nancy and I hadn't much talked in the last few weeks; she and my mother hung out more, they tap danced. And Nancy wanted to dye her hair red too. The police sighed and took notes, leaning back as I spoke. They asked me what I thought my mother's interest in Nancy was. If I'd noticed anything peculiar in the way she behaved toward her, anything inappropriate. My father took a quick look at me and stared at the cop who'd posed the question with the same sort of expression my mother wore that afternoon in the living room, somewhere between pain and mystification. Finally they turned to my father and inquired as to whether he thought my mother might have a lover somewhere. Normally that would be the first question, the cop explained, but this is a little less usual. My father shook his head no and began to cry, head rocking side to side in his hands, fingers buried in his hair, his chest jerking quietly.

Nancy's mother called twice after the police left wanting to know if we'd heard anything. She called again that night. She cried through the phone at my father, screamed so that I could hear her from my chair. "What kind of man can't control his wife," she said and hung up.

It was less than a week before someone turned my mother in. Nancy had stolen the keys to the family's convertible and the two of them took a leisurely drive to Vegas. When they got to town they went to the Tropicana so that Marion could apply for a job as a dancer in one of their shows. She and Nancy, mother and daughter, sat in a lounge talking with the manager who couldn't make Marion understand he didn't hire showgirls. That was a whole 'nother department, he told her. The lounge television was turned to the news, sound off. Marion pulled out her scrapbook, explaining she really could dance, if she could just get an audition. He let her go on, jabbering like her freakin' life depended on it, he said. He looked away, thinking she was too old to start dancing, that maybe he'd offer her a cocktail job, when he glanced up at the TV screen and saw pictures of my mother with her straight blonde hair and Nancy with hers, bold print stating Marion Adler, aged thirty, grand theft auto and kidnapping of Nancy Donner, aged eleven. Both redheads now, the manager recognized them instantly, aided by the fact that my mother had given Donner as their family name. Apparently, she didn't see the television or if she did, she didn't absorb the content. Nancy sat with her head down counting nickels she'd won at slots. The manager excused himself a moment and called security and the police. Turned out his own wife had run off with his son the year before and as much a looker as this Donner broad was, he told police, he didn't have any kind of sympathy for it.

Once home, Nancy and the car were handed over to the Donners. My mother was delivered by the Nevada State Police to the local authorities, who charged her and put her behind bars to await trial. I saw her only on the news; no one would post her bail, they said.

After the second day of news, we turned off the television altogether and didn't leave the house unless we ran out of food, not for school or work, not until the trial was over and my mother had been convicted. My father stayed away from work so long, they eventually had to let him go. I stayed away from school so long, my father agreed to let me switch, take the bus to another to avoid the looks and whispers. We lived on unemployment insurance. My father mortgaged the house.

I saw Nancy twice before the Donners moved: once on the news, the back of her head bobbing as she walked down the courthouse steps, her parents ducking away from the press and into their cars, and once at the corner store.

I had just picked up some milk and bread and canned stuff my father'd written down on a list. On her way in, she stopped, faced me with a shaken look as though I were a car accident. "Hi."

"Hi," I told her and she stood there blocking my way out. Trying to go around her, she reached out for my arm and I winced back like a burnt hand.

"Wanna go play or something," she asked me, "like maybe go with my brother and his friends to the water slides?"

"Go to hell," and I walked past her out of the store, the bell jingling summer-clear behind me.

It was two years before my father came out of his stupor. My mother was released on parole about the same time. There must have been a correlation. He started to leave the house more regularly again, never walking anywhere, only driving. He would disappear all day, just driving, he said. I don't think it calmed him exactly. I think it woke him up, or maybe it would be more accurate to say that it got him breathing. Like a shark, continuous movement kept him alive. Soon he applied for a job as a courier, driving packages all over town.

My mother showed up after school one afternoon, a couple weeks after she was released. She waited outside, scanning the crowd of kids until she caught sight of me. I saw her first and felt a bit sick as if the school bully were waiting. She took a couple nervous steps and stopped. Her hair was back to blonde and she looked as though she'd aged suddenly. I walked in the other direction toward the swings and monkey bars and she followed. Sitting down on a swing, I watched her come closer, her feet delicate in heels, crunching and wobbling on the pebbles, her trench coat flapping in the breeze. She eyed the swing beside me but kept her distance, hands worrying over a gnarled-up Kleenex. I wished she would turn and vanish. I sat in the swing turning myself instead.

"Audrey?" Her voice cracked. She sounded fragile, uncertain. I closed my eyes, spinning the chains of my swing to knots. "Audrey, will you let me talk to you just for a minute?" She stuffed the Kleenex in her pocket, then rubbed her fingertips at her forehead the way my father used to when they fought. Finally she said, "I must've started a hundred different letters wanting to write but I just didn't know what to say. I just –"

I let the swing unspin from its tangle and caught the earth with my feet, dizzy, the ground breathing under me.

"Hey, I, uh, I enrolled in university while I was away, you know. I'll have a Bachelors of Arts degree soon." I didn't speak. "Are you okay? Is everything okay for you?" I opened my eyes at the ground. "How about Nancy? Do you still see Nancy?"

"Nancy can go to hell," I said, matter-of-factly, the way you might give someone directions or a weather forecast.

She was quiet a moment. "You've gotten so old in two years." She tisked to herself and looked away. "I just want you to know that a day hasn't gone by where I didn't . . . I just thought I should tell you that I'm going to be in the phone book. Under Donner. For when you're ready. I thought you should know."

Tipping my head at the sky, I took in all the air I could swallow and still felt as if I might suffocate. Seeing the hem of her coat out of the corner of my eye, I turned my head and got off the swing, walked across the football field and through the opening in the chain-link fence. I walked across town instead of taking the bus, walked up and down the streets in our neighbourhood, long past dark. It was after eleven when I wandered up our driveway. My father was sitting in his car staring straight ahead with the windows down, no motor running. His elbow balanced on the bottom of the window frame, fingertips touching the top as though a Sunday breeze was playing at them. I headed for the house, touching his shirt sleeve as I passed.

About the Authors

Kevin Armstrong was hired as first mate aboard the sailing yacht *Wendy Lynne* while travelling through the Kingdom of Tonga in July 1997. In the ensuing fifteen months, he visited nine countries and sailed eight thousand miles. The stories in his forthcoming collection, *Inside Passage* (Penguin Books Canada, spring 2002), including the one reprinted here, are products of this journey. First published in *Event* magazine, "The Cane Field" won the Booming Ground/Chapters Scholarship and the Best Short Story Award at the Western Magazine Awards. He lives in Vancouver.

Mike Barnes is the author of *Aquarium* (The Porcupine's Quill), which won the 1999 Danuta Gleed Award for best first collection of stories in English. His poetry collection, *Calm Jazz Sea* (Brick Books), was shortlisted for the Gerald Lampert Memorial Award. His poetry and stories have appeared in numerous magazines and anthologies, including *The Journey Prize Anthology 11* and *99:Best Canadian Stories*.

Heather Birrell, a poet and fiction writer, is a recent fellow of The MacDowell Colony in New Hampshire, U.S.A, and the Fundación Valparaiso in Mojácar, Spain. "The Present Perfect" and "Machaya" are from an as-yet-unpublished collection of stories, tentatively titled *Congratulations, Really*. She lives in Toronto.

Craig Boyko was born in Saskatchewan and currently resides in Calgary, where he is studying English at the University of Calgary. He is currently working on his first novel. "The Gun" is his first published story.

Vivette J. Kady grew up in South Africa, and now lives in Toronto. Her short fiction has appeared in numerous journals and anthologies in Canada and the United States, including *Coming Attractions:00* and *93:Best Canadian Stories*, and has been shortlisted for a National Magazine Award and a Western Magazine Award. She is currently working on a collection of stories.

Billie Livingston's first novel, *Going Down Swinging*, was published by Random House Canada in the spring of 2000. Her first book of poetry, *The Chick at the Back of the Church* (Nightwood Editions), hit the shelves in May 2001. She is currently working on a short-story collection and is researching a second novel.

Annabel Lyon is a Vancouver writer and a graduate of the M.F.A. program in creative writing at the University of British Columbia. Her first book, *Oxygen*, a collection of short stories, was published by The Porcupine's Quill in 2000. She is currently working on a novel and more stories. "Fishes" was also nominated for a Western Magazine Award.

Lisa Moore is a St. John's writer and a graduate of the Nova Scotia College of Arts and Design. Recently, her stories have appeared in *The Malahat Review*, *00:Best Canadian Stories*, and *The Fiddlehead*. Her first collection of short stories, *Degrees of Nakedness*, was published by Mercury Press. Her second collection will be published by House of Anansi in the spring of 2002.

Heather O'Neill is the author of the poetry collection *Two Eyes Are You Sleeping*. She lives in Montreal, where she is currently completing her first novel.

Susan Rendell has a B.A. from Memorial University of Newfoundland. "In the Chambers of the Sea" won first place in the 1999 Newfoundland and Labrador Arts and Letters Competition and *TickleAce*'s inaugural Cabot Award. It is her first published story. She lives in St. John's, where she works as a freelance writer, editor, and researcher.

Tim Rogers is currently a postdoctoral research associate at the Cognition and Brain Sciences Unit in Cambridge, U.K. After five years of graduate work in Pittsburgh, he is getting very confused about how to spell the word "colour." "Watch" is part of an ongoing cycle of short stories. "Scars and Other Presents," an earlier story from the same cycle, appeared in the tenth volume of *The Journey Prize Anthology*.

Margrith Schraner was born in Switzerland and came to Canada when she was twenty-two. She is the in-house editor of New Orphic Publishers. "Dream Dig" is her first published short story and has been selected for inclusion in *The Flat Earth Excavation Company: A Surreal Fiction Anthology* (New Orphic Publishers, 2002). She is the co-author, with Ernest Hekkanen, of *Black Snow: An Imaginative Memoir* (1996). She is currently translating selected chapters of a new novel by Eveline Hasler for the Spring 2002 Special Swiss Issue of *The New Orphic Review*.

About the Contributing Journals

For more information about all the journals that submitted stories to this year's anthology, please consult *The Journey Prize Anthology* Web site: www.mcclelland.com/jpa

Event is published three times a year by Douglas College in New Westminster, B.C. It focuses on fiction, poetry, creative non-fiction, and reviews by new and established writers, and every spring it runs a creative non-fiction contest. *Event* has won regional, national, and international awards for its writers. Editor: Cathy Stonehouse. Assistant Editor: Ian Cockfield. Fiction Editor: Christine Dewar. Submissions and correspondence: *Event*, P.O. Box 2503, New Westminster, British Columbia, V3L 5B2. E-mail (queries only): event@douglas.bc.ca Web site: http://event.douglas.bc.ca

filling Station magazine has been published on a non-profit basis by a volunteer editorial collection in Calgary for almost seven years. The *filling Station* editorial collective strives to strike a balance among new, emerging, and established writers, and among local, national, and international writers. *filling Station* encourages submission of all forms of contemporary writing (poetry, fiction, one-act plays, essays, and book reviews). All submissions must be original and previously unpublished, and simultaneous submissions are acceptable. Submission deadlines are March 15, July 15, and November 15 of each year. Managing Editor: Darren Matthies. Submissions and correspondence: *filling Station*, Box 22135, Bankers' Hall, Calgary, Alberta, T2P 4J5. E-mail: editor@fillingstation.ca

The Malahat Review publishes mostly fiction and poetry, and includes a substantial review article in each issue. It is open to dramatic works, so long as they lend themselves to the page; it welcomes literary works that defy easy generic categorization.

Editor: Marlene Cookshaw. Assistant Editor: Lucy Bashford. Submissions and correspondence: *The Malahat Review*, University of Victoria, P.O.Box 1700 Stn. CSC, Victoria, British Columbia, V8W 2Y2.

Matrix is a Montreal-based literary and cultural periodical that publishes three times yearly. Along with a focus on Montreal and Quebec poetry, fiction, non-fiction, photography, and art, *Matrix* casts its net widely enough to include work from Europe, Australia, Asia, and the U.S. We are interested in innovative work of all kinds and from all places, and in the last few years have edited special sections on translation, the g/Gods, travel writing, underground comix, and lost and found art. We specialize, too, in long poems, novel excerpts, multi-media work, experimental texts, etc. *Matrix* will look at unsolicited work of any and all kinds. Editor: R.E.N. Allen. Submissions and correspondence: *Matrix*, 1400 de Maisonneuve Blvd. West, Suite 502, Montreal, Quebec, H3G 1M8. E-mail: matrix@alcor.concordia.ca Web site: http://alcor.concordia.ca/~matrix

The New Orphic Review is published semi-annually by New Orphic Publishers in Nelson, B.C. It focuses on fiction, poetry, plays and essays up to 10,000 words in length. Each issue contains a Featured Poet section. Payment is in copies only, for the magazine isn't subsidized by government grants or money from institutions. *The New Orphic Review* publishes authors from around the world as long as the pieces are written in English and are accompanied by an SASE with proper Canadian postage and/or U.S. dollars to offset the cost of postage. Editor-in-Chief: Ernest Hekkanen. Associate Editor: Margrith Schraner. Roving "Featured Poet" Editors: Chad Norman and Catherine Owen. Submissions and correspondence: *The New Orphic Review*, 706 Mill Street, Nelson, B.C. V1L 4S5

The New Quarterly publishes poetry, fiction, interviews, and essays on writing. A two-time winner of the gold medal for fiction at the National Magazine Awards, with silver medals for fiction, poetry, and the essay, the magazine prides itself on its independent take on the Canadian literary scene. Recent issues include an interview with and new work by Mike Barnes (featured in this anthology), and "Wild Writers We Have Known: a celebration of the Canadian Short Story in English." Editor: Kim Jernigan. Submissions and correspondence: *The New Quarterly*, c/o St. Jerome's University, 200 University Avenue West., Waterloo, Ontario, N2L 3G3. E-mail: newquart@watarts.uwaterloo.ca

Prairie Fire is a quarterly magazine of contemporary Canadian writing which publishes stories, poems, and literary non-fiction by both emerging and established writers. *Praire Fire*'s editorial mix also occasionally features critical or personal essays, and interviews with authors. *Prairie Fire* publishes a fiction issue every summer. Some of *Prairie Fire*'s most popular issues have been double-sized editions on cultural commmunities and individual authors. *Prairie Fire* publishes writing from, and has readers in, all parts of Canada. Editor: Andris Taskans; Fiction Editors: Heidi Harms and Susan Rempel Letkemann. Submissions and correspondence: *Prairie Fire*, Room 423 – 100 Arthur St., Winnipeg, Manitoba, R3B 1H3. E-mail: prfire@escape.ca Web site: www.prairiefire.mb.ca

PRISM international, the oldest literary magazine in Western Canada, was established in 1959 by a group of Vancouver writers. Published four times a year, *PRISM* features short fiction, poetry, drama, creative non-fiction, and translations by both new and established writers from Canada and from around the world. The only criteria are originality and quality. *PRISM* holds four exemplary competitions: the Annual Short Fiction Contest, the Earle Birney Prize for Poetry, the Maclean-Hunter Endowment Award for Literary Non-fiction, and the Residency Prize in Stageplay. Executive Editor: Michael Kissinger. Fiction and Poetry Editor: Abigail Kinch. Submissions and correspondence: *PRISM international*, Creative Writing Program, The University of British Columbia, Buchanan E462, 1866 Main Mall, Vancouver, British Columbia, V6T 1Z1. E-mail (for queries only): prism@interchange.ubc.ca Web site: www.arts.ubc.ca/prism.

This Magazine is a thirty-four-year-old national magazine focusing on politics and culture. Some of Canada's best-known journalists and creative writers have been involved with the magazine, and we continue to publish original fiction in every issue, and poetry three times a year, plus an annual special literary supplement in our September/October issue. *This Magazine* is put out by the Red Maple Foundation, and publishes six times per year. The magazine does not accept unsolicited literary submissions. Editor: Julie Crysler. Submissions and correspondence: *This Magazine*, 401 Richmond St. W. #396, Toronto, Ontario, M5V 3A8. E-mail: thismag@web.net

TickleAce is a semi-annual literary magazine that publishes fiction, poetry, book reviews, interviews, and visual art. Now in its twenty-fourth year, this award-winning magazine focuses on the words and images of contributors in its own province but also includes a fine selection of good work from across Canada and beyond. Decidedly eclectic in subject, form, and flavour, *TickleAce* offerings include pieces by the internationally renowned, the emerging artist, and the talented first-timer. Editor: Bruce Porter. Submissions and correspondence: *TickleAce*, P.O. Box 5353, St. John's, Newfoundland, A1C 5W2.

Submissions were also received from the following journals:

Algonquin Roundtable Review
(Nepean, Ont.)

The Amethyst Review
(Truro, N.S.)

The Antigonish Review
(Antigonish, N.S.)

The Capilano Review
(North Vancouver, B.C.)

The Dalhousie Review
(Halifax, N.S.)

Descant
(Toronto, Ont.)

The Fiddlehead
(Fredericton, N.B.)

Grain
(Regina, Sask.)

Green's Magazine
(Regina, Sask.)

Other Voices
(Edmonton, Alta.)

Pagitica in Toronto
(Toronto, Ont.)

Parchment
(Toronto, Ont.)

Pottersfield Portfolio
(Sydney, N.S.)

Prairie Journal
(Calgary, Alta.)

Queen Street Quarterly
(Toronto, Ont.)

Queen's Quarterly
(Kingston, Ont.)

Storyteller
(Ottawa, Ont.)

sub-Terrain Magazine
(Vancouver, B.C.)

Taddle Creek
(Toronto, Ont.)

*The Toronto Review of
Contemporary Writing
Abroad*
(Toronto, Ont.)

The Windsor Review
(Windsor, Ont.)

The Journey Prize Anthology
List of Previous Contributing Authors

* Winners of the $10,000 Journey Prize
** Co-winners of the $10,000 Journey Prize

1
1989

Ven Begamudré, "Word Games"
David Bergen, "Where You're From"
Lois Braun, "The Pumpkin-Eaters"
Constance Buchanan, "Man with Flying Genitals"
Ann Copeland, "Obedience"
Marion Douglas, "Flags"
Frances Itani, "An Evening in the Café"
Diane Keating, "The Crying Out"
Thomas King, "One Good Story, That One"
Holley Rubinsky, "Rapid Transits"*
Jean Rysstad, "Winter Baby"
Kevin Van Tighem, "Whoopers"
M.G. Vassanji, "In the Quiet of a Sunday Afternoon"
Bronwen Wallace, "Chicken 'N' Ribs"
Armin Wiebe, "Mouse Lake"
Budge Wilson, "Waiting"

2
1990

André Alexis, "Despair: Five Stories of Ottawa"
Glen Allen, "The Hua Guofeng Memorial Warehouse"
Marusia Bociurkiw, "Mama, Donya"
Virgil Burnett, "Billfrith the Dreamer"
Margaret Dyment, "Sacred Trust"
Cynthia Flood, "My Father Took a Cake to France"*
Douglas Glover, "Story Carved in Stone"
Terry Griggs, "Man with the Axe"
Rick Hillis, "Limbo River"

Thomas King, "The Dog I Wish I Had, I Would Call It Helen"
K.D. Miller, "Sunrise Till Dark"
Jennifer Mitton, "Let Them Say"
Lawrence O'Toole, "Goin' to Town with Katie Ann"
Kenneth Radu, "A Change of Heart"
Jenifer Sutherland, "Table Talk"
Wayne Tefs, "Red Rock and After"

3
1991

Donald Aker, "The Invitation"
Anton Baer, "Yukon"
Allan Barr, "A Visit from Lloyd"
David Bergen, "The Fall"
Rai Berzins, "Common Sense"
Diana Hartog, "Theories of Grief"
Diane Keating, "The Salem Letters"
Yann Martel, "The Facts Behind the Helsinki Roccamatios"*
Jennifer Mitton, "Polaroid"
Sheldon Oberman, "This Business with Elijah"
Lynn Podgurny, "Till Tomorrow, Maple Leaf Mills"
James Riseborough, "She Is Not His Mother"
Patricia Stone, "Living on the Lake"

4
1992

David Bergen, "The Bottom of the Glass"
Maria A. Billion, "No Miracles Sweet Jesus"
Judith Cowan, "By the Big River"
Steven Heighton, "A Man Away from Home Has No Neighbours"
Steven Heighton, "How Beautiful upon the Mountains"
L. Rex Kay, "Travelling"
Rozena Maart, "No Rosa, No District Six"*
Guy Malet De Carteret, "Rainy Day"
Carmelita McGrath, "Silence"
Michael Mirolla, "A Theory of Discontinuous Existence"
Diane Juttner Perreault, "Bella's Story"
Eden Robinson, "Traplines"

5

1993

Caroline Adderson, "Oil and Dread"

David Bergen, "La Rue Prevette"

Marina Endicott, "With the Band"

Dayv James-French, "Cervine"

Michael Kenyon, "Durable Tumblers"

K.D. Miller, "A Litany in Time of Plague"

Robert Mullen, "Flotsam"

Gayla Reid, "Sister Doyle's Men"*

Oakland Ross, "Bang-bang"

Robert Sherrin, "Technical Battle for Trial Machine"

Carol Windley, "The Etruscans"

6

1994

Anne Carson, "Water Margins: An Essay on Swimming by
    My Brother"

Richard Cumyn, "The Sound He Made"

Genni Gunn, "Versions"

Melissa Hardy, "Long Man the River"*

Robert Mullen, "Anomie"

Vivian Payne, "Free Falls"

Jim Reil, "Dry"

Robyn Sarah, "Accept My Story"

Joan Skogan, "Landfall"

Dorothy Speak, "Relatives in Florida"

Alison Wearing, "Notes from Under Water"

7

1995

Michelle Alfano, "Opera"

Mary Borsky, "Maps of the Known World"

Gabriella Goliger, "Song of Ascent"

Elizabeth Hay, "Hand Games"

Shaena Lambert, "The Falling Woman"

Elise Levine, "Boy"

Roger Burford Mason, "The Rat-Catcher's Kiss"

Antanas Sileika, "Going Native"
Kathryn Woodward, "Of Marranos and Gilded Angels"*

8
1996

Rick Bowers, "Dental Bytes"
David Elias, "How I Crossed Over"
Elyse Gasco, "Can You Wave Bye Bye, Baby?"*
Danuta Gleed, "Bones"
Elizabeth Hay, "The Friend"
Linda Holeman, "Turning the Worm"
Elaine Littman, "The Winner's Circle"
Murray Logan, "Steam"
Rick Maddocks, "Lessons from the Sputnik Diner"
K.D. Miller, "Egypt Land"
Gregor Robinson, "Monster Gaps"
Alma Subasic, "Dust"

9
1997

Brian Bartlett, "Thomas, Naked"
Dennis Bock, "Olympia"
Kristen den Hartog, "Wave"
Gabriella Goliger, "Maladies of the Inner Ear"**
Terry Griggs, "Momma Had a Baby"
Mark Anthony Jarman, "Righteous Speedboat"
Judith Kalman, "Not for Me a Crown of Thorns"
Andrew Mullins, "The World of Science"
Sasenarine Persaud, "Canada Geese and Apple Chatney"
Anne Simpson, "Dreaming Snow"**
Sarah Withrow, "Ollie"
Terence Young, "The Berlin Wall"

10
1998

John Brooke, "The Finer Points of Apples"*
Ian Colford, "The Reason for the Dream"
Libby Creelman, "Cruelty"

Michael Crummey, "Serendipity"
Stephen Guppy, "Downwind"
Jane Eaton Hamilton, "Graduation"
Elise Levine, "You Are You Because Your Little Dog Loves You"
Jean McNeil, "Bethlehem"
Liz Moore, "Eight-Day Clock"
Edward O'Connor, "The Beatrice of Victoria College"
Tim Rogers, "Scars and Other Presents"
Denise Ryan, "Marginals, Vivisections, and Dreams"
Madeleine Thien, "Simple Recipes"
Cheryl Tibbetts, "Flowers of Africville"

11

1999

Mike Barnes, "In Florida"
Libby Creelman, "Sunken Island"
Mike Finigan, "Passion Sunday"
Jane Eaton Hamilton, "Territory"
Mark Anthony Jarman, "Travels into Several Remote Nations of
    the World"
Barbara Lambert, "Where the Bodies Are Kept"
Linda Little, "The Still"
Larry Lynch, "The Sitter"
Sandra Sabatini, "The One With the News"
Sharon Steams, "Brothers"
Mary Walters, "Show Jumping"
Alissa York, "The Back of the Bear's Mouth"*

12

2000

Andrew Gray, "The Heart of the Land"
Lee Henderson, "Sheep Dub"
Jessica Johnson, "We Move Slowly"
John Lavery, "The Premier's New Pyjamas"
J.A. McCormack, "Hearsay"
Nancy Richler, "Your Mouth Is Lovely"
Andrew Smith, "Sightseeing"
Karen Solie, "Onion Calendar"

Timothy Taylor, "Doves of Townsend"*
Timothy Taylor, "Pope's Own"
Timothy Taylor, "Silent Cruise"
R.M. Vaughan, "Swan Street"